ONSLAUGHT

ONSLAUGHT

A Steve Flynn Thriller

Nick Oldham

Severn House Large Print
London & New York

This first large print edition published 2016
in Great Britain and the USA by
SEVERN HOUSE PUBLISHERS LTD of
19 Cedar Road, Sutton, Surrey, England, SM2 5DA.
First world regular print edition published 2016 by
Severn House Publishers Ltd.

British Library Cataloguing in Publication Data
A CIP catalogue record for this title is available from the British Library.

ISBN-13: 9780727894885

Severn House Publishers support the Forest Stewardship Council™
[FSC™], the leading international forest certification organisation. All
our titles that are printed on FSC certified paper carry the FSC logo.

Typeset by Palimpsest Book Production Ltd.,
Falkirk, Stirlingshire, Scotland.
Printed and bound in Great Britain by
T J International, Padstow, Cornwall.

Dedication
This one is dedicated to Belinda, my love
– now incredibly
my wife – and to three brilliant young
people, no longer kids,
Philip, Jessica and James.

One

Steve Flynn knew a wolf pack when he saw one.

He could instantly identify the grizzled, grey-haired older leader, the strategist, the alpha male; the one with the ever thinking, ever moving, ruthless, black intelligent eyes; the one moving with the easy grace that came with the power and confidence of the position, never putting a foot wrong.

He knew the type: as old and wise as this wolf might be, he was more brutal and dangerous than any of the pack members following in his wake. His physical speed might not be what it once was, but he more than made up for that deficiency with his thought process and the viciousness with which those thoughts were transformed, without hesitation, into action.

Flynn could also recognize the underlings for what they were, the pack members. Maybe of the same family as the leader, siblings or sons, who would one day vie for dominance themselves and challenge for the top dog position. Initially they would fail and have to lick their wounds, but they would eventually come back stronger and more cunning each time, learning from experience, and ultimately displace, or even kill, the leader.

But that time had yet to come for the wolf pack he was now observing carefully.

This leader was still very much in charge and would be for some time to come.

There were only three members in this pack, but Flynn knew that somewhere there would be others; this was merely the hunting party, searching out prey to identify, hunt, then bring down in a frenzy of blood-lust for the benefit of the other pack members who would later be able to feast on the carcass.

Flynn could even imagine the victorious return home to their lair.

He had seen it on so many wildlife documentaries. The way the snivelling pack would welcome the returning hunters, cowering submissively, abasing themselves, licking the blood-stained faces and then gorging themselves on the remains of the victim. Then they would all lounge around, dissolute, full-bellied, until it was time to hunt again, go out and kill once more.

Except, he reflected as his eyes shifted from one to the other, these were not wolves running wild on the Canadian tundra or the steppes of Russia. These were their human equivalents, out for their pound of flesh in Flynn's domain.

He was also glad there were only three of the bastards.

Despite this, and despite his inner rage at the intrusion on to his peaceful chunk of turf – because he knew they would spill blood some-time, somewhere – an electric frisson of excitement zipped up and down his spine as their presence fired up that latent part of him that revelled in the challenge of dealing with such people. This feeling stopped abruptly, however, when Flynn

2

found himself looking at the prey in this scenario and demanding, 'What the hell are you doing with this lot?'

Flynn had been alerted to the presence of the wolf pack before they actually arrived on the quayside, although at that moment he had assumed they were just simple businessmen, not predators.

He had been aboard *Faye*, the forty-five foot sportfishing boat he part-owned, moored in the Puerto de Escala side of the marina in the resort of Puerto Rico on the south-west coast of Gran Canaria. He had been busy cleaning and doing some running repairs on the boat which, mid-way though a long, hard season, was showing signs of wear and tear. *Faye* hadn't been a new boat when Flynn had bought her and as he worked on her he realized he needed to find a gap of time in order to haul her shapely body out into dry dock and give her some much required TLC to set her up for a few years to come.

Even though Flynn lived to be out on the ocean, the prospect of having *Faye* out of the water for a couple of weeks warmed his soul; he would be able to mollycoddle his baby and give her, and himself, a well-deserved break.

It had been pretty full-on for the last year or so since he had emerged relatively unscathed from an encounter that had found him slap-bang in the middle of a blood-splattered race between rival factions of gangsters for a fortune worth millions in uncut blood diamonds. Not that he had seen a cent of that treasure. It had all ended up in the hands of the authorities.

From then it had been all go as far as business was concerned. He was *Faye*'s skipper; with a somewhat disreputable crew of one he took out daily or weekly charters to fish the Atlantic waters south of Gran Canaria.

It had also been a pretty full-on year as far as Flynn's personal life was concerned.

Or had been until very recently.

He stood up stiffly from his scrubbing duties, wrung out the sponge over the side of the boat and squinted across to the quayside booking office. In reality this was nothing more than a garden shed with a sliding window where day trippers who fancied a go at sportfishing booked their charters. In it sat Karen Glass, the kid sister of Flynn's boss, Adam Castle (although she had grown well beyond the term 'kid'), the lady Flynn had been seeing for almost the best part of twelve months now.

His sharp eyes were a touch sad and he sighed down his nostrils with frustration.

When they had struck up their relationship, Karen had been on the verge of quitting the island and returning to the UK to go to university as a mature student and resume her degree in media studies. When she fell in love with Flynn – and he with her – she decided not to go home but to stay here and make a life with him. But Flynn saw the cracks start to appear when she began to realize that sitting in a booking kiosk was not what she wanted to do with her life. It had all been great at first, but when the prospect of spending her working life without any real chal-lenge hit home, Flynn could tell the end was nigh. He knew he didn't offer enough of anything to make her stay.

She glanced over at Flynn, caught his eye and gave him a tiny, dejected wave, which gave his usually hard heart a bit of a flip. He squeezed out the sponge again – as if it was someone's neck – dropped it into an empty bucket and walked across the gangplank to speak to her.

'Hi.'

'Hey.' She looked at him.

His mouth twisted cynically, then tightened into a thin line as he recalled the sequence of events leading up to falling in love in the first place. The two of them had held off from anything happening between them – such as sex – ever since Karen had landed on the island at the beginning of the previous year. That was in spite of the obvious two way attraction which, from Flynn's perspective, had been very intense. But they'd eventually fallen into a relationship (a word Flynn despised with a passion) by reassuring each other it could work. And perhaps it could have done had they followed a parallel pathway.

He had gone to great pains to point out to her that in him she would get what she saw, and she seemed to accept this. He had no pretensions, no subterfuge, although he did find it hard to reveal his inner self to anyone. When it all started to disintegrate he almost felt he had been cheated into opening up, laying himself bare, then being chucked away. He carried a lot of baggage and he knew Karen did too, but he'd been willing to give it a shot and it hadn't worked out because, as it transpired, he couldn't give her what she

5

needed to fulfil herself – which was more than sun, sea and sex.

Now they had regressed into acrimony and petty sniping and, despite Flynn's toughness, he didn't have the heart to carry on with it.

He knew it was big decision time.

They hadn't seen each other for three days. He had been out on a two night charter to fish the waters around El Hierro, the most westerly of the Canary Islands, and on the third he'd crashed in a villa belonging to one of his regular customers.

Their eyes locked, but even then, with all that was churning up inside him, he was forced to admit she had the most amazing honey-coloured eyes.

'How are you doing?' he asked.

She nodded, sighed, shrugged. There was a lot of sighing going on this morning.

Flynn would rather be bludgeoned or hunt sabre-toothed tigers than experience this sort of pain.

'What's happening?' he asked stiltedly.

She shrugged again.

'Any bookings for today? Boat's as good as ready.'

'No, nothing so far. I would've told you.'

'Yeah, course you would.' He hesitated. 'Erm . . .'

Fortunately her mobile phone rang at that precise moment. She raised a forefinger at him to be silent, picked it up from the counter and answered it.

Flynn backed away from the hatch, feeling uncomfortable. Over the past year he would have been leaning in, listening to her take calls, messing about, pulling his face, trying to make her giggle. But that bird had flown. Now he did not feel able to keep his eyes on her because it hurt so much.

He turned away, his eyes narrowed against the early sunshine. The heat was already rising on what looked like becoming another scorching day in Flynn's slice of paradise. He looked across the marina, then up the valley, so tightly packed with apartment blocks and hotels, that was the tourist resort of Puerto Rico.

No one could say that this brash, loud place was pretty any more. There was no room left for further development, but it was a place Flynn had called home for the last decade since his uncomfortable departure from marriage and a career in the police. It was here that his boss and now business partner – and Karen's older brother – Adam Castle had kept his promise to Flynn. When he'd turned up virtually penniless on Castle's doorstep all those years ago, clutching a kit bag, rucksack and very little else, Castle had given Flynn a job on one of his sportfishing boats here in Puerto Rico. Flynn had repaid the gesture by becoming one of the most sought-after skippers on the islands, guaranteeing satisfied and returning customers year on year.

He now co-owned *Faye* with Castle, just tipping the balance at fifty-one per cent, and this past year had been one of the most successful, financially and fish-wise.

So now Flynn half-owned a boat, but still little else.

He folded his muscled, bronzed arms, blinked at the sun and tried not to feel too bitter.

Get a grip, he remonstrated internally with himself. Wuss!

'Flynnie!' Karen called, using her pet name for him.

Adjusting his frown, he turned, giving her a fabricated smile.

She waggled her mobile phone. He sauntered back, leaned on the sill of the hatch and tried to smile properly, but found it a struggle. Leaning there now seemed too intimate, as if he had no right to do it any longer.

'That was Adam,' she said of the phone call. 'He wants *Faye* today – bringing a special party with him. Be about an hour.'

'OK, I'll get her ready.'

An hour later Adam and his special party still had not arrived. Flynn was beginning to get annoyed because Karen had been obliged to say no to two prospective clients, cash in hand, who had turned up on the wharf on someone else's recommendation. They simply walked on to other fishing boats further down the quay, Flynn's business rivals. As far as he was concerned, it was money chucked down the drain. One of the customers had wanted a full day's fishing, 900 euros. Important income Flynn knew he would not see if Adam had the boat for a day, entertaining people.

He jumped off the boat, leaving his crew – a rather grand title for the curmudgeonly Spaniard called Jose – on board. He strutted over to the kiosk.

Karen saw him coming, recognized the look on his face and raised her hands placatingly.

'I know, I know,' she said.

'In that case I'm going to get a coffee and something to eat across the way.' He jerked his thumb in the direction of the small commercial centre on the opposite side of the marina.

'OK, whatever.'

'I'll keep an eye out, but I'll be back in half an hour, either way,' he promised. Karen nodded. Flynn hesitated again, wondering if he should say something, make a plea, maybe prostrate himself at her feet. He decided against it, then set off around the marina; he found a table which overlooked it at a good café on the first floor of the commercial centre. He ordered a large cafetière of strong Kilimanjaro coffee and a full English breakfast, because when he was upset he liked to fill himself with comfort food.

It was excellent. The couple who ran the place, and whom Flynn knew well, could certainly do an authentic breakfast, and the food helped to calm him down, although his ventricles might have argued differently.

As he sipped his second mug of coffee, replete after the meal, he spotted a large car crawling along the Doreste y Molina, stopping just below where he sat on the balcony of the café. All vehicles, other than those with authorized access on to the quayside itself, had to stop at the rising barrier so a security man could check them out. Quite often the barrier didn't even work and was left up, as was the case today. This meant the guard had to stand in front and stop all vehicles he didn't recognize – if he felt that way inclined. Today, it seemed, he did, and he held up his hand to this car, which was a big old silver blue

Rolls-Royce bearing Spanish number plates. The driver was a young man with a severely shaved head and he leaned out to speak to the security guy.

Flynn had a bad habit of stereotyping people. He knew that, despite what do-gooders said, stereotyping existed in all walks of life; it wasn't a problem so long as, ultimately, people were treated fairly. But when this young man leaned out of the driver's window of the Rolls, Flynn instantly thought he looked completely out of place and would have been more at home behind the wheel of a souped-up banger, not driving some stately old lady on her last legs. He also thought the young man – a buck – looked like trouble.

But what did he know?

From where he sat he could hear a raised, intimidatory voice coming from the driver to the guard, who wasn't for letting the Rolls on to the quayside. All credit to him, Flynn thought, that he stuck to his guns and did not allow it through. He could hear the driver obviously cursing in a language he did not understand, but still the Rolls had to reverse away and be driven into the crowded car park opposite the commercial centre where, much to Flynn's satisfaction, he heard a metallic scraping noise as it was manoeuvred into a space just a bit too tight for it to slot in comfortably.

Flynn continued to watch, with the peak of his sun-bleached baseball cap pulled down over his eyes. Its once deep red colour had now faded to a dirty pink.

Four people squeezed out of the Rolls.

And one of them was Adam Castle – who,

ironically, did own a vehicle with the necessary authorization to drive on to the quayside.

Flynn slowly placed his mug down and his heart started to beat just a little bit more quickly, but not because of the grease-laden meal he'd just devoured. Because this was his first glimpse of the wolf pack surrounding their prey.

Even then, in those first few moments, he made them: identified their roles and, with perhaps just a gut feeling at that time (to be confirmed later), knew that Adam Castle was in deep trouble.

A tiny facial tic made his upper lip twitch.

Then he sat back and finished his coffee with one gulp, stood up, left cash on the table and sauntered down to ground level, keeping his distance from the four people while trying to get a better measure of the situation – who was who, what was what – as they made their way around the marina towards *Faye*.

He was certain of one thing: they were not businessmen, at least not in the civilized sense of the word.

Castle seemed to be trying to impress the alpha male of the pack, talking volubly, expressing himself with big hand gestures. Flynn could not hear what was being said, though. Castle and the leader were walking ahead of the other two pack members, who actually loped like body-building werewolves, their heads lolling from side to side, always checking around themselves like the bodyguards Flynn suspected they were. One turned, spotted him, tapped his companion on the shoulder, said something – a warning, possibly – and he also turned and glared.

11

Flynn kept walking, paying no heed to their attention, but still scrutinized them from under the ragged peak of his cap.

He really did not like what he saw.

Adam Castle obviously dealt with lots of different types of people in his lines of business. He ran two pubs, two nightclubs, a travel agency, a jeep safari business and the fishing boat, all on Gran Canaria. These interests were pretty much replicated on Lanzarote and Tenerife. This meant his clientele and associates were diverse, from rogues to straight-ahead businessmen, but Flynn knew him as a pretty canny guy, streetwise (as anyone running nightclubs had to be); throughout the recession he had kept his head just above water and, as far as Flynn knew, was once again thriving after a few shaky years.

But the men he was with that morning were different from the usual crop.

They walked with the cocky roll of people not strangers to violence, who welcomed it, revelled in it . . . lived and died by it. It emanated from their pores. Flynn knew the type.

The two younger guys slowed their pace purposely to allow Flynn to draw level with them, which he did, nodding affably as though they were his next door neighbours and at the same time getting a good close-up of their features and physiques.

Both were very obviously into weight training. They had small bullet heads sitting on thick necks and unnaturally broad shoulders narrowing to slender waists, but thighs like ham hocks. Both wore tight T-shirts and carried jackets, and their skin was covered in tattoos, swirls and symbols which meant nothing to Flynn. They eyed him through tiny, beady eyes as he strolled past. He noticed that one of them had something heavy in the pocket of his jacket.

Then he was alongside Castle and the older man, the leader.

'Adam,' he said, greeting his business partner and friend.

'Hey, Steve, didn't notice you sneaking up behind,' Castle said, his bonhomie somewhat forced. The three of them stopped at the water's edge and Castle turned to the other man. 'Can I introduce Steve Flynn? He's the co-owner of *Faye*.' He looked at Flynn and said, 'Steve, this is Aleksander Bashkim.'

Flynn nodded, staying affable.

'Mr Flynn, I've heard a lot about you.' Bashkim looked down his nose and held out his hand. With reluctance Flynn shook it, finding the palm large and smooth, but the back of it thickly hairy. It gave him an extra moment to weigh up this man, who, Flynn knew, was doing the same in the opposite direction: he too was being assessed.

Bashkim was as tall and wide as Flynn, but nowhere near as misshapen as the two younger men, who were probably on steroids. He was a good ten years older and dressed casually but well, his head closely shaved; Flynn could see the greyness of his hair at the temples and he almost wilted under the intense scrutiny of Bashkim's penetrating, laser-like eyes, set close together like a sniper's. They were the eyes of a predator, someone with the extremely good hand-to-eye coordination that was necessary to gain just that slight advantage over others. He was a man to be wary of, to avoid if at all possible, Flynn thought. His face was gaunt and angular but strikingly handsome, and the roguish effect was enhanced by the two scars on his jawline on the right side of his face – knife slashes from many years before.

Bashkim smiled – a smile designed to charm – at Flynn's appraisal of him.

'Well, Mr Flynn – what do you see?'

He smiled back. 'A wolf.'

'Yes, yes, yes,' Bashkim said appreciatively. 'You are a good judge of character. Adam tells me you were once a Royal Marine, then a policeman.'

'Both a long time ago.'

'But still,' Bashkim said with a little gesture – the splaying of his fingers; Flynn noticed that his left little finger had been snipped off at the knuckle. 'And now the best sportfishing captain on the islands?'

'On a good day, when the fish throw themselves at me.'

By the time this brief exchange and weighing up had taken place – so little said, so much learned – the two younger men had drawn up, making a very friendly-looking group.

'Allow me to introduce my sons,' Bashkim said. Flynn had noticed the Eastern European accent, maybe Russian, he thought, but could not have said for certain because he was no expert, even though since moving to the Canaries he had heard many accents. He assumed he would learn where these dangerous-looking men came from

14

in due course. He angled slightly to look at the fruit of Bashkim's loins. Both were in their early twenties and were taller and (probably due to their body building) also much wider than Flynn, which was saying something. He was six-two and years of hauling in fish heavier than men had kept all of his muscles naturally big without recourse to drugs. The sons did not smile at him, despite his pleasant grin of acknowledgement. Like their father, Flynn suspected, they had already pegged him. 'Pavli and Dardan.'

'Nice to meet you guys,' he said, keeping friendly, deciding that the best course of action, until he knew what exactly was going on, was to be charming and gracious to this trio. He guessed this was likely to be an attitude that would be tested to the extreme if he was around them for any length of time.

They had their father's eyes, which pierced into Flynn's skull, but he just acted all innocent and smiled boyishly.

'Pavli means Paul in your language,' Bashkim explained. 'And Dardan is from the name Dardani, a proud tribe who once lived on the Balkan Peninsula.'

'So what is your language?' Flynn asked, though he had started to narrow down the field.

'Albanian,' Bashkim said.

Internally, Flynn said, Oh shit.

Aloud, and hoping he wasn't speaking with a tremor in his voice, he said, 'Well, gentlemen, it is a pleasure to meet you. I'm assuming' – and here he glanced at Castle – 'that you're here for a few hours of fishing.'

15

Castle nodded. 'If you don't mind us commandeering *Faye*.'

'No, no problem . . . no customers today,' Flynn lied.

'You do not need to worry, we will pay,' Bashkim said, pronouncing his Ws as Vs, though not outrageously so. 'And if we catch anything, there will be a bonus in it for you.'

'And my crew?'

Bashkim nodded. 'And your crew.'

'Then let's go.'

He went ahead of them up the quayside, frowning at Karen as he approached the booking office and mouthing, 'What the fuck?' He turned left and hopped aboard *Faye*, saying to Jose, 'Let's get ready to roll.'

Jose had watched the party walk along the quay. He said, 'I don't like the look of them,' and spat something horrible over the side, scowling.

'Treat 'em nice, could be a good payday,' Flynn advised.

'Or a bad one,' he said, with an uncanny ability to see into the future.

Jose was a black-skinned barrel of muscles. He had been with Flynn over six years and was almost his equal when it came to catching fish, but was definitely on a par with him when it came to judging others.

Neither one of them needed a sixth sense to know that this party was very bad news.

Ten minutes later Flynn was steering *Faye* out of Puerto Rico. He was at the wheel and Jose was keeping himself busy preparing outriggers and bait and doing his best to avoid the party.

Castle and Bashkim were in deep conversation on the rear deck, both men moving easily with the roll of the boat on the swells. It was a conversation that made Flynn uneasy, even though he could not hear a word of it.

The sons were slouching in the air-conditioned cabin. Flynn took occasional peeks down the companionway at them, grinning to himself to see that Dardan had gone a pale shade of green and was not enjoying the ride, which did not bode well for him in the coming hours.

Jose had also noticed this.

'The proud tribesman of the Balkans looks peaky,' Flynn said to him in a stage whisper.

'Sick as dog,' grunted Jose.

'Aye,' Flynn said, and concentrated on aiming *Faye*'s bows over as many whitecaps as possible in the hope of debilitating both brothers, thinking that having them out of action and honking up for the duration, or maybe demanding a quick return to shore, would be good options for this trip. But Pavli looked fine as he rummaged through the fridge and pulled out a bottle of chilled lager. Seasickness did not seem to run in the family. 'Let's fish,' Flynn told Jose, and the Spaniard began to feed out the bait lines.

'What will we catch?'

Flynn glanced over his shoulder and shrugged at the question posed by Bashkim, who had left Castle sitting in the fighting chair, staring backwards.

'Blue marlin are still running. We've had some good catches over the last month, and a few super-large bigeye tuna . . . good chance of either.'

17

'I hope so.'

'Maybe you should sit ready in the fighting chair.'

'I think I will.'

Then Jose screamed, 'Boss – fish!'

Flynn craned his neck, peering through the bright glare reflecting off the ocean like silver mist, and instantly caught sight of the object of Jose's excitement. A single blue marlin ranging the surface, the ocean wanderer, slicing like a scimitar through the swell, maybe 200 metres from the back of the boat.

Flynn's stomach did its usual backflip because he never wearied of this 'laying of eyes', as they called it in almost religious terms on this boat. With an Atlantic record of over 600 kg (and the only way of catching this marvellous beast was by fast-trolling baits to it), it was a great adrenalin rush.

'Where?' Bashkim demanded, shading his eyes.

'There,' Flynn said as the fish reappeared like a surfer emerging from a wave. Bashkim saw the fish and yelled enthusiastically. He rushed to the fighting chair, now vacated by Castle, and Jose harnessed him into it. Bashkim's voice was almost lost on the wind, but Flynn clearly heard him promise a bonus of 1,000 euros each if he managed to get into the fish.

Flynn hurtled up the ladder into the flying bridge, the permanent raised steering platform over the bridge itself which gave Flynn a better all-round view of everything, including the trolling baits and, of course, fish. Jose began to deal with the rod and feed out the bait – a hook threaded with Spanish mackerel that moved in the water like a living creature in the hope of enticing the fish – and the trolling began. Flynn put to use all his years of experience and instinct to position the boat and bait in exactly the right place to coax him to lunge and bite. His heart pounded with exhilaration.

This, he thought, was one great way to make a living.

Attracted by the commotion, the two sons emerged from below to see what was happening. Pavli stayed up but Dardan soon rushed down below and threw himself back on to the sofa, moaning.

Jose and Flynn worked hard for Bashkim, their relationship having fused into a team that could communicate through thought alone.

Flynn teased the fish.

Then it struck.

There was a scream of the heavy line from the PENN International reel as the fish dived. Bashkim, under Jose's instruction, hauled back to embed the forged steel hook into the fish's mouth, then – under Flynn's shouted instructions, too – he began to play the monster.

And all credit to him, he kept with it, the sweat pouring from him. The marlin leapt spectacularly half a dozen times as it tried desperately to shake the hook free, until three-quarters of an hour later Bashkim, exhausted, had won. Under more careful instruction (because this is one of the most delicate times, when an angler, thinking he or she has done everything necessary, relaxes for an instant, the fish takes advantage of this and suddenly – no fish), Bashkim brought the fish to the side of the boat. Flynn, timing it to perfection, caught it by its dangerous beak.

Flynn took the usual photographs with the digital camera, then with Jose's assistance tagged and released it before turning back to Bashkim who, standing there with his hands on his hips, looked like a man who had just beaten a lion into submission.

'Well done,' Flynn congratulated him genuinely.

'Thank you,' he said, pronouncing it *Zank yous*.

'Six hundred and ten kilos is my estimate . . . best fish of the season, no lie.'

'Now I want catch one,' Pavli demanded.

Flynn gave him his best crooked grin. 'I'll do my best.'

Flynn's best was not good enough. As so often happens, there was neither sight nor sign of any other fish that day. Even some bottom fishing in the hope of bringing up a thornback ray was a dismal failure. The atmosphere on board became increasingly tense, but Flynn could not give a damn because that was how it went sometimes. The fish of the season followed by zilch. He was getting weary of Pavli's childish petulance and was glad when it was time to head home and Jose started to wind in the lines, clean and stack the tackle.

About four miles out of Puerto Rico, *Faye* was joined by a school of bottle-nosed dolphin, probably about a dozen of the magnificent creatures, giving everyone on board a view of one of nature's spectacles, one of which Flynn never tired.

Pavli edged down the side of the boat, went to the bow, sat with his legs dangling either side of a stanchion.

Flynn assumed it was in order to get a better view of the dolphins, which swam right alongside the boat giving an intimate, playful display.

That was until he saw the gun in Pavli's right hand – a semi-automatic pistol of some sort – and he realized what the heavy 'thing' was he had spotted earlier on the quayside. He was using the rail to steady his forearm and aim at the dolphins.

He fired. Missed. Fired again.

Flynn did not know whether he missed the second time because by then he had slammed *Faye*'s engine into neutral, had left the cockpit and was scrambling along the side of the boat towards Pavli, who fired another round at the dolphins.

Flynn was behind him before he could fire a fourth time. He wrestled the gun from him and hurled it into the sea.

'Just what fuck you think you are doing?'

Pavli, still seated, jerked his elbow up into Flynn's groin. He saw it coming and doubled back, grabbed the thick wrist and twisted Pavli's arm into an unnatural angle, just about resisting the temptation to tear his shoulder out of its ball joint. Flynn hauled him back from the edge, realizing just how muscled and powerful Pavli's arms were as the Albanian, having recovered from the initial shock of the intervention, slowly, inexorably eased his arm out of Flynn's grip. It was like trying to hold on to a python.

Flynn was strong but here, in the short term, Pavli was the stronger man – and, judging by the

21

triumphant look on his face, knew it. Bit by bit his arm came free, finally flipping out of Flynn's fingers. Pavli scrambled to his feet and both were then facing each other on the foredeck, having adopted wrestlers' stances.

If *Faye* had rolled at that moment, both of them could have been somersaulted over the rails into the cold sea.

Pavli wiped his rubbery lips with the back of his hand.

'I'm going to kill you for touching me,' he said.

Flynn believed him. At least he believed he would try.

The boat did roll because there was no power to steady her. Pavli was taken by surprise. He lost his balance slightly and staggered, his thick arms flapping to compensate for the movement, and his head reared back. That was the moment Flynn struck.

He drove his right fist hard into Pavli's exposed throat, just above the Adam's apple. It was a good, well-delivered jab. Pavli clutched his throat and sank to his knees, making a horrible gagging sound.

'Mr Flynn, back away.'

Flynn stopped himself, which was a great effort because of his rage. He was about to kick Pavli as hard as he could in the testicles – if the steroids hadn't shrunk them to the size of frozen peas. It was his intention to drive them right up into his throat so that while his hands were massaging his windpipe he could also rub his balls better.

He turned at the voice.

Bashkim was behind him on the foredeck. He

22

too had a gun in his hand – a Makarov, Flynn guessed, this time – and it was pointed squarely, unwaveringly at Flynn's body mass in spite of the roll of the boat. Bashkim was steady, confident and balanced.

Behind him, wearing a horrified expression, was Adam Castle and behind him was Dardan. Jose brought up the rear.

Flynn eyed them all, running fast through the conjecture he'd mulled over, how they were the human equivalent of a wolf pack, and it was at that moment he said to Castle, 'What the hell are you doing with this lot?'

'He was taking pot shots at dolphins,' Flynn protested vehemently. Just Flynn and Castle were in the cabin. All the others were on deck. Jose was up in the flying bridge, steering *Faye* from there. 'He brought a gun on board, as did daddy Bashkim.'

'And you didn't?' Castle countered weakly.

'That is not the argument and you know it,' Flynn bristled. He once did have a gun hidden on board, a hunting rifle, but it wasn't for shooting dolphin – it was for shooting pirates.

'Did he actually shoot one?' Castle demanded.

'Y'know, I don't know and I don't care . . . and I say again, Adam – what the hell are you doing with that bunch of gangsters, because I'll bet my share of this boat that is what they are. Albanian at that. The worst sort . . . dangerous, *dangerous* men.'

'I know what they are,' Castle gulped.

Flynn made a 'Tell me' gesture by waggling his fingertips.

Castle shook his head. 'You don't need to know.'

'Right, OK,' Flynn said, flabbergasted and struggling to find the words. 'Let's just get back to Puerto Rico, get this lot off the boat and leave it at that. You may be involved with them somehow, though fuck knows why, but I'm not. I do not ever want to see them anywhere near *Faye* again.' He leaned meaningfully towards Castle and drove home his point with a jab of his finger. 'You get that?'

Flynn drew back then, puzzled by Castle's sheepish reaction – the eye avoidance.

'What?' he asked suspiciously.

'You will be seeing them again,' he whispered.

'You'd better run that one by me.'

'I'm selling my share of *Faye* to them.'

Two

Flynn pounded off his fury on the bubbling hot streets. He ran across the cliff-hugging pathway to Amadores Beach, past the Punta de la Hondura, then returned via the punishing steep slope to the rear of Puerto Rico before dropping back into the resort by way of the snaking road from the Europa Centre until he was on the Playa de Puerto Rico, the manmade beach built with Saharan sand adjacent to the marina.

At the water's edge he kicked off his ragged trainers – he hadn't bought a new pair in years

– divested himself of his running gear, top and shorts, under which he was wearing swim shorts (not Speedos). He plunged into the warm water of the bay and swam hard crawl back and forth, parallel with the breakwater, for twenty minutes until he felt as though his arms would drop off.

Afterwards he lay in the tide line to get his breath back, allowing the surf to massage him gently, and revelled in the declining heat of the day. He was bronzed to perfection but took great care of his skin and this was the only time of day, around the five p.m. mark, that he ever did any sunbathing at all. He had never lain out in the midday sun and had turned the colour he was simply because he lived in this climate and worked outdoors. He never purposely set out to get a tan; it was just a bi-product of the life.

The life he liked.

Reluctantly dragging himself out of the water, he bundled up his belongings and padded barefoot and dripping up into the town park right behind the beach. On the outer edge of the park, with the Doreste y Molina running right behind it, was the semi-detached villa, in a row of similar properties, in which he lived – for the time being. It belonged to one of his regular clients, a rich German guy, who Flynn knew would not be back on the island until next year. Flynn had permission to use the villa and had done so, on and off, for a few years now. The owner was just glad someone trustworthy was keeping an eye on the place in his absence. Although Flynn had been virtually living with Karen in her apartment further up the resort, he still kept the majority of his gear in the villa simply because there wasn't much space at Karen's.

At least that is what he told himself.

Now he was beginning to wonder if, subconsciously, he had kept this little pied-à-terre against the event of things turning sour between him and Karen.

As they had.

Now he wished he had moved everything he owned into her place. That would have made it much harder to move out, rather than just chucking a few bits and pieces into his old kit bag.

He pummelled himself mentally. Had he gone into the relationship with the expectation of failure?

What was it? he thought. A self-fulfilling prophecy?

Expect the worst and, lo and behold, look what happened.

Letting himself into the raffia-screened garden, he stopped sharply when he saw that Karen was stretched out on a sun lounger on the tiny terrace. He could tell she wasn't on a romantic mission because she was still in her work gear – shorts, T-shirt – and her bag was on the ground next to her. Also the villa doors weren't open. She had a key but now she obviously did not feel comfortable enough to let herself in any more.

Flynn surprised himself by recognizing the signs. Clearly he had now become a soft-arse, an old romantic; not the hard-edged guy he used to be. This woman had chipped away at that veneer and now, after tearing out his heart, was doing a runner.

She sat up. Her eyes quickly crossed Flynn's dripping, brown body, before she pulled her

26

sunglasses down from her forehead – another sign Flynn picked up on. Because he was now unable to look directly into her eyes, he would be unable to weaken any resolve she might have had. His well-practised deep meaningful look, he kidded himself, could melt the heart of any female.

But not this one. She had come with a ring of steel around her heart.

He closed the gate slowly behind him. 'Karen,' he said.

'Steve.' Her lips were pursed tight, nothing sensuous about them.

'What can I do for you?'

'I thought we should talk.'

Flynn's wrath began to boil over instantly. 'I just want to point out that you were the one who said I should take a chance on "lurv",' – and here he made air speech marks by tweaking his fingers on *that* word, which he also said as cynically as possible. 'And I did – and now you've pulled the plug on it, Karen, not me. So thanks a bunch.'

'Steve,' she whined.

'Nah.' He shook his head, finding it difficult to speak any more. He began to withdraw back into his shell, like a fisherman hauling in trawl nets, and put up the shutters around his feelings. 'If it's done, it's done. I don't want a post-mortem. I wasn't enough for you.' He shrugged. 'I get it and so be it. You're going back to the UK in a couple of weeks, so let's just be as polite as we can to each other in the circumstances.'

He almost blurted the word 'bitch', but refrained – because she wasn't, and he would have regretted that single syllable for as long as he lived.

27

'If that's how you . . .' she started to say as she pushed herself up from the sun lounger.

He felt a tinge of shame that he wanted to get hold of her and give her a good shake. He would never have done anything like that, nor condone anyone who did, but he was pretty bloody angry.

'No,' he said, grinding his teeth. 'That's how you want it.'

She scooped up her bag, slapped her sun hat on and stalked across the small garden past him, the tension in her body very evident from the stilted way she moved.

It was all he could do not to call her back and plead. Instead he said, 'And tell your brother that if he thinks he's selling me into fucking slavery, he can think again.'

She stopped at the gate. 'You don't know the half of it, Steve,' she said, then was gone.

He watched her turn towards the town before slamming the gate shut – inasmuch as a gate made of raffia can be slammed – and then went into the villa. He poured himself – and drank in one – a shot of Talisker whisky before heading for the shower, where he stood under the hot jets, head bowed, letting the water power away the sea salt and sweat. He emerged feeling fresh, as though he had stepped through a portal of some sort. In the bedroom he rummaged through a stack of old, clean clothing and found exactly what he was searching for. Karen had weaned him out of his usual rags into nice shirts, shorts and loafers, but as he pulled on his very worn and torn Keith Richards T-shirt – still showing faint bloodstains from a previous 'encounter'

28

– and baggy three-quarter length cargo pants, a transformation of sorts was starting to take place. He regarded himself in the full length mirror on the wall.

It was getting back to how Steve Flynn should look; and with this reversal, his old attitude also seemed to slot back into place. He knew exactly what his plans were for the night ahead – and they included drinks and ladies.

These plans were almost instantly scuppered, however, as he set foot in the living room and saw who was sitting there, waiting for him.

They lounged indolently as if they owned the place, sneering, challenging expressions on their faces.

Flynn stopped at the living room door and took in the very dangerous-looking pair that was Pavli and Dardan Bashkim, one sitting on the armchair, the other on the settee.

'So,' Pavli said. His voice croaked harshly as if an emery board had got stuck in his windpipe – much to Flynn's satisfaction: his knuckles had had their desired effect and Pavli's right hand was continually kneading his throat. Flynn's only regret was that he hadn't been able to kick his testicles up into it. Pavli continued, 'A cop and a Royal Marine.'

'Like I said, a long time ago.'

And that was no lie. Time had galloped by.

He stepped into the room, seeing for the first time that Dardan, the brother on the chair, was holding a semi-automatic pistol in his right hand. It dangled loosely in his grip down the side of the piece of furniture. He saw that Flynn had clocked the firearm, so brought it up into plain sight and, probably just to prove a point of manliness, he cocked the gun while keeping his piggy eyes firmly focused on Flynn. The gun looked like the one his father had brandished on the boat, but Flynn wasn't certain.

'You come to kill me – bit extreme, isn't it?' Flynn asked. His voice was steady, though at the same time he would readily have admitted to anyone that he was scared. He wasn't going to let that fear show to these guys. Already he had begun to calculate angles, distances, times, speeds, abilities and, of course, the odds. Dardan would have to be the first one down if it came to it because he had the gun, but Flynn thought that Pavli was actually the more dangerous of the pair, armed or otherwise. Flynn cursed the whisky he'd just had, knowing that any alcohol, no matter how small the amount, would slow him down. His only hope was that, slow as he might be, these two great lumbering body builders were even slower, physically and mentally.

He raised his eyebrows, always willing to try a charm offensive first, rather than a violent one.

'Maybe,' Pavli answered.

Flynn looked pointedly at him.

'Our problem is,' Dardan said, resting the pistol on the chair arm, 'our father is going to need you, once he owns half of your boat.'

'He won't own half,' Flynn corrected him.

'No, you are correct, he will own fifty-one per cent, because you will sign over two per cent of your holdings in order that he has a controlling interest.'

'And how much does he intend to pay for that two per cent? Because I can assure you, he won't be able to afford it.'

Pavli shrugged his huge shoulders. 'He will pay nothing . . . you'll be making a gesture . . . all legal and above board, obviously.'

'I don't think so.' Flynn shook his head, his eyes scanning one brother, then the other, and back again. Dardan saw him weighing them up and moved the pistol from its resting place into a new position, holding it between his monstrously muscled thighs and pointing it generally at the centre of Flynn's body mass.

Two metres away, a distance Flynn could cover in the blink of an eye, but not necessarily before Dardan could jerk the trigger back and send a nine mm slug flying across the room. Flynn shifted uncomfortably, then gave a tiny shrug. 'I probably need to discuss this with daddy, then, don't I? Not his puppies.'

Pavli's face reacted to the insult. He did not like it. He moved fast, but to reach Flynn he had to launch himself across Dardan's line of fire. Flynn did not expect the immediate assault, but instantaneously saw the split-second advantage it gave him.

As Pavli rose from the settee with his arms extended, Flynn did a little sidestep and at the same time pivoted his torso like a matador and drove the point of his left elbow hard and accurately into Pavli's face, just on the lip below his nose. As the bone connected, he jerked his elbow up at a slight angle, dislodging Pavli's septum and separating it from his top lip. Flynn knew

31

he had to be careful because, though it would have given him intense pleasure, he did not really want to drive the shard-shaped piece of gristle up into the front lobe of what little brain Pavli had. He did not want him dead on the tiled floor, so all he did was break Pavli's nose and knock him senseless for a few precious seconds.

Unsighted by the blur of movement and bodies, Dardan half-rose from the chair, trying to aim at Flynn and miss his brother.

Flynn swirled round and caught Pavli's head, holding it like a medicine ball, twisting it so it hurt him, then with a surge of power he ran him backwards into Dardan, which must have been like having a rhino charge backwards into him. He went with Pavli, then released his head to one side and knocked Dardan's gun sideways with his right forearm and tried to grab his wrist at the same time as he smashed his left fist into the side of Dardan's surprised face.

But Dardan managed to rear back, avoid the punch and keep hold of the gun – so Flynn did not have much success with any of his efforts.

As Pavli staggered away clutching his face, which spouted bright red blood between his fingers, Dardan and Flynn were virtually face to face, with Flynn desperately trying to keep a grip on Dardan's wrist, like a couple with very bad timing trying to learn a ballroom dance – a position that became much more intimate when Dardan slid his thick left arm around Flynn's neck like a python and started to squeeze as he drew Flynn closer and closer to him. At the same time Flynn felt his head start to tilt inexorably backwards as the grip tightened, his neck muscles screaming as they fought back, and Flynn knew he was trapped by someone far stronger than himself and without much wiggle room, because his left hand was trapped down between their torsos and his right was still doing its best to hold on to Dardan's left hand to keep the pistol pointing away.

Unless Flynn could manage to rotate his trapped arm and get his hand around Dardan's gentleman parts and rip them off.

It was like a macabre tango, but whereas sex was the driver for that dance, death was the driver for this one. It wasn't as though Flynn had ever danced a tango in his life, but he had been subjected to weekly doses of a popular ballroom dancing competition on TV on which all the contestants had, at some stage, to dance a tango. So he knew that legs were entwined, and this actually gave him the idea. Flynn wormed his left arm between himself and Dardan's lower belly and grabbed what turned out to be excessively tiny testicles. Their eyes met, Dardan's widening as he realized what was happening.

Flynn squeezed with all his might and at the same time turned his wrist as if he was tightening a stopcock, then yanked downwards as if he was pulling a toilet chain, and also forced his lower leg around Dardan's calf muscle, jerked back and drove the top half of his body into him to knock the Albanian off balance.

He screamed as Flynn crushed his delicate organs, then tried to writhe out of the grip. He let go of Flynn's neck and fell back, but Flynn was still concerned about where the gun might end up pointing. He took advantage of the pain shooting up through Dardan's groin, let go of his wrist and grabbed the barrel of the gun instead. At the same time he released the balls, jerked his left arm free, pushed Dardan away from him and, with a flip of the right wrist, managed to tear the gun out of his hand.

He was free and he had the gun.

Dardan doubled over clutching his balls and sagged to his knees, hissing like steam escaping from a boiler.

Flynn spun the gun into the palm of his hand and backed away from the brothers.

Pavli was still on his hands and knees, his head between his arms, trying to stem the blood pulsing out of his nose.

Dardan was just on his knees, his face purple as he cupped his testicles, grimacing in agony. He still managed to stare malevolently at Flynn, who caught his breath, letting the gun rest on his outer thigh . . . but then, as much as he tried to resist, he could not hold himself back from delivering a double *coup de grâce*.

He booted Pavli between his legs, sending him sprawling across the tiled floor. In the same movement he side-swiped the pistol across Dardan's face, knocking him sideways. Then he stood back and surveyed the pitiful tableau.

'Time to go, boys.'

Flynn was furious he had to change his clothes again. His T-shirt and three-quarters had been splattered with blood from both Bashkim brothers. Now he was wearing an even older pair of

34

three-quarters and a very ragged T-shirt he had bought on a trip to Florida just because it had a picture of a marlin on it.

Once he had swilled the blood off the tiled floor of the villa and ensured he had locked up properly, he sauntered down to one of the restaurants lining the back of the beach. He found a table in the sand and ordered a blind paella and a large Cruzcampo beer because both his thirst and hunger were fierce. While waiting for the paella he drank the lager, ordered another, and munched thoughtfully on a couple of portions of tapas – a dish of Canarian potatoes and a bowl of olives – and considered his predicament.

Double-dumped, he thought.

By his girlfriend and his business partner, who happened to be his girlfriend's brother. He assumed the dumpings were unconnected.

He felt he was innocent of charges on both counts.

He sighed heavily and sat back in the deeply cushioned cane chair and raised his face to the sky, still enjoying the heat of the early evening, wondering if the events of the day had been designed to tell him something – that maybe it was time to move on.

A few years ago it would have been easier to do. Then, emerging from a dark place that was his ignominious exit from Lancashire Constabulary – a process of grieving, guilt or something that had taken him several years to get through – he hadn't got much in the way of clothing, savings or material things. He did not have a property or a share in one (having handed his house in

Blackpool over to his ex-wife) and always crashed out in other people's places. He lived out of bags and relied on his income from skippering the boat – money that was unpredictable, varying from non-existent to rolling in cash. That was how he had liked it. He had been a cop for twenty years so was due a pension, but wouldn't be able to touch it until he was fifty-five, which, he thought thankfully, was some years away yet.

About that time he had also just about recovered from losing the woman he had fallen in love with – Gill Hartland. She had died from injuries sustained from an assault because she had been unfortunate enough to be with Flynn when he was attacked by two merciless enforcers seeking to prise money from him which he did not have, nor ever had.

It had taken him a long time to get over Gill, and his murderous revenge in her name had not made his recovery any less painful.

He had slipped into a life of one night stands, or holiday flings, which suited him and, he hoped, the ladies concerned. He did not want to be emotionally connected to anyone.

That was the point at which he could have left the island, maybe returned to the UK, but then a change of mind made him realize this place had become his home, so he got his head down and, living tight, managed to save enough money to buy a controlling interest in *Faye*, the one darling in his life; then, falling in love with Karen had crept up on him. He thought he had been on the verge of settling down for good until she had yanked the carpet from under his feet.

36

So now he was back to where he had been, more or less. Not much money, few possessions – but still with fifty-one per cent of *Faye*, which he was not about to lose to some half-baked gangsters.

'And do you know what?' he asked the sky. He rocked forward on the chair as the waitress delivered the paella to his table in the sand.

'Sorry?' She smiled.

He grinned back. 'It feels good,' he answered his question to the stars.

He watched her sway curvaceously back to the bar, catching her eye as she glanced coyly over her shoulder. He gave her a little tinkling wave, then started to spoon out the rice and seafood from pan to plate. As he shovelled the first aromatic forkful into his mouth he decided he would simply enjoy himself that night and leave everything else until morning.

Tonight was for fun.

Three

He surfaced slowly from a swirling series of lurid dreams, visions of his own flesh and female skin and urgent, pounding sexual intercourse . . . and then blackness.

Although he knew he was awake he kept his eyes tightly closed because there was a ferocious headache crashing around the inside of his skull and behind his eyeballs. He tried to swallow but his mouth was completely dry, his tongue wedged into the cavity as though a dishcloth had been stuffed in.

Coming back to life was a very slow process until that very last moment when it became instantaneous as his brain clicked into gear and he realized the severity of the situation he was in.

His eyes shot open and he discovered he was handcuffed to the bed on which he lay. He was spread-eagled, naked, each wrist zip-tied to the iron bedhead, and his ankles were similarly tied to the foot board. It was also true that he had something very much like a dishcloth stuffed into his mouth – it wasn't his tongue as he had thought – and it was held in place by a strip of duct tape over his mouth.

He tried to shout and writhe against the zip-ties, but his voice was just a muffled sound and he was completely secured so that, despite his strength, he was pretty much unable to move.

He raised his head, looking desperately around the bedroom. It was in semi-darkness, curtains drawn, though he could see it was actually daylight outside.

His head flopped back on to the bed – no pillow, just a mattress – and he tried to piece together what had happened to him the night before when, after the paella, he had trudged up to the commercial centre and hit the bars and clubs.

He recalled everything – up to the point where he recalled nothing.

He had spent time in a couple of his favourite bars, mingling with a few people he knew – friends, former lovers – and it had been a good laugh after the stressful day he'd had.

After the bars, he gravitated to the Electron, one of the two nightclubs owned by Adam Castle in Puerto Rico. That had been fairly quiet with no sign of Adam or Karen. He chatted to the staff, including the doormen, but no one seemed to have any idea about anything concerning gangsters or Adam's business dealings.

About one a.m., having had his fill of beer, he moved on to Adam's other club, the Paris Nitro. This place was heaving with bodies, but still no sign of Adam or Karen or the Albanian goons. He recalled being slightly disturbed by the lack of Adam or Karen. Adam usually made his presence felt in the clubs, so his not being there was slightly unusual. But he shrugged his shoulders, edged his way through the ululating throng, ordered a double Glenlivet with a drop of water, no ice, and as he scanned the crowd from the bar, caught a woman's eye. She was standing just a little further along the bar.

She was mid-to-late-thirties with a nice angular face, blonde hair trimmed in a bob and very nice lips. She sidled up to him without any encouragement, touched his arm and said, 'You seem to be alone.'

'Not now,' he responded with meaning, very encouraged by his alcohol intake. At that point he had probably drunk way in excess of his usual night out amount, which was a couple of pints and a couple of chasers. He tried to drink as little as possible mostly because Puerto Rico is one of those places where it is very easy to become an alcoholic.

The woman smiled coolly, calculatingly at him,

then the two of them swirled over to the tightly packed dance floor. Flynn began to gyrate in a way he believed to be über-cool, bringing a smile to her face which, fleetingly, Flynn thought was one of contempt.

A taxi took them to one of the numerous, samey, holiday apartment blocks clinging to the valley that made up the resort of Puerto Rico. They stumbled drunkenly through the front door of her apartment, tearing off what little clothing they wore to start with. Flynn lifted her into his arms and carried her easily through to the bedroom, where they unleashed themselves on each other.

The last thing Flynn recalled was sitting propped up on the pillows, sipping a cocktail she had mixed for him while he watched her head bob up and down slowly further down his body. His second coming was the last thing he actually remembered.

He tugged at the zip-ties which dug into his flesh. Only now did he realize he had been led into a trap and he fully expected the two Albanian mafia brothers, Pavli and Dardan, to appear at the bedroom door and wreak havoc with him for kicking their backsides out of his villa and hurling their dismantled gun after them.

It had been all too easy: the seductive look, the pick-up, piling into the taxi and the sex. And now here he was about to face the consequences of not keeping his guard up.

A brutal death at the hands of two murderous gangsters.

He gave up struggling. His head flopped back and he awaited his fate.

'Hi, Steve – that's your name, isn't it?'

His head jolted back up.

The woman he had picked up in the club was leaning against the bedroom door frame, a half-smile playing on her lips. She was completely naked, unashamedly so, and was holding something in her hand: Flynn's debit card. 'Stephen J. Flynn, it says here.'

He attempted to reply, but could only manage a muted sound. She smiled, flicked the card across the room and walked over to him. She eased herself over him, straddling him, looking down at him still with that smug, condescending smile on her face. She leaned over and placed a fingertip on the tape covering his mouth.

'No one can hear you,' she whispered.

Flynn breathed through his nostrils.

'Puzzled?' she asked.

He glared at her.

'You want to talk? Nod if you do.'

He nodded.

'I'm going to slowly strip back this tape, Steve, but if you speak to me in anything other than a nice whisper, I'll just refit it, OK?'

He nodded, watching her.

She inserted a fingernail between the corner of the tape and his skin and drew it back slowly and painfully, then left it hanging as if on a hinge. She pulled the J-cloth out of his mouth and dropped it on the pillow. Flynn gulped air down greedily.

'Where are they?' he demanded.

She sat upright, arching her back and displaying her breasts for him. He did remember them. 'Where are who?'

41

'The brothers Grimm.'

She frowned, mystified. 'I don't know who you mean.'

'Yeah, course you don't. Why am I here, then?'

An evil gleam came into her eyes. 'Because I despise a man who thinks he can look at a woman in a pub or club, talk glibly to her and then expect to sleep with her. I despise men like you.'

Flynn blinked, easily detecting the madness in that gleam and wondering what 'glibly' meant. 'I think you'll find it was a two way street.'

'You arrogant piece of shit,' she sneered.

'OK, OK, you've made your point . . . time to let me go,' he suggested reasonably. 'I won't do it again.'

'Promise?'

'Promise.'

'You must think I'm an idiot.'

'I'm not sure what to think. I'm just a confused man tied to a bed.'

'You think I'm a bunny boiler?'

'No, no way,' he said hopefully, gently tensing his arm muscles against the zip-ties.

'I'm not.'

'Good . . . look, I'm really sorry about what happened,' he began, feeling no need to apologize, but not stupid enough to maintain a point of view that could be detrimental to his health.

'No you're not,' she said.

She clambered off him, stood by the bedside for a moment, weighing him up with undertaker eyes.

'It is time to let me go,' Flynn said. 'Fun's over, whatever your name is.'

As soon as he'd said those last four words he wished he could rewind, swallow them back and never say them again.

A chilling expression came over her face. 'Exactly my point. You don't even know my name. You never bothered to ask.'

'Two way street,' he reiterated hopefully.

'I'll be back in a moment.' She flounced out of the bedroom. Flynn could hear her moving around in the lounge area, humming contentedly to herself.

His head was clearing now.

He pulled on the zip-ties and looked along his arms up to them. They were around his wrists and also around the vertical iron bars of the bed frame. Flynn tested them for strength again and thought there could be some possibility of bending the bars. When he heard her padding back from the other room he stopped moving instantly and waited for her to reappear.

She leaned in on the door frame, still naked.

'You telling me you didn't enjoy it?' Flynn posed to her.

'What, the sex?'

'Uh – yeah.'

'It was great,' she admitted.

'So your problem is what, exactly?'

'Everything else, Steve, everything else,' she said pityingly. She held up a felt tip pen and came over to the bed, her eyes weighing up his torso as she removed the pen lid and said, 'Indelible ink.'

'OK,' he drawled, confused.

'Now, let me see.' She placed the tip of her left forefinger in the centre of his chest, on his

43

sternum, then slid it across an inch to the right, leaned over and carefully drew the shape of a love-heart on his ribcage, just above where his heart was actually beating – *thumping* – in his chest. Then she drew a jagged, diagonal line across the heart and also a broken arrow through it. She stood back, checking if she was accurate, then smiled.

'Inasmuch as you have a heart, that should be just about where it can be found.'

He knew for sure he did have one, because it was pounding, fit to burst. His stomach suddenly cramped up and he winced.

'Icky tummy?' she asked.

'Rohypnol?' he guessed.

She nodded. Flynn knew one of the after-effects of Rohypnol, the date rape drug, was often an upset stomach (coupled with a fucked-up life). 'I thought you drugged people to have sex with them, not after you'd had sex with them?'

'Role reversal,' she said. She angled forward and drew two large delta shapes over his chest, representing where his lungs were situated. With his chin pressed into his neck, Flynn watched more artwork as she drew a map of the rest of his internal organs. Under the right side of his ribs she drew a triangular shape – the liver – which at that moment, because of his alcohol intake, felt like a brick inside him. Flynn was starting to look like one of those diagrams of a cow he remembered seeing when he was a kid going to a butcher's shop with his mother, showing the different cuts of meat, although in this case it was a map of his own internal organs.

44

She drew in his stomach and bladder, then carefully lifted his very shrunken penis upright, using her thumb and forefinger on his foreskin; once it was perpendicular, she drew a circle around its base, in his pubic hair. Then she let his cock drop back into place.

After this final piece of artistry she stood back to admire her work.

'You certainly know where things are,' he commended her.

'I should do,' she said. Flynn did not really want to know the reason why, but she told him anyway. 'You'll be the fifteenth.' She folded the duct tape back over his mouth.

She seemed to be in no particular hurry. She had her victim and he was going nowhere. Flynn got the impression she had to get herself in the right frame of mind before she did anything. She moved in and out of the bedroom, around the apartment, always naked. He heard a lot of clattering of cutlery in the kitchen as she rummaged through drawers, making cursing noises.

Eventually she came into the bedroom bearing what Flynn thought were items of clothing. When she unfolded them he saw the first thing was a white paper forensic suit. Then a skull cap and elasticated slippers.

'I have a slight problem,' she admitted.

Flynn watched her coldly, his eyes half-lidded.

'Tools of the trade.' She sighed irritably. 'This cheapo flat is so badly equipped . . . I need to nip out . . . half an hour tops . . . popping down to the shopping centre.'

'Don't rush back,' he mumbled under the duct tape.

'And don't you go anywhere.' She wagged a reproving finger at him, then gave him a tender smile and looked wistfully at his manhood, transferring the target of her finger to his penis. 'I'm so looking forward to slicing you off, little feller,' she informed it, then eyed Flynn again. 'One of those little things that mean so much.'

She spun and left the room. Flynn heard her moving around again, presumably getting dressed. A door slammed and there was silence.

Flynn strained his hearing, wondering if she had really gone or was just teasing him. If she had gone he knew he would not have long, depending on whether she had transport down to the centre or was on foot. The latter would give him a bit more time – it was about a ten minute walk, mainly down steps, ten minutes back and, say, ten minutes in the centre itself. That time could be halved if she had a car.

He looked up across his right shoulder, along his arm to his wrist bound to the bed frame by the zip-tie. Such fastenings were easy enough to get out of if both hands were tied together at the front. There was a fairly straightforward technique of breaking free, but it required the use of both arms. It was much more difficult with the hands separated and tied to what was essentially a vertical post. He pulled and realized there was no way of easing his hand out through the tie, so he twisted his wrist in an effort to bring the cable fastener to the front so that it lay across the soft inner part of his wrist. The weak point of zip-ties – as with any type of cable, wire or rope when used to bind people – was the knot, or the point where they were fastened. Knots could be worked loose, though the fastening of a zip-tie was pretty much immovable – but there was always a tiny degree of 'give' in them with time and effort.

Flynn did not have the time to stretch it, to work it loose.

The time he had available meant he had to break free in one instant.

With painful slowness, as the plastic cut into his skin, he managed to work the fastening to the front and found he was panting at the exertion.

He estimated four minutes had passed.

He was operating on a worst case scenario and calculated he might have ten minutes at most.

He tried to focus along his arm to the tie. He could see it was a heavy duty one of a similar type to those he often used for binding things on the boat. It consisted of a nylon tape with small teeth running all the way along it from one end and a ratchet on the other, through which the plastic cable was threaded; when the teeth of the tape aligned with the ratchet, the zip-tie locked. The tie could then be tightened even more as the tape was passed further through the ratchet.

Flynn tensed his wrist muscles, expanding them.

His problem was that because of his spread-eagled position on the bed he had very little momentum in any of his muscle groups. His deltoids and biceps were virtually locked in place, giving him virtually no leverage, which is what he needed.

47

Somehow he was going to have to compensate for this.

It was akin to hitting a golf ball with a driver – being asked to place the head of the club just behind the ball on the tee and hit the ball 200 metres down the fairway, but not being allowed to use a backswing.

In the minute space of movement that he had, he would have to magic up the same amount of power as if his arm had been free to move.

It did not help that his other hand and both feet were similarly tied.

He ensured the ratchet in the cable-tie was at the centre of his wrist.

He took some breaths to fill his body and bloodstream with oxygen.

Then he braced himself, closed his eyes, gritted his teeth, focused his mind and began a count-down in his head.

'Three . . . two . . .'

On 'one' he went for it. With a surge of strength backed up by the instinct for self-preservation, he tried to rip his hand free from the zip-tie.

It might have worked if the bed had been securely fastened to the wall, but instead of simply tearing his hand free he twisted the thin metal bar and the whole of the bed collapsed as the cheap bolts that fastened the headboard to the bed frame snapped. The top end of the bed crashed to the floor and Flynn found himself lying with the headboard on his head. His feet remained fastened to the bottom of the bed, which had stayed intact, and his left hand was still tied to the other side of the headboard.

48

Flynn swore, looking up through the bars of the headboard as if out of a prison cell, but at least he knew he had found another weakness, because the bars were not good quality but were made of tubular, pliable, soft metal and by working his wrist he started to bend the metal, even though the cable dug deep into his skin, drawing blood.

It was agonizing but he kept going, turning, twisting, bending, keeping at the metal until it finally broke and his arm came free.

'Eight minutes,' he said to himself as he contorted his right arm across his chest and, using his thumb to shimmy the teeth on the zip-tie holding his left wrist, easily released it. A few seconds later he was freeing his legs.

He found his clothes stashed in a carrier bag in the kitchen and dressed quickly, finding his phone and wallet in there. As he rose, he sensed a movement behind him.

It was the woman.

She turned and fled. Flynn went after her, tearing down the short hallway to the front door of the apartment through which she had shot, slamming it behind her. By the time he had opened it and stepped out on to the walkway, there was no sign of her.

Flynn rubbed his cut wrist, still panting. Then he raised his T-shirt and looked at the map she had drawn on his torso. At least his internal organs were still in place, and he knew exactly where they were now if he didn't before.

There were missed calls on his mobile phone, all from Karen, making him sneer. She hadn't seen fit to leave a voicemail message, so Flynn did not phone back. Instead, he set off down the steps of the valley, through the commercial centre, down through the town park and to his villa.

He half-expected to find it trashed by the two brothers, but it was intact, in exactly the same condition in which he had left it.

Ensuring that the doors and windows were locked, he stepped into the shower and stood under the hot jets, attempting to scrub the pen diagram off his front, but with only a modicum of success. It was indelible and would probably take a few washes to remove all traces. He cleaned his cut wrist and tried to recall everything about the night before, but it still remained a hazy blur of excess booze, stupid dancing, pounding music, great sex (he thought) and then, after the glass of pink champagne/Rohypnol cocktail, nothing. Until he awoke, apparently about to be butchered.

Unless the woman was having one big nasty practical joke at his expense, he could only be grateful that the apartment was so poorly kitted out in the cutlery department, otherwise the killer-lady would be feasting on his liver and cheap Canarian wine by now.

Whether or not it had all been a big joke, Flynn decided she would be having a very sober revisit from him in the near future if he could find her again.

She was not, however, at the top of his to-do list that morning.

He dried off, treated his wrist with antiseptic cream, dressed in even more scruffy attire and made his way down to the marina with his iPad, phone and charger. He had a few online enquiries to make.

Once more he found he was ravenous and went to his favourite breakfast time café on the first floor of the small commercial centre by the marina, the one from which he had witnessed the arrival of the wolf pack the previous morning.

He sat at a table overlooking the bay. Over on the far side of the marina he was pleased to see *Faye* was still moored and Jose was busying himself with various chores. Flynn knew the Spaniard would have been on the boat since six a.m. The booking kiosk was closed, the security panel in place, and there was no sign of Karen.

Flynn ordered a full English breakfast, plugged his phone into the charger and logged his iPad on to the free Wi-Fi provided by the café. He sent a couple of emails, then went on to a search engine to check on some things.

Results came in thick and fast.

He tabbed through various ones thoughtfully and one item caught his eye. A wicked smile came to his face and made him sit back and smirk.

His breakfast arrived, accompanied by a pot of strong filter coffee.

He ate and drank, thinking about what he had just found, then went back to his emails, getting a reply from one he'd just sent. He bunched his fist in a tiny gesture of triumph and replied immediately.

In the short term, he knew it was for the best.

After breakfast, he dawdled over the second

mug of coffee, paid up and made his way across the marina.

'You look like shit,' was Jose's truthful, but hurtful, appraisal of Flynn's appearance. 'And what fuckin' time you call this? Where you been?'

'Having breakfast.'

'Hey – I seen you having breakfast . . . I mean before that,' Jose said accusingly. He made a big show of inspecting his fake Rolex. He tapped it with a thick brown finger. 'We got a boat to run, you know?'

Flynn held himself back from the obvious flippant remark about being 'tied up' and just shrugged his shoulders. He was actually the boss and did not have to answer to Jose, but felt uncomfortable not doing so. Flynn was rarely late and liked to set a good example, usually beating Jose to work. He loved being on *Faye* at dawn with a coffee in hand – always a special time of day. Although, even if he hadn't ended up being tied to a bed, he would have been late anyway today by virtue of having drunk too much.

He looked at Jose, who did not yet know what Adam Castle had revealed the previous day about the sale to gangsters of his forty-nine per cent share in *Faye*. Jose had been working with Flynn for a long time. He was a good fisherman with a nose for big specimens and over the years he and Flynn had become good friends, particularly after the previous boat had exploded and a chunk of flying shrapnel had almost sliced the top off Jose's head. The resultant scars and medical work on Jose's bald dome of a cranium were still visible nearly five years on – though he did bear them like badges of rank now.

'And what has happened with those gangsters from yesterday?' Jose demanded, seemingly reading Flynn's mind. 'And don' tell me they weren't gangsters, 'cos I can tell these things. Guns is a good way of telling.'

Flynn's expression changed: awkward. Jose said, '*Qué?* What?'

'Adam wants to sell his share of the boat to them,' Flynn said bluntly.

'Shit,' Jose said, looking up at the sky. 'Why?'

'I don't know. Not got to the bottom of that yet.'

Jose leaned over the rail and spat into the water. 'What does that mean to us?'

Flynn knew what Jose was getting at. The boat was his life as much as Flynn's and he depended on it for his livelihood.

'I still have a controlling interest.'

Jose scowled at Flynn under the overhang of his dark bushy eyebrows that met in the middle. 'That does not always mean you have control,' he said intuitively.

'I'm aware of that,' Flynn replied, already imagining how unpleasant the future would be in bed with the Albanian mafia. Marginally less pleasant than being in bed with a female serial killer, he guessed.

'You need to speak to Adam. To stop this madness.'

'Aware of that, too.' Flynn held up a hand to halt what he predicted would be a tirade from Jose. 'I intend to see him later.' He glanced at the booking kiosk – still closed – then back at Jose. 'Have we anyone booked in for today?'

'No.'

Flynn nodded. 'In that case – first things first . . . is she fuelled up?'

Jose said, '*Sí.*' As if she wouldn't be.

Flynn reached into his pants pocket and pulled out his car keys, lobbed them over to Jose who caught them easily.

'You go and pick up the Nissan, then drive up to Puerto de la Aldea. I'm going to take this lass up there and leave her for a couple of days until I see what's really happening. I've just emailed the harbour master and he says that's OK. You meet me up there, bring me back, then I'll go see Adam.'

With yet another strong coffee in his hand, Flynn, sitting in the flying bridge, felt good to be nudging *Faye* out of her mooring, then out of the marina into the open sea where, basically, he turned right and sailed in a north-westerly direction. He followed the coast of the island, past Puerto de Mogán – the last decent-sized harbour on the stretch up to Aldea, which was a tiny harbour nestling under a mountainous cape on the western side of Gran Canaria.

The heat was starting to rise, but the wind in his face made him feel very much alive as he piloted *Faye*, ploughing her steadily through the swell, feeling her roll under him as she pushed on, revelling in the power surge from her engines; she was doing the job she was designed for, and loving it.

He kept fairly close to shore, able to see a series of almost inaccessible beaches and enjoying the view.

He took his time because he knew Jose would not be hurrying in the Nissan on the sixty kilometre journey from Puerto Rico, particularly since the road beyond Mogán was winding and bendy, and Jose was not the greatest of drivers.

With uncertainty simmering inside him, Jose had watched Flynn manoeuvre *Faye* out of the marina before turning and walking around it. He paused for a quick espresso, throwing it down his throat in one, then went to the villa.

Flynn's Nissan Patrol was parked at the back, tucked into a narrow driveway just long and wide enough for the vehicle to fit into, with just enough room for the driver to squeeze in and out. Jose opened the gate and climbed into the very battered old vehicle and reversed out on to the road, bringing all traffic on the Doreste y Molina to a horn-blasting halt.

With a middle-finger jerk at the other drivers, he set off out of town.

Flynn arrived in Aldea long before Jose. He found the harbour master, whom he knew quite well, and fully explained his plan to leave *Faye* in the tiny harbour for a few days. It was no problem, and after the appropriate number of euros had changed hands, Flynn strolled round to one of the fish restaurants on the promenade and found a table from which, if he craned his neck, he got a view of the GC-200, down which Jose would be coming at some stage in the near future.

He ordered coffee and a churro, sat and waited,

while his mind churned over all sorts of possibilities.

The diesel engine in the Nissan was sluggish at best. It was no mean machine but was great for driving tourists on safaris over Gran Canaria's rugged landscapes, which was mainly what Flynn used the vehicle for. He ran holiday makers up into the mountains on excursions for Adam Castle's jeep safari business when Castle's other cars were overbooked or one of the other drivers was sick. It was a marvellous vehicle for rough terrain and for bouncing tourists around to shrieks of delight. But it was not so great on the open road.

This lack of performance did not bother Jose. He enjoyed dawdling along, taking in views, none of which he ever tired of seeing. As he reached the very last part of his journey, the final drop towards Aldea nestling below, Jose was treated to the magnificent spectacle that was Mount Teide over the water in Tenerife. It was at its best that morning, completely cloudless, pin-sharp clear, the summit visible for probably a hundred miles in every direction. Once again, Jose found he was in awe of the great beauty of the Canary Islands, the place where he had been raised, then married.

The snow-capped mountain peak on the neighbouring island was the last thing Jose ever saw, the thought of his wife the last one ever in his mind.

Flynn had just checked his watch, thinking Jose should not be far away now. He glanced across at Mount Teide at the exact moment Jose did. Then the boom that blasted his ears was followed by the whomp of air that almost lifted him bodily out of the chair he was sitting on.

The waiter standing close to him had the tray balanced on his splayed-out hand flipped from his grip, and his apron blew up into his face.

Flynn jumped to his feet, staggering against the powerful gust of air now filled with grit and smoke.

A mushroom of dirty smoke rose in a cloud from a point on the main road, about a kilometre from Flynn.

And he knew. *He just knew.*

Four

Flynn stood by the roadside staring with numb horror at the devastation that was the remains of his vehicle and of the man who had become a great, trusted friend.

In essence, nothing remained of the Nissan. It had been blown to oblivion. The engine block and transmission were still recognizable as such, as were the wheels which had been flung to each side of the road – three of them, that is. The fourth wheel had been hurled bouncing like a Barnes Wallis bomb down the road towards Flynn as he had sprinted towards the explosion. He'd had to dive sideways to avoid it, otherwise it would have mown him down. But there was very

57

little else left of the vehicle. It had been torn open and shredded in a similar way to Jose, who had been blasted apart.

Flynn knew enough about explosions to know that what had destroyed the car and Jose was a bomb. He had first learned about explosives in 1982 when, as a raw recruit to the Royal Marines, he had been taught many things very quickly on his first ever deployment – on a troop ship bound for the Falkland Islands. Much of that knowledge had left him now but, looking at the scene in front of him, he could tell that whatever the bomb had been made from, it had been located directly underneath the driver's seat. And he was certain this was a bomb, because cars do not simply explode.

The blast had ripped Jose in half. The force of it had scorched up through the underside of the car and the Spaniard's backside. One half of him still remained and was recognizably human, though burned and charred; nothing remained of his right half, which was completely shredded.

Flynn gaped dumbly at the smoke-billowing carnage, still able to feel the heat of the blast which wafted against him like a furnace, depending on how the breeze caught the air.

For a transitory moment he was reminded of an Airfix kit of a model car he had once lovingly constructed as a kid, painstakingly glued together and painted, even the little plastic driver. It had been an E-type Jaguar – a car he still coveted. He'd taken the finished model to school to show it off proudly to his teachers and mates. At the end of the school day it had been stomped on gleefully by a school bully, cheered on by that lad's cronies. The little driver had been made of two halves, the line running vertically down his body from head to groin. He had been split open by the foot of the bully. One half had survived intact, the other crushed to pieces by the pounding of the lad's Doc Martens shoes.

The bully, at a later time, date and location chosen by Flynn, lived to regret his actions.

The image, the memory, was fleeting, as Flynn's mind returned to the present.

He knew he could do nothing, standing there with one hand on the back of his head, the body language of someone in complete shock. He inhaled the aroma of the blast, the acrid smoke, the diesel oil, the burned flesh and somewhere, in amongst it, the smell of linseed oil.

Other people had begun to gather, most having rushed up from the port, as well as drivers from other vehicles as traffic jams started to develop in both directions. Fortunately – if that was the correct word – it seemed that the Nissan was the only vehicle affected and Jose the only casualty of the bomb. The only piece of luck in the whole scenario. No one else was involved.

Somewhere, distantly, Flynn heard the sound of sirens.

He swallowed something with the consistency of a lump of cold porridge, double-swallowed to keep it back, and ran a hand over his shocked features.

Flynn was a hard, tough man. He had seen and experienced many awful things in his life, mainly via the professions he had chosen to enter – the armed forces and the police – but now even he could not help turning away, sagging to his knees and vomiting, having realized he could no longer keep things down.

In his mind were dual thoughts.

First, his friend had met a dreadful end.

Second, it was he, Steve Flynn, who should have been at the wheel and should, by rights, have been torn apart by the blast, a body in the mangled wreckage.

Someone touched Flynn's back – the waiter from the restaurant.

'*Amigo?* Are you OK?'

Flynn nodded, wiping his mouth with the back of his hand. '*Sí, sí, gracias.*'

The waiter gently assisted him back up to his feet.

'*Gracias,*' Flynn said again, turned away and walked back towards the little port of Aldea, then started to jog, then run as tears streamed from his eyes.

He spun *Faye* out of the harbour, gritting his teeth as he pushed the throttle forward and applied power to the inboard Volvo diesel engine. Her nose rose majestically as she responded to the requirement. The boat picked up her skirts and went for it without hesitation, slicing through the water as if she knew Flynn was on a mission.

He wasn't sure how long it took to return to Puerto Rico. He was in a furious trance most of the way, steering by instinct and experience, noticing little of what was going on around him, but he powered right down well before reaching the harbour entrance and motored in sedately, mooring single-handedly in his usual spot.

It was then his mind clicked back into gear. Ensuring *Faye* was properly secure and the intruder alarm set, he had a quick word with a couple of the neighbouring sportfishing skippers and asked them to keep an extra eye out for him. He didn't explain anything and neither skip asked for details. Though they were in commercial competition with each other, they looked out for one another too.

As he hurried along the quay, Flynn checked his phone for the first time in a couple of hours. It had been on silent because he had not wanted to answer any calls from Karen. When he looked at the screen he saw there were numerous texts from her and three missed calls.

Now he definitely wanted to speak to her – and her brother.

He stopped at the water's edge. The fish in the clear water scattered away from his shadow, then three barracudas appeared from nowhere, dangerously harassing the smaller specimens. He took in the little drama for a few seconds before concentrating on his phone and wading through Karen's messages.

The first couple were the ones of interest to Flynn, all the others just designed to gee him up to respond.

Having expected the texts from Karen to be about their break-up, he was surprised to see that the first one read, 'S – please call. Adam needs help.' The next one: 'S – call Adam, even if you don't call me. K. X.'

The remainder were simply variations on that theme.

Flynn began to wonder if Adam was having second thoughts about his new found friends and needed some muscle to back him up . . . but it was only speculation on Flynn's part so, to end it, he tabbed through his phone's menu, found Castle's number and called him while standing by the water, his mind cluster-fucked by the image of the explosion, his dead friend and the certainty that Jose had died in his place. And that it was all connected to Albanian gangsters. Flynn knew he had enemies, old and new, but he found it too much of a coincidence that Bashkim and his brood had appeared on the scene and bad things started to happen to good people.

The call went straight through to voice mail. Flynn ended it with a frustrated jab of his thumb.

'Fuck,' he cursed.

He turned away from the quayside and his phone rang, Adam's number on the screen.

'Adam,' Flynn answered immediately. 'We need to talk . . . I have some bad news and I think it's connected to the Albanians.'

A harsh laugh came down the line.

'Mr Flynn,' said a heavily accented voice. Flynn's guts tightened as he recognized Aleksander Bashkim's gravelly tones. 'Seems you are still with us.'

'Where's Adam?' Flynn demanded.

Bashkim laughed again.

'Put him on,' Flynn said, his voice lowering an octave.

'Somewhat late for that . . . how should I phrase it? Our business dealings have reached a conclusion.'

'What's that supposed to mean?'

'The situation has moved on, shall we say? Things have got messy.'

'Put Adam on,' Flynn insisted.

'OK.'

There were rustling noises, echoing footsteps, then, 'Flynn?'

'Adam, what's going on? You know Jose's been murdered?'

'What? God, no!' Castle cried. Then, 'Flynn – run, fucking run. Find Karen—'

'That will do,' Bashkim intervened after another rustling noise. 'Now then, Mr Flynn,' he said, 'our business transactions can be done easily or under duress . . . that will be your choice . . . but I suggest we meet very soon, don't you agree? In spite of my sons' desire to exterminate you, I feel that you have skills from which I can benefit. Now, just so you know we are businessmen who mean business, you may wish to listen to this . . .'

Flynn stopped breathing, listened hard, his hand covering his free ear to eliminate the background noise of the marina.

There were two bangs as if someone was knocking on a door.

Gunshots.

Just as Flynn knew a wolf pack when he saw one, he also knew the sound of a gun being fired when he heard it.

The moments waiting for Bashkim to speak again were terrible, standing on the quayside, phone pressed to his ear, normal life going on all around him.

'Is your imagination running riot?' Bashkim

asked eventually. Flynn did not reply. 'Let me tell you now, what you are imagining is reality, Mr Flynn . . . your friend Adam Castle now lies dead at my feet, his brains oozing out of his head, his feet twitching the last dance of death . . . his price for awkwardness.'

'Liar. Put him back on.'

'Not something I can do with a dead man, unless, of course, you have the ability to converse with the spirit world. Now then—'

'Now then nothing, you fucker,' Flynn blasted, 'whether you have killed Adam or not, you tried to kill me but killed my friend by mistake.'

'Ah, ah,' Bashkim interrupted. 'I sense a threat coming. I implore you not to make any promise you will not be able to make good. I am a reasonable man . . . somehow you are still alive and I – we – can work with that. My sons can forgive you for their humiliation—'

'Their humiliation?' Flynn said. 'They stuck a bomb under my car because I kicked their arses?'

'You insulted them,' Bashkim said calmly. 'And they are steeped in the culture of my country. Insults have to be responded to.'

'Fuck you,' Flynn said, thinking, *they did it*. The angrier he got, the faster his heart pumped and the more his voice rose. He tried to control himself, become cold and calculating, because he knew to be rash and reactive would only end badly. 'And trust me, I make good my promises,' he said, although even to himself it sounded empty.

His head had been down at that moment, one hand still covering his ear, his whole world inside the cage of this conversation with an Albanian

64

gangster, and so deep was he embroiled in this horrific world that he failed to notice the Toyota Land Cruiser that had just driven on to the quayside, past the raised barrier where there should have been a security guard. The vehicle had driven across the southern edge of the marina, turned left and stopped for a moment before beginning to accelerate towards Flynn.

It was on him, just metres away, the engine shrieking, before he glanced up and saw it was about to strike him down.

He glimpsed the driver but all he saw was a pair of eyes because whoever was at the wheel was wearing something that, in that flash, reminded him of a burka, but he had no more time to consider this because his survival instinct overruled everything else. He considered the choices available to him. He either took his chance on being hit and living or tried flinging himself one way or the other. To his left was not an option. That was simply on to the quayside and all the Toyota would need to do to connect was swerve. He had to hurl himself to his right into the water between two moored boats.

That was the way he went.

He dived sideways, as though he was the only member of a synchronized swimming team, but he hit the water more like a boulder than a rapier, feeling the air zip past him as the Toyota crossed the exact spot he had been on only a millisecond earlier.

Flynn went under. The air was driven out of his lungs by the impact of hitting the water and then being enveloped by it, because here in the marina it was several degrees colder than the water in the shallow bay lapping the beach.

He thrust upwards, wiping his face, gasping, hearing the sound of the Toyota as the vehicle reversed and manoeuvred on the quayside.

Flynn trod water, shaded by the hull of one of the daytrip boats.

The vehicle appeared in his line of sight and stopped at the point where he had gone into the water, facing the direction it had come from.

Since the vehicle was left hand drive, the driver was on the far side, but Flynn could see the figure at the wheel looking in his direction. He could tell it wasn't a burka over the head but a baseball cap with the peak facing backwards and a scarf tied across the face, covering the lower part of it. He could also tell the driver was female. And he could see her eyes.

The car lurched and accelerated away. Flynn heard it roar off into the distance. He finned around and caught a glimpse of it through the boats, speeding back towards town.

He swam to one of the safety ladders hanging over the edge of the quay and hauled himself out, turning and sitting, dangling his legs over the side to let some of the water drain off.

The only good thing to come from the incident was that when he had jumped out of the way he'd let go of his mobile phone and it hadn't gone into the water with him. Good in that it wasn't now wet, not so good in that as it hit the ground it had burst into three sections, front, back and battery.

Flynn winced to see that the screen was badly

cracked like a drunken spider's web, but he managed to reassemble it and turn it on.

It powered up, seemed to be working.

Just to test it Flynn tapped the Candy Crush icon and the game opened, which was good. At least he could now try to progress on to level three.

Then it rang and he answered. 'Steve Flynn.'

'Steve . . . Steve . . .' It was Karen's voice, speaking in a barely audible whisper.

'Karen, what the hell's going on?' he asked with impatience.

'Steve . . . I'm hiding . . . they don't know I'm here. Please, oh God, please help me . . .'

Five

Karen Glass could not even begin to describe the incredible guilt she felt at dumping Flynn.

The relationship had taken off at her instigation. There had been the simmering mutual attraction between them as well as their friendship but things had gone no further than that for a long time because neither of them wanted to spoil a good thing. They had thought that sex would do just that – but when it came, it made a good thing even better.

Karen had escaped to the island following the messy break-up of her marriage to a teacher in Lancashire. She had fled there as soon as her brother, Adam, had suggested he might have a 'bit of a job' for her that might tide her over, give her time to lick her wounds.

It had not been a greatly taxing occupation – staffing the quayside booking kiosk for Adam's sportfishing boat in Puerto Rico – but it was ideal for what she needed at the time and it did have its compensations – sunshine, sand, paellas, a good tan and Steve Flynn.

She had met and instantly liked him. He had the outer layer of an alley cat, the inner core of a soft-arse, and the truth was Karen fell in love with him almost instantly when he flashed his sea blue eyes at her and laughed uproariously at one of her pathetic jokes.

The crunch time came when she was dithering about returning to the UK to restart her education, but convinced herself and Flynn to take a chance on each other.

He had been reluctant. He'd grown used to keeping women at arms' length, emotionally speaking. He had gone through a torrid break-up with his wife years before – something that still haunted him; he was also still reeling from the death of a woman he had fallen in love with on the island, hence his double-edged reluctance to become involved with anyone else – other than in the sack.

Karen had dismantled his barriers, made promises, said it would be OK, exposed him to be hurt again – and then hurt him.

She felt cruel and nasty and the truth was – as the guilty one always says – it wasn't him, it was her.

In spite of his reservations about getting into

something again he had been marvellous and loving but the situation had started to stifle her, and Flynn's warnings before they embarked on the relationship (which she had failed to heed), in which he cautioned her that life on the island would not be enough for her in the long run, had come home to roost.

She found herself thinking more and more about her degree and discovered there was a place at Manchester Met, and a friend who worked at the BBC's Media City in Salford promised she would get her a part time job at a small TV production company. It was all too much for Karen and the days spent inside the booking office on the quayside began to feel like a prison sentence. The thing with Flynn started to suffer, until it came to a head after much bickering and sniping.

After Flynn had returned with Adam's so-called fishing party the day before and she had waited to catch him after his daily run and swim, just to talk, she had never seen him so angry.

Correction. She had seen him killing angry – but that had been different. She had seen him go up against violent men, coldly and brutally. But what she saw in him yesterday was a different kind of anger. The anger of disappointment and broken dreams.

She had stormed away from the villa after their brief argument, up to the commercial centre and straight into one of Adam's bars, lined up three vodka shots, necked them one after the other and bought a bottle of cheap red wine, which she had taken out on to the sun terrace to consume while crying behind her big sunglasses.

This was where Adam found her a couple of hours later, on the verge of opening a third bottle and close to being very regally pissed up.

She did not remember much after that.

Adam helping her to her feet, almost carrying her to his car, easing her across the back seat, then, vaguely, the journey up to his villa in the hills behind Puerto Rico. There was then another hazy recollection of Adam laying her out on a bed in one of the top floor bedrooms and having to lift her legs back on to the bed repeatedly because, for some unaccountable reason, they had developed a mind of their own and kept sliding off.

She did remember him kissing her forehead, then leaving her with the blinds drawn.

During the night she did manage to make it – just – to the en suite bathroom, where she hurled up most of her insides before crawling back to bed and falling asleep muttering, 'Steve . . . Steve . . . Steve . . .'

Her morning headache was the most intense pain she had ever experienced, as if an axe had been embedded in her skull.

She rolled into the shower, which ran cold after three minutes, then checked herself in the mirror to see a dreadful dragon confronting her.

Bitch, she remonstrated with herself.

She was still dressed in yesterday's clothes, but by discarding her underwear she thought she could manage for another hour. She went down one flight of steps to the middle storey of the villa, where she found Adam sitting out on the small balcony adjacent to the kitchen at the back, looking towards the mountains.

Karen stood unsteadily at the sliding door, blinking at the blinding daylight for a moment before having to cover her eyes with her sunglasses.

'Hi, sis.' He turned slowly towards her.

'Hi, bro.' She thought he looked anxious.

'Won't ask how you're feeling,' he said. 'Coffee's on, there's a warm croissant in the oven.'

She would have nodded but believed this would have moved the axe in her head. 'Ta.'

She went into the kitchen, poured the coffee, buttered the croissant and came back, sat at the small table across from her brother.

'I heard you murmuring "Steve",' Adam said.

'That's about all I remember,' she admitted, and took a swig of the coffee: black, unsweetened, designed to kill hangovers. She almost groaned with pleasure.

'So it's really over and you're going back?'

She was glad she was wearing her sunglasses. At least Adam could not see the shame or sadness in her eyes. Or could he? she wondered. She nodded. The axe moved slightly.

Adam sighed. 'Shame.'

She looked up quickly, pain lancing through her skull. Adam raised his hands defensively. 'I'm not judging, love. He's a good man and I think we've both let him down now. You in the world of "lurv", me in the world of business.'

Karen continued to sip the coffee. It was strong, but not bitter. Then, despite the laser-like strength of the morning sun, she raised her sunglasses off her face and looked directly at her brother.

'What's going on?'

* * *

71

Since it was a very tall villa – ground, middle and upper floors – it was possible to strip naked on the top balcony, stretch out on one of the sun loungers without being seen by any of the neighbours and catch some serious rays. That was what Karen decided to do after speaking to Adam. Not that she had a lot of options about what to do anyway. Adam had said he needed to work on some figures; her own car was parked outside her apartment in Puerto Rico and it was too far to walk. She would have loved to call Flynn to come and pick her up in that wonderful beat-up old Nissan he drove around in with a kind of stupid pride. But that was not possible now that it was over. Her only option was to wait for Adam to finish up, then run her home. In the meantime she decided to take a bottle of chilled water up to the balcony, strip down and catch the sun.

Her mind was also in real turmoil now that Adam had explained exactly what was happening in his business life. She had already had her suspicions, but Adam confirmed them all. He was in severe straits and, to put it mildly, in his desperation to get out of a self-inflicted mire had got into bed with the wrong crowd.

After advising Adam of her plan to sunbathe so he would not stumble across her to the acute embarrassment of them both, she settled on the sun lounger. He said he would rattle his keys if he was coming up so she could cover up. She then checked her mobile phone, blinking with stupid disbelief when she saw the number of texts she had sent to Flynn over the course of her drunken binge.

She didn't even recall sending one.

'Shit,' she gulped quietly, reading through a series of messages that began legibly and comprehensibly, gradually becoming blubbering and incoherent shite. She also saw she had made three actual calls to him. Tellingly, Flynn had not responded to any of them. Fuming with herself, she sat back and let the sun caress her body, then had a thought.

Now she was more or less sober she decided to text him again, but this time only in relation to Adam. Her brother was in deep; he needed help and was clearly too proud to ask for it. She wasn't sure what Flynn could offer, but moral support would be nice. She closed her eyes and waited for a response.

Nothing landed.

Although she tried to relax, Flynn's lack of communication – basic texting manners – began to irk her, so over the course of the next hour she sent more: short, curt ones, ordering Flynn to call Adam. Again, none elicited a response.

In the end she placed her phone down on the floor and said, 'Fuck you.'

She closed her eyes, let the sun do its work.

She was dozing when she heard the smooth sound of a car engine on the road outside the villa. This wasn't unusual in itself, but the villa was situated at the end of a gated cul-de-sac, although the gate itself was rarely locked, and few cars other than those belonging to residents came down. Karen did not open her eyes but listened to the progress of the vehicle as it drove past the villa, then up on to the driveway at the back. The car obviously stopped. There was a

73

little squeak of brakes. The engine ticked over for a few moments, then was turned off, and the day resumed its silence until three car doors slammed. There was a murmur of voices, the sound of footsteps up the staircase leading to the front door of the villa. Then loud knocking on the door. Lots of it.

Karen listened.

The front door opened, then was closed; whoever it was had entered. She sat up, then crept to the balcony rail and looked down at the driveway, where an old blue Rolls-Royce was parked behind Adam's Audi.

Adam Castle knew they were coming. He had checked through his paperwork and accounts and had made his decision by the time the knock came on the front door.

He was not going to deal.

He'd found some money buried in a long-forgotten account which, although not a huge amount, would be enough to get him and his businesses through this very rough patch.

It was a harsh rap on the door, not a knock. Insistent, loud, demanding.

Adam straightened his papers, braced himself, stood up and walked to the door. He opened it and tried to smile and appear confident.

Aleksander Bashkim wasn't a man who could easily be smiled at and he knew it. He did not seem to have any warmth in him — just a cold, tough man who wanted to take over every aspect of Adam Castle's small business empire and consume it.

Adam stood aside as Bashkim and his two sons trooped into the living room. He noticed the battered features of both young men and was slightly puzzled. They looked as though they were usually the ones who did the dishing out and he wondered who could have done such damage to their faces.

'Flynn,' he whispered, and grinned.

Then he inhaled deeply and said, 'Gentlemen,' as Bashkim turned to face him. 'I fear you've had a wasted journey. I've reconsidered everything and I no longer wish to relinquish any part of my businesses to you, and that includes selling my share of the sportfishing boat.'

He hoped he came across as business-like and assured. Inside his heart was hammering against his chest as though a nasty alien was trapped inside, trying to break out.

Bashkim smiled.

At least his lips curled, but it wasn't a pleasant thing and all it did was distort the old knife slashes on his cheek obscenely.

Bashkim shook his head sadly, raised his eyes to his sons. They moved in, grabbed Adam.

'I was willing to step in and assist, to help you rise from your . . . predicament,' Bashkim explained. 'We would have worked as partners . . . in a way. I would have protected you.'

Pavli and Dardan had moved quickly and efficiently; they had obviously come prepared for the eventuality that they would have to resort to violence. Pavli had stepped in behind Adam and enfolded him in a bear hug while Dardan had swiftly covered Adam's head with a polythene bag, instantly blocking his mouth and nose. Adam thrashed in panic but he was no contest for the brothers, who then hauled him bodily down the steps to the ground floor of the villa; they sat him down on a plastic chair in the lower kitchen and whipped the bag off his head.

He sucked in air greedily and tried to stand up. Pavli backhanded him, knocking his jaw hard but not breaking it. Adam slumped back on to the chair, tasting the salty blood inside his mouth where his teeth had cut his inner cheek.

Pavli took up a position behind him, Dardan to one side.

Bashkim stood in front, leafing through Adam's paperwork with disinterest. He slid it on to a worktop, then unfolded a sheet of his own that he produced from his back pocket. 'I suspected you might prove difficult, which is why I had this drawn up by my lawyer so that all our dealings will be watertight. Signed, sealed . . . all that.' He smiled at Adam. 'All I require is your signature.'

'No,' Adam said. 'Where is your lawyer anyway?'

'Please,' Bashkim said patronizingly. 'He works in an office. He doesn't do home visits. Now . . . just sign this document and we will be on our way.'

'No,' Adam said resolutely, a challenge in his face.

Bashkim raised his eyes to Pavli.

His son swooped quickly, grabbed Adam's left hand with his own, pinning it to the arm of the chair, then selected Adam's ring finger, bent it back and squeezed it in his fist, the implication obvious. Pavli glanced at his father for approval.

'Break it,' Bashkim said.

Six

Karen knew the Albanian guys were trouble from the moment they entered Adam's life. They reeked of it, but all her brother did when she warned him was redden up indignantly and tell her to mind her own business. He knew what he was doing and up to a point she trusted his judgement and ability, but now he had got in too deep and was trying to extract himself from a horrible business deal, terrified it was too late. He had told her that Bashkim would not respond kindly to the snub.

'If I go down, I want to go down fighting – that's what I've decided,' Adam had declared. 'But I won't be rescued by going into a business deal with criminals, and nor will I drag Flynn into this. I need to keep control and deal with it all legitimately . . . if I can,' he concluded bleakly. Then he had pointed at her in a brotherly way. 'And do not say "I told you so".'

And then they had arrived in that stupid old car the father cruised around in.

After they had entered the villa Karen quickly pulled her shorts and T-shirt back on, then stood silently on the landing at the top of the stairs that led down to the middle floor lounge.

She listened, but could not see what was happening. She heard a few lines of conversation, mumbled, but was unable to work out the content. Then there was the sound of a scuffle and she just caught a glimpse of the men bundling Adam down the stairs to the ground floor, with a plastic bag over his head.

She paused, holding her breath, suddenly aware of every beat of her heart, then went down a level to stand at the top of the steps to the ground floor.

Moments later, Adam screamed – a pain-wracked howl, like a wounded animal, that made her jump; then she was filled with terror and horrible images. She covered her mouth to stifle a gasp.

For a few seconds she did not dare to move.

She sank slowly to her haunches, now shaking in fear but summoning enough courage to slide one bare foot down on to the first step; maybe she could try to see what was going on.

Adam's mobile phone then rang, playing his all-time favourite track, about which she had mercilessly ribbed him over the years: the Bee Gees singing 'Islands in the Stream'. Then there was silence, followed by the sound of Bashkim's voice, evidently on the phone, although she still could not quite hear what was being said.

She slid down another step, crouched over, attempting to stay hidden but also trying to see into the kitchen where she was sure they were congregated. The problem was that the stairs dropped to a small landing, then dog-legged around on themselves; she needed to get on to that landing to have any hope of seeing into the kitchen.

She moved slowly down, then was on the landing, and now if she stretched her neck she would be able to see. Then she recoiled as she heard Adam's frantic, shouted words, realizing there was a message in there for her.

'Flynn – run,' he yelled. 'Fucking run . . . Find Karen—'

Her name was shouted even louder than the other words.

She stretched, extending her neck to try and see over the banister without revealing herself, and glimpsed the tableau in the kitchen.

Bashkim senior had his back to her, holding a mobile phone pressed to his ear.

Adam was seated on one of the plastic garden chairs, one of the brothers standing behind him, another to his side. With horror she noticed Adam's left hand, the ring finger hanging back across his hand at an unusual angle. She realized instantly the reason for Adam's unearthly scream. They had broken his finger.

Once more she tried to stifle a gasp with her hand. Her eyes widened with even more dread as Bashkim held the phone away from his ear, turning it towards Adam – presumably it was Flynn at the other end of the line. He nodded at one of his sons, who pulled a snub-nosed revolver out of the waistband of his tracksuit bottoms, placed the muzzle to Adam's left temple and pulled the trigger twice in quick succession. Adam's head jerked obscenely and blood fountained out of the wound as the son stepped back so as not to get splattered. Adam slumped off the chair, dead.

Bashkim put the phone back to his ear and

started talking. Karen could not hear the words, but they were still at a conversational level as if nothing had happened, as if no one had just been murdered in front of him.

It was then that the other son – Karen thought his name was Pavli – spun sharply and looked in her direction.

She ducked, hoping she had been quick enough not to have been spotted. She scrambled back up the stairs to the living room, ran across to the front door, dragged it open and ran out on to the outer landing before hurtling down the steps close to where the Rolls-Royce was parked. She flattened herself against the villa wall, took one quick look behind her and saw the front door opening.

She turned and ran along the back wall of the villa towards the pool area, pausing at the corner as panic rose in her like a living thing. Behind, she heard a shout. Someone was coming down the front steps.

Keeping low, she dashed diagonally across the pool terrace and towards the brick built construction by the back garden wall, not much bigger than a small shed, which was the pool house. It contained the water pumps and electronic motor that served the pool itself. She knew it was always unlocked and she ducked in through the door, pulling it closed behind her, sealing her in darkness.

She pulled her phone out of her back pocket, dialled Flynn.

'. . . help me . . .'

They were the last words Karen spoke before the connection failed.

Steve Flynn glared at his phone, demanding an answer, as people do when mobile phones suddenly go dead. The signal was still strong and his phone appeared to be OK, still working after he'd dropped it and cracked the screen.

He stood on the quayside, drenched, staring stupidly at the device, stunned and confused, almost paralysed, trying to compute everything in his brain, but it did not seem to be working at all well at that exact moment. He spun 360 degrees, everything in a slow whirl.

He wasn't sure how long he stood there.

It felt like an hour.

In reality it was just seconds.

He stopped turning and then it all became clear. He ran back to *Faye*, leapt on board and – driven by instinct – grabbed a large bait knife from on top of the tackle box, shoved it up his sleeve, then jumped ashore again. He set off running, although he wasn't completely certain as to where, but as he pounded his way around the quayside he knew his first port of call would be Adam's office on the outer edge of the commercial centre. That was where he assumed Adam and Karen would be, their place of work.

He weaved between strolling tourists, running around as if he was on a slalom, past his villa, up through the town park, across the main road and up the steps into the commercial centre through its south entrance, then veered right on to Avenida del Valle and up to Adam's office. It was just the one room, and it was instantly clear that neither Adam nor Karen was there, just the lady who did the admin.

'Adam! Where is he?' Flynn demanded breathlessly. He had just run about half a mile at his top speed.

The young lady gawped open-mouthed at his drenched, dishevelled appearance.

'Where the fuck is he?' he screamed.

The words seemed to jolt her back into life. She knew Flynn well, but not as the person who had crashed through the office door. Normally he was cool and charming and friendly – not demonic.

'I . . . I . . . he's not here yet,' she stuttered.

'I can fucking see that. Just tell me where he is.'

'Villa . . . his villa . . . why?'

'I need a car . . . one of the jeeps will do.' Flynn used the generic term to describe any of the small fleet of four wheel drive vehicles owned by Adam and used for the safari side of the business.

'They're all out,' she said meekly.

Flynn saw she was starting to cry.

'I need transport to get up to see him.'

'I don't know,' she whimpered, somewhat nonsensically.

Flynn swung out of the office door and saw that one of the open-topped safari jeeps was actually parked a little further up the road in a layby. Josh, one of Adam's regular driver/guides, was standing next to it, chatting to a cluster of people. This was one of the pick-up points for the safaris and Josh was obviously talking to clients before taking them up into the mountains for the ride of their lives.

'That'll do,' Flynn muttered. He took a step

towards the jeep, had a thought, pulled himself back into the office and said, 'Sorry, Lil.' Then he was gone.

Josh had started herding the clients on to the back of the jeep when Flynn ran up to him.

'All right, mate,' Josh said. He was a young, good-looking beach bum of a guy, all muscle, bronze tan and smiles, and always a big hit with the lady clients but not so much with their boyfriends. He scowled with incomprehension at Flynn's bedraggled appearance.

'I need the jeep,' Flynn said.

'Uh?'

'I need it. I need it now,' Flynn growled, and turned to the four clients staring dumbfounded at him. 'Off,' Flynn ordered them. 'Get off.'

'Oi!' Josh stepped in front of him, a finger raised. 'They are my customers.'

'And I need this vehicle urgently. Trust me, Josh, I don't have time to explain.'

'Sorry man, no can do. These folks've paid.'

'Like I said,' Flynn replied dangerously, 'I don't have time to explain. They can get refunds from the office.' Flynn jerked his thumb in the direction of the office, where a scared-looking young lady was peeking out of the door. He turned to the clients. 'Sorry folks, pop down to that lady there and get your money back. Say Steve Flynn sent you.'

'Adam's not gonna like this,' Josh warned him.

Flynn's face went up to Josh's. 'Adam's too dead to care,' he growled. Then back to the holiday makers. 'Off, now, before I drag you all off.' And back to Josh again. 'Keys.'

83

The clients filed off, disgruntled, muttering and a little afraid, and Josh handed the keys over. 'This better be kosher.'

Flynn snatched them from his fingers and dashed to the driver's door. Moments later he was pulling out, ignoring irate horn blasts from other drivers – they were only normal anyway. The jeep was newer than his now extinct Nissan Patrol, but the large diesel engine was just as sluggish and slow to respond to his foot jammed down on the pedal. He had to coax it in low gears to get any performance out of it at all.

He flung it through the narrow streets, out of town, and headed up the valley to where Adam's villa was located in a new development between Puerto Rico and Tauro. He drove recklessly through the narrow streets, forcing the jeep through impossible gaps, overtaking – and struggling to do so since, again like his Nissan, the jeep was ideal off road but not great for speeding on it.

It wasn't a long journey. Within five minutes he was pulling off the main road on to a sprawling estate of new villas of all shapes, sizes and costs. Adam's place had set him back around three-quarters of a million euros but other properties surrounding it were double, sometimes triple that.

Just on the outer edge of the development was a row of shops and a restaurant. He pulled on to the car park adjacent to these, stopped and got his thoughts together, wondering how best to approach the situation.

A huge part of him wanted to bowl in like a Spanish bull, but he knew that would be a move of folly. Like a bull he'd end up dead with blood gushing out of his nostrils. On top of that, other than the bait knife up his sleeve he was not armed in any way. Sitting there in the jeep he cursed his brainless stupidity. He was here, virtually defenceless apart from his own physique and skills, most of which were blunted by the ageing process and lack of use.

He thumped the steering wheel in frustration, knowing he had to make some sort of move.

The entrance to the estate – a huge, wrought-iron arch – was to his left. He glanced at it and saw the regal nose of a large luxury saloon car emerge from it.

Bashkim's Rolls was leaving. Pavli was at the wheel, Bashkim in the front passenger seat.

Flynn slid quickly down in the driver's seat of the jeep, hoping the Rolls would sail past without the occupants noticing him, although Flynn thought there was little chance of that with Adam Castle's business logo emblazoned on the jeep doors, which was a bit of a giveaway. If they did see it, they might not make any connection to him, he prayed. He slithered right down under the steering wheel, keeping his eye-line just above the dash. Through narrowed eyes he watched the car sail past like some regal Victorian lady in a big skirt. He tried to see if there was anyone else in the car, but all he could make out were Bashkim and Pavli, making him wonder where Dardan might be.

They appeared to pay no heed to him, but he still remained wary, deciding the best approach to Adam's villa would be with caution and stealth.

He got out of the car and started off on foot,

trying to work out how best to get there. He had only been to the villa once before and knew it was on the far side of the development, one of the latest to be built, and its grounds abutted an area of scrubland that had been bought by the builders for further development.

Flynn began to jog-trot, feeling the blade of the bait knife pressing against the soft inner skin of his left forearm.

He did not want to go into this situation with assumptions that would bite him on the backside. The fact that he had not seen Dardan in the Rolls made him extra wary. He upped his pace a little, now having virtually dried out from his drenching. He reached the entrance to the cul-de-sac in which Adam's villa was to be found. He paused behind one of the gate posts, caught his breath, glanced down the road. The villa was the last one on the right, past half a dozen others. It was surrounded by a high stone wall which offered some cover to his approach. He had already dismissed the idea of knocking on the front door. Always best to come unannounced through the back entrance, a philosophy that had served him well as a cop and a marine.

He went past the entrance, then cut across a landscaped grassy bank and worked his way on to the scrubland behind the villas where he crouched low and surveyed his approach.

On the outer edge of this tract of land were eight partially completed villas which seemed to have been abandoned for the time being. There were no workmen about, not a sign of anyone, in fact, no one to see him make his way along the rear of the line of villas in the cul-de-sac.

Underfoot it was quite treacherous, full of builders' debris and waste garden materials from the villas themselves. He had to make his way over boulders, bricks and steel rods that poked out dangerously while keeping low and attempting not to look conspicuous if someone did spot him.

Finally he was at the back wall of Adam's villa. He peeked over and could see the rear and one side elevation – a gable end – of the property, and also on to the driveway where Adam's Audi TT was parked in the shade.

The house seemed still. Normal.

He could see the window of the ground floor kitchen. Next to it was a set of sliding patio doors and behind these a lounge.

Flynn edged along until he reached the point where the wall became a waney-lap fence. Over it was the pool house and the pool itself, which looked calm and serene, no bodies floating face down in it. It looked inviting and Flynn winced mentally at the memory it evoked. His first and only visit to the villa was for a house-warming party thrown by Adam soon after he'd bought the place. He and Karen had stayed on after all the other guests had dispersed and when a very drunken Adam had finally gone to bed, Flynn and Karen sneaked out to the pool for a three a.m. skinny-dip. That led to sex in the pool and Flynn's hope that the filter mechanism worked well. Whether it did or not hardly mattered. It had been a wonderful night and after the pool encounter the couple sneaked up to the top balcony where further fun took place under a full moon and the stars, on a sun lounger.

Flynn blinked at the memory, then realigned his brain.

He ducked down on to his haunches and waddled along using the fence for cover until he came to a large bush that had spread from the garden, up and over the fence. He scrambled over at this point, using cover provided by the shrub. He was now at the back wall of the villa. There were no windows at this level so he strode across and put his back to the wall and sidled along to the car port. Here there was a door giving access to the ground floor, which was locked. It was a substantial door and he knew he could not just kick it open in one.

His face twitched as he swore internally, then continued to edge his way around the villa, under the arch of the staircase that led up to the front door. Then, still crouching at the bottom step, he looked up to the small terrace by the door.

Still no sign of movement, occupation or danger.

He took the steps three at a time, then flattened himself against the wall by the door and stretched for the handle, which he pulled slowly down and pushed.

The door was unlocked, swung gently open. He paused, holding his breath, then peeked quickly into the living room. It was empty.

He exhaled, then squeezed into the room, closing the door behind him.

On the face of it there was nothing out of place. The dining table where Adam had been working held his papers spread out around his laptop. His chair was there, not upturned.

Again, all normal.

Flynn stood still, listening hard. His senses told him he wasn't alone. Just that almost imperceptible movement of air and maybe the experience he'd accumulated after twenty years as a cop entering houses in which people were often hiding or already dead.

Although it was coming up to ten years since he'd been a cop, they were senses that had never quite left him.

He moved silently across the room and glanced down at the papers on the table. Adam's accounts with a lot of red highlighter pen on the figures, plus marks in red pen, and a calculator.

Adam must have been poring over them that morning.

But where was he now? Was the phone call just a sick ruse by Bashkim?

In his heart, Flynn knew what he had heard was for real.

He breathed slowly and drew the bait knife from his sleeve. He held it upside down with the blade concealed and lying up his inner forearm. It wasn't a practical weapon, though brilliant for gutting fish.

He moved across to the kitchen and glanced in, then the lounge area. Off here was a door leading to the main double bedroom and en suite shower room. Flynn entered slowly, knowing this was Adam's room, but there was no sign of him or Karen. He knew Adam, who was divorced, was 'between ladies', as he liked to say (and he always added 'metaphorically speaking'). There was no sign of any female friend either.

From there Flynn went up to the top floor,

where there were two double bedrooms, each with an en suite shower room. One of the rooms had been slept in and Flynn caught his breath when he saw Karen's shoulder bag hanging from one of the bed posts. The bed was ruffled and unmade and Flynn guessed she'd spent the night here.

The other bedroom was pristine.

He stepped out on to the balcony, saw Karen's sunglasses on one of the loungers. He stooped to pick them up, turning them over between his fingers, recalling how he had last seen them on her face, covering her eyes: a barrier, so Flynn could not see through the lenses.

He dropped them back on to the sun lounger and, feeling frustrated, went back down to the middle floor, stopping as he reached the living room. He sniffed the air. An odour he recognized. Just a hint of gun smoke. He became more tense. Like the aroma of cannabis smoke, cordite was something once sniffed, never forgotten.

Then he wondered if he heard something on the floor below. A scrape. A breath. A click. He was not certain what it was, but he was now positive he was not alone in the villa.

Putting his back to the wall, he shuffled the bait knife down so that he was holding it properly in his right hand and started to descend the stairs, one quiet step at a time until, after the dog-leg, he was halfway down the second flight and could see clearly into the ground floor kitchen.

Adam lay sprawled on the tiled floor next to a plastic chair, face down in a pool of thick blood, horrific gunshot wounds in his head.

Flynn did not move or breathe.

With extreme caution he took one further step down, then another and another until he was at the bottom of the stairs, the kitchen door to his left.

He stayed there, his senses still telling him that he was not alone, that he was walking into some kind of trap – because where was Dardan?

Was he still here, waiting?

The kitchen was ahead of him down a short hallway with the ground floor lounge next to it. Directly across was the door to a room used as a storage area. Further back along the hallway was a shower room and toilet and the door to the car port.

Flynn moved along the hallway and checked the shower. Before he got to Adam he wanted to confirm there would be no surprises in store. The shower was empty. Next along was the storage room, the door of which was locked. From there he stepped across to the kitchen door and stopped on the threshold, his eyes, ears, nose, feet, trying to pick up anything. A noise. A waft of air. A vibration.

The bait knife hung in his hand by his outer thigh.

He looked at Adam's dead body with blood still oozing from the head wounds, pooling like black oil underneath him. Flynn could see he had been shot twice.

Flynn had to fight to control the grief that threatened to engulf him for the man who had been there for him when he'd most needed help, provided him with a living and kept promises and who had now, somehow, got in too deep with people he could not even begin to control – and Flynn had not been there for him.

He forced himself to remain calm.

The grief could come later. He had found Adam and now had to find Karen, although he truly believed she too was dead.

He stepped into the kitchen and looked down into Adam's eyes. One was still open – glassy, unseeing – the other closed as if he was giving Flynn a wink.

'Jesus,' he breathed.

And then, despite his fighting it, that grief grabbed him. He went down on to his haunches by Adam's side with his back to the kitchen door. That was the moment Flynn realized he had allowed his guard to slip, and was vulnerable.

Behind him came the unmistakable sliding noise of a semi-automatic pistol being cocked. One of those sounds Flynn knew as well as the reek of cannabis.

He spun on his heels, flipping the bait knife into a throwing grip, a move he had mastered so many years before. It had been drilled into him on his first ever sea voyage and the skill remained with him to this day. As he rotated, it all slowed down and became ultra-definable: the swivel on the heels, the throwing arm arcing backwards and then the throw itself as the knife left his fingers. In concurrent thought, he also realized that this knife was not made for throwing, so as he lined up on the target he made minute adjustments to accommodate this fact. It was for gutting, not throwing at targets. It did not have the balance. But there and then Flynn had to make it a throwing knife, compensate for its failings and make it into a deadly weapon as it went from his fingers, cartwheeled once and flew through the air at the target, another thing that Flynn's brain had had to compute as he had spun around and released the blade.

It flew towards the surprised figure of Dardan Bashkim, who was there with a semi-automatic pistol in his hand, the slide that cocked the weapon still between the fingers of his left hand, mid-cock, because he simply had not anticipated how quickly Flynn would react. He had turned as soon as he'd heard the sound and dispatched the bait knife before Dardan could react himself.

To be fair, Dardan probably only saw the blur of Flynn's reaction and quite possibly his brain did not even manage to compute the titanium-coated blade zinging towards him. The first he probably knew about it was when the 43/8 inch blade embedded itself in his throat, in the soft cleft just below his chin. It sliced cleanly through his trachea, cutting his windpipe in half.

Then Dardan really did look surprised.

He dropped the gun with a clatter, clutched and clawed at his throat which pulsed blood from the thick carotid artery the knife had also managed to sever.

He sank to his knees, gurgling horribly, his mouth popping like a fish, making bubbles of blood.

Dardan's right hand curled around the handle of the knife and Flynn watched in curious horror as the muscled man slowly extracted the blade from his own throat, then looked across at Flynn with ferocity. With his left hand clamped around the wound, he stood up, forcing himself up on to his feet, and came at Flynn with the knife, uttering a terrible, blood-coated roar.

Flynn leapt sideways and at the same time lashed out with both feet, kicking Dardan's legs from underneath him. He stumbled and crashed to his knees again on the floor alongside Adam. Flynn jumped as Dardan slashed the knife pathetically at him. He was weakening as blood gushed out of his neck, between his fingers.

Flynn circled away from him, out of range of the knife, until the waving subsided and Dardan's head drooped. He let go of the knife and fell forward on to his face, hitting the tiled floor with a sickening crunch and, in a final ignominy, breaking his nose.

At first there was a lot of blood from Dardan's throat, mingling with Adam's, and a lot of convulsive death twitching. A minute later Dardan was still and dead.

Gasping, Flynn swiped the back of his trembling hand across his mouth.

Seven

'I told you to sit in the car.'

Flynn turned slowly and looked towards the man, the detective – Ramos Romero – who had taken charge of the scene. He and Flynn had met before, not in auspicious circumstances – and

94

they did not like each other. It was probably just one of those personal things, not really based on any evidence, but sometimes people either gelled or did not and usually first impressions stuck, as in this case.

'I'm not going anywhere,' Flynn said. He raised his eyes over Romero's shoulder at the other detective on the scene, who had introduced herself as Maria Santiago. She was in her mid-thirties, very dark-skinned with flashing brown eyes, shimmering long black hair and a beauty that passed Flynn by. In other circumstances he would have been more attentive but now nothing interested him but justice.

Both detectives wore forensic suits that billowed unflatteringly on Santiago and clung unflatteringly on the more portly Romero.

'I can't just sit. I need to stand and think, not be cooped up in the back of a cop car.'

Romero's eyes narrowed, then he relented. 'OK.'

He moved closer to Flynn, who was hovering by the gate of Adam's villa, leaning on the wall and looking in an unfocused way at the rough scrubland behind. A long line of police vehicles was parked up all the way along the cul-de-sac, including crime scene, plain and liveried cars, a dog handler and also an ambulance, which was fairly useless under the circumstances.

'You need to tell me again what happened, Señor Flynn.'

'I've told you three times.'

'Tell me again . . . you must remember that although I speak, read and understand English

95

very well, it is not my first language and some-times I miss the . . .' He grasped for the word.

'Subtleties?' Flynn hazarded.

'Exactly . . . I turn up, find two dead bodies, blood everywhere – *and you*. Details and subtle-ties are important.'

'Well the subtlety that you need to grasp is that I was here. I stayed until you arrived. I didn't touch anything.'

'But you admit killing that man.'

'In self-defence, yeah. Guy was pointing a gun at me.'

Romero sniffed, unimpressed, his dark Spanish eyes assessing Flynn, who was now beginning to regret calling the police and waiting for them to arrive.

But as he had stood over the two bodies, one dead by his own hand, he realized he had no option but to call them. Things had gone too far and although he had no desire whatsoever to get involved with local law enforcement and possibly the Spanish justice system, he realized there was no choice. His predisposition was to take the fight to Bashkim and find out for himself where Karen was – because, despite what he had told Romero, he had searched the villa and its outbuildings from top to bottom again, every drawer, every cupboard, and found no sign of her. He had to believe that Bashkim had taken her, probably in the boot of the old Rolls, and Dardan had waited to ambush him, for whatever reason, when he turned up at the scene. His gut told him Bashkim had Karen.

'Mmm, self-defence,' Romero said doubtfully,

his thick moustache and slug-like mono brow twitching madly.

'And I think they've got Karen, Adam's sister. I know they have.'

Romero rolled his eyes. 'So, these supposed Albanian gangsters—'

'Supposed?' Flynn interrupted sharply, eyeing the detective with suspicion and not liking the implication in the tone of his voice. And it wasn't because of his accent. As he'd said, Romero's English was excellent and he never had to revert to the 'how you say?' cliché. He could speak and use inflections just as effectively as most British people Flynn knew (and better than many) in spite of his claim about subtleties. It was his use of the word 'supposed' that Flynn did not like. 'These guys were moving in and pressuring Adam. Obviously he decided to stand up to them and got killed for it.'

'Mmm.' The expression of doubt was used for the second time by the Spaniard, who was unimpressed by Flynn. Flynn's eyes flicked over to Santiago, the woman detective, who gave him a blank look. 'You have no evidence of what you allege – and you have killed one of them, it seems.'

Flynn shifted uncomfortably, not happy with the direction of this conversation. His insides contracted.

Romero's mobile rang. He fished it out of a pocket in his jacket underneath the forensic suit, glanced at the screen, then at Flynn, and moved away to answer it, leaving Flynn and Santiago standing two metres apart. For just an instant, Flynn thought he saw her expression change

– sympathy, he wasn't certain – but then she refitted her professional po-face.

Flynn turned away from her and stared moodily across the scrubland again.

Inwardly he cursed himself. He knew he'd done the right thing by calling the cops, but already the Spanish justice system was making him anxious. It could still be as unforgiving as it had been in the days of fascism. Despite being an EU member and signing up to all parts of the Human Rights Charter, Spain still sometimes dealt harshly with people in the system. People might not end up facing firing squads any more, but they often faced judicial delays and incarceration that were throwbacks to a bygone age.

Flynn hoped he could sidestep all that, but having killed someone was not a great start.

He turned back to Santiago. 'I'm really worried about Karen Glass, Adam's sister.'

She just nodded. 'I know.'

'You need to be moving on it. She has to be found.'

'I'm sure your friend will be OK.'

'I'm not,' Flynn said, tight-mouthed.

He squinted in Romero's direction. The detective had moved well away to take his phone call, out of sight around the corner of the villa. He reappeared with two uniformed cops who had fallen in behind him, striding purposefully towards Flynn. The three stopped a few feet away and the uniforms fanned out either side of Romero's shoulders, their hands resting ominously on the butts of their holstered pistols.

Romero looked serious.

Flynn swallowed drily. 'What?'

'Señor Flynn . . . it seems you have had a busy morning.'

'You could say that.'

'Two dead men at your feet and now, I am informed, another dead man, blown to pieces in your vehicle on the road to Puerto de la Aldea. You, sir, seem to drag death with you.' Romero glanced at the two uniformed cops and nodded almost imperceptibly. They drew their weapons and aimed them at Flynn.

Flynn backed away, raising his hands, palms out, defensively. 'No need for that.'

'A bombing – something you neglected to tell me about . . . your involvement in it, that is.'

'I wasn't involved.'

'Your vehicle, your crew member, I believe. The plot thickens. I have a witness who puts you at the scene. Do you deny that?'

'No . . . but my crew member was meeting me in Aldea.'

'Why, exactly? Why was he to meet you there? So he could drive in your car carrying a bomb you planted . . . so you could murder him!' Romero declared like a TV detective.

'Utter bollocks,' Flynn retorted. 'And you know it. The Albanians—'

Romero slashed his hand down through the air like an axe. 'Albanians, Albanians, Albanians,' he said contemptuously. 'A ruse to deflect blame, to deflect your guilt.'

Flynn was already weighing up how he could take and disarm the two uniformed cops, leap over the fence and escape. For a moment it was a real possibility in his head, then he dismissed it. He neither wanted to hurt the guys, nor get a bullet between the shoulder blades. Romero and Santiago would be armed and it would be just his luck for the woman cop to be a small arms shooting champion.

'Your hands,' Romero said.

Flynn frowned, then understood.

Slowly he extended his arms, wrists together.

Romero nodded at one of the uniforms, who holstered his gun and took his handcuffs out of the pouch on his belt. They were the old style, chain-link type as opposed to the newer rigid cuffs, but when they encircled his wrists and tightened up, they hurt just as much.

'I'm arresting you for triple murder,' Romero said proudly. 'Do you wish to say anything?'

'You need to find Karen Glass.'

Romero sidled up to Flynn and said, 'You're right, I probably do . . . but I suspect she is your fourth victim of the morning and you are trying to wriggle out of adding her to your already substantial tally.' He shook his head. 'Albanians my arse.'

The interview room was squalid and a little oppressive. Flynn sat at the table on an uncomfortable plastic chair, his still-cuffed hands resting in front of him and a cup of coffee clasped between his palms which, despite its bitterness, actually tasted half-decent to him. It was also a surprise, because he had not been afforded anything else by Romero, such as access to a lawyer or a toilet.

He had been here before, locked up in the tiny police station in Puerto Rico. On that occasion he had not stayed long, had been swiftly transferred to the more substantial one in Playa del Inglès. He wondered why that wasn't the case this time, because this cop shop was not really built for dealing with serious prisoners, certainly not ones accused of multiple murder who could be due for a long stay. He seemed to have been here for a long time now, either in the one and only cell – more a drunk tank than anything – or here in the interview room, waiting for something to happen. Almost three hours, he estimated, being pushed from room to room and back again by grim-faced cops who refused to converse with him other than to bark orders.

Valuable time, he thought. Time he should have spent finding Karen and then – only then – involving the cops once he knew she was safe, or otherwise. Sitting there brooding, he now deeply regretted not punching the lights out of the two cops up at Adam's villa and running.

Then he thought about Adam and found himself grinding his teeth and flaring his nostrils, steeling his inner resolve to get real justice for the man who had given him so much.

The interview room door opened.

The detective called Maria Santiago stood there. Having divested herself of her forensic suit she was now in her normal work attire – smart blazer and slacks with a brown blouse underneath buttoned just below her neck line, and flat shoes. It was severe, practical clothing but it did a poor job of disguising her figure, which was slim and lean.

She stood at the door staring intently at Flynn. He thought there could have been some kind of message in her look. She glanced over her shoulder down the corridor and grimaced with frustration. Flynn heard voices approaching – Romero talking loudly to someone else. Then the male detective appeared behind Santiago and whoever he had been talking to walked by.

Santiago stepped aside to allow Romero in, then she too entered and closed the door softly.

Romero settled opposite Flynn, Santiago sat on a chair in the corner of the room. Romero was balancing two coffees in disposable mugs with plastic tops in his right hand and a folder under his right arm, a small paper sack in his left hand. He pushed one of the cups across to Flynn, then, placing the sack on the floor by his feet, he put the folder on the table top and opened it. Flynn saw his name scribbled on the inner leaf.

Flynn released the original coffee and wrapped his hands around the new one. If he knew anything about being in custody – and in his time he had incarcerated many criminals – it was never to refuse food or drink, however awful.

In the slammer, energy was everything. It kept you alert, able to think, work things out, and the only way to get it and keep it up to a high level was by consumption. He had a premonition he was going to need every ounce in the next few days.

'Milky and sweet,' Romero said, nodding at the drink.

'Thank you. Have you found Karen yet?'

'Not as yet. My officers are still looking.'

Flynn took a sip of the coffee through the

flip-back hole in the lid. It was frothy and sweet, exactly how he did not like coffee, but under the circumstances this was how he had asked for it. It was also hot and gave him a nice sensation.

'We need to have a little talk,' Romero said. 'I want to discuss your background . . . go back to the beginning . . . just so I have a big picture of you, the man I am dealing with.' He glanced at his watch.

'It's not me you need to know about,' Flynn informed him.

'I think that is a decision I should make,' Romero countered, his eyes steely and determined. Flynn realized that the man was not going to be derailed from any route he chose to take. 'I have found a man standing over two dead bodies, two people who have died violent deaths. Oddly, I wish to know something about that man.'

'Seems you have quite a lot to begin with.' Flynn nodded at the file.

'Mm,' Romero muttered, sifting through the papers. He raised his eyes. 'Tell me about yourself.'

'Not much to tell.'

'How about the fact that you were once a Royal Marine Commando?'

'In the very distant past. I left in the mid-nineteen eighties.'

'But you were trained in weaponry and killing techniques. How to fire a gun. *How to throw a knife.*' Romero stressed the latter statement.

'As I said – long time ago.'

And it was, but Romero was correct. He had been taught those skills as a callow seventeen-year-old youth. He had just completed basic training and selection and then found himself on a troop ship leaving huge, well-wishing crowds at Southampton and heaving 8,000 miles to the Falkland Islands, via Ascension. It was on the deck of that commandeered merchant vessel that he really learned to love the sea. Becoming ultra-fit under the harsh, intense regime on deck, he also acquired skills and arts which he would put into practice immediately when he set foot on the island. Within minutes of disembarkation his unit found themselves in a firefight with the Argentine military. It was a short, brutal battle the British troops won when they overpowered two machine gun nests and then engaged in ferocious hand-to-hand combat, during which Flynn first drove a knife into the heart of another human being – in that case belonging to a young man his own age. To this day, Flynn could recall how it felt and the terrified face of the other soldier as his life ebbed away.

'Some skills are embedded, some skills do not leave you, some skills lurk below the surface only to be reignited when conditions demand,' Romero said. 'And some are lost for ever.'

'Very poetic.'

'*Gracias* . . . and then you became a police officer, uniform at first, then a detective like myself.'

'Sort of,' Flynn assented.

'And according to this' – the Spaniard held up a few sheets of paper from the file, pinned together; Flynn saw the Lancashire Constabulary crest on the top right of them and groaned inwardly. 'You left the police in . . . uh . . .

unclear circumstances . . . something to do with missing drug money?' Romero smiled.

Flynn shook his head, actually amazed – and distressed – that Romero had got his grubby hands on this information. He sighed. 'Nothing was ever proved.'

'Mm, but a cloud is a cloud, isn't it, Señor Flynn?'

Flynn glanced at Santiago. She averted her eyes.

'And then you came to Gran Canaria where you have lived ever since.' Romero continued to sift through the paperwork. 'I see that your sport-fishing boat exploded in mysterious circum-stances several years ago and a lady you knew died as the result of an assault she suffered at the hands of two unidentified men . . . in fact, I recall all that quite well.'

Clasping the coffee tightly now, almost crushing the cup, Flynn felt his insides jar.

'And on top of that you were somehow involved in diamond smuggling and you actually did kill a man not very long ago.'

Struggling to keep his voice level and calm, Flynn said, 'A matter that was fully investigated jointly by your authorities and Lancashire Constabulary, resulting in no charges being brought and a verdict of self-defence at a very thorough inquest and a subsequent criminal trial in the UK.' That had been a very long drawn out, complex affair, including a murder in the north of England and links to the US underworld as well as to African blood diamonds. 'The man I killed – *had to kill* – was trying to murder a British police officer.'

Romero inspected his paperwork. 'Ahh, Detective Superintendent Henry Christie.'

Flynn nodded. His mouth became dry at the mention of that name. 'That's the one.'

'So you're saying you're a hero?'

'I'm saying the only men I've ever killed were trying to kill either me or another person. They were justified. I'm not proud of any, nor do I see myself as a hero, detective.' Flynn leaned forward. 'You let me out of here now so I can find Karen Glass and when I do – because you are obviously not even trying – I'll walk back in here and you can do whatever you feel you have to do to me . . . but just at the moment, all this shit is wasting valuable time.'

'That is not an option, Señor Flynn, nor is it something I would trust you to do.' Romero sat back, checked his watch, calculated something, an action Flynn found slightly odd.

'So,' the detective said, 'we have ascertained that you are a man with certain skills, a violent past, the necessary attitude to deploy those skills, a propensity to become involved with the seedy side of life . . . and now you have two dead bodies at your feet, and more.'

'Are you looking for Aleksander Bashkim?' Flynn asked stubbornly.

Romero shrugged. 'Maybe.'

'Fuck, this is a joke.'

'When I say maybe, I mean it, but not in the way you mean it.'

Flynn gasped with exasperation.

Romero's lips rubbed together. His thick moustache seemed to crawl across his top lip. 'I believe that yesterday you had an argument with Dardan Bashkim.'

Flynn shifted uncomfortably. Again. Still not sure whether this was an official interview or not, he knew enough about conducting them, from the cop's side, to be aware that prisoners often felt compelled to answer, to speak, to fill gaps, to ramble on, often resulting in just what the interviewing officer wanted: incriminating statements.

So he remained silent, even though his mind began to slot the pieces together: to have the knowledge that Romero had just revealed meant that the Spaniard must have been in contact with the Bashkim clan.

'It seems that you took the Bashkims out on your boat yesterday and a trivial argument you had on board spilled over into the evening, when you lured Dardan and Pavli Bashkim to your villa and there assaulted them. Is that not so?'

'You tell me.'

'The evidence speaks for itself.' Romero picked up the paper sack by his feet, opened it and fished out a clear plastic bag. It contained Flynn's Keith Richards T-shirt, which he knew was stained with the blood of Dardan and Pavli Bashkim. 'Although this has to be established scientifically, I believe we shall find bloodstains on this piece of clothing belonging to Dardan Bashkim and when that is shown, we begin to have a motive for murder developing, don't we?' Romero touched his head and then flicked his fingers towards Flynn as if he was trying to send him an idea by telepathy. 'Now then, as regards Señor Castle, the man who co-owns your boat . . .'

Flynn's jaw dropped in disbelief.

'I believe you were very angry with him,' Romero said.

'You can believe anything you want,' Flynn said petulantly.

'He wished to sell his share, some forty-nine per cent, I believe, to Aleksander Bashkim. You did not wish this to happen, did you?'

'You're saying I killed Adam now?'

'I'm saying what I said before. You were found with two dead bodies at your feet and the more I investigate – even in such a short space of time – the more I dig up worms, cans of them.'

Flynn closed his eyes. His chin sagged on to his chest.

Romero looked along his wide nose at Flynn. 'And with regard to the so-called "missing" Miss Glass . . . where exactly is she? Where have you buried that body?'

Very slowly, Flynn's eyes opened.

'Yes, I ask myself,' Romero went on, 'where is she? The woman who, I understand, has just' – here Romero did have to think for a moment to find the correct word – 'ditched you.' He paused. 'Someone else you have a grievance against, Señor Flynn.' He smiled triumphantly, then said, 'I have yet to find a reason for you to have murdered Jose Galvez by putting a bomb underneath a car you knew he would be driving. But I will.'

'Hey, you're good – good at twisting everything,' Flynn said.

'I am simply investigating and finding out things, all of which you will have ample opportunity to answer.'

'You're wrong about everything, though,' Flynn said, feeling the sides of a mantrap starting to spring up around him.

'All I do is present evidence,' Romero said. 'It is for other people better than me to draw conclusions from it. That is my job, as you will know, having been a detective yourself once.'

Romero sniggered.

Following this, Flynn was left alone again for what he estimated was another half hour back in a cell.

When they came for him he was sitting on the concrete bench/bed, leaning forward with his elbows on his knees, staring blankly at the floor, recalling the number of times in his police career he had tampered with evidence to suit a prosecution and realizing that Romero didn't have a lot of altering to do, at least in terms of circumstantial evidence. If Romero could prove that he and Dardan had come to blows, that Adam was going to sell his stake in *Faye*, that Karen had dumped him, all those things plus the actual evidence – the blood, the knife, the 'bodies at his feet' that Romero harped on about – would be very compelling in court.

The icing on top would be for Karen's body to turn up, a thought that petrified Flynn.

Please don't be dead, he'd said to himself a few times.

It seemed that the Albanian family Bashkim had really set him up, but, to Flynn, this also begged the question – was Romero involved? He hoped not.

The cell door opened.

It was Santiago.

'Come on, Señor Flynn.' She beckoned him.

'To where?'

'We have to take you to Playa del Inglès. We have more facilities there.'

Flynn rose.

Two uniformed cops were in the corridor behind her.

'Why has it taken so long?' Flynn asked. 'I could be out on bail now if you lot had pulled your finger out.'

'I don't know,' she admitted, 'but bail would be doubtful in the circumstances anyway.' She swung her handcuffs on her finger and Flynn extended his arms. Then she stood aside as Flynn edged past her, their faces only inches apart.

Her lips were nice and wide and as he went by she whispered the words he longed to hear without them even moving.

'I'll try to help you.'

Then he was past and standing between the two cops in the corridor. They led him down to the rear door of the police station and were buzzed through to the yard. He was pushed ahead of the officers and into the back seat of a plain police car, a SEAT Toledo.

'Sit this side,' one of them instructed: the seat behind the front passenger. Flynn doubled up to fit his height and bulk in and the door slammed. He looked through the window and watched Santiago saying something to the officers. Flynn realized they were the ones who had pointed their guns at him at Adam's villa.

Santiago walked around the car and slotted herself in the back seat alongside Flynn. The two officers then got into the front.

Flynn looked sideway at Santiago.

Again, almost without moving her lips, just pursing them slightly, she said, 'Shh,' and made an almost imperceptible shake of her head.

Flynn nodded and said, 'You're coming along for the ride, then?'

'Romero wishes it.' She held Flynn's gaze for a long moment, then said, '*Vale*' to the driver and smacked the back of his seat. 'Let's go.'

Eight

It is not a long journey from Puerto Rico to Playa del Inglès, some twelve kilometres by way of the autopista – the motorway – the GC-1. Flynn settled back for the ride and closed his eyes, feeling overwhelmingly tired.

After a few minutes he slowly opened them and looked sideways at Santiago's profile, noting the slight bump on her nose, maybe the remnant of its having been broken once and a defect which, if anything, made her more attractive. He glanced down at her hands clasped on her lap, saw no wedding ring.

'Has anyone been to see Jose's widow?' he asked.

'It's in hand. Now please do not talk. Keep it for the police station.'

'I don't see myself chatting much in there.'

She shrugged. Flynn's eyes dropped again and he saw the semi-automatic pistol in the holster at her waist, just peeking out from under the flap of her blazer. He wondered how easy it would be for him to take it, kill her and the cops in front.

Easy, he concluded. But stupid.

He tore his eyes away, watching the backs of the heads of the two officers in front and through the windscreen. They had reached the junction with the GC-1 and the car was accelerating up the slipway and moments later speeding east.

'I didn't kill anyone – with the exception of Dardan. I did kill him. I had to.'

'*Por favor* . . . please, say nothing, Señor Flynn,' said Santiago.

'OK, OK.'

She turned to face him then, square on. 'I know,' she whispered so only he could hear. 'I believe you.'

She held his gaze for a few seconds, then faced forward again.

Now they were at the junction for Arguineguín and Flynn was mildly surprised when the driver signalled to exit the motorway – as was Santiago.

'Why are we turning off?' she asked in Spanish, leaning forward to the driver's shoulder.

'There are hold-ups ahead, there has been an accident,' he replied.

She sat back, frowning. 'An accident,' she said to Flynn in explanation, but he could see she was mystified by this.

They drove down to the GC-500, the original

road that connected most of the towns along the south coast of the island. The driver turned in the direction of Maspalomas and Playa del Inglès, but then almost immediately turned left again on to the GC-505 and headed north up the road that ran towards the centre of the island, following the Barranco de Arguineguín which was basically a valley or gully running up from the coast as far as Soria on the Risco Grande, well up in the mountains.

It was a road Flynn knew well. As a licensed safari guide with the requisite permission, he often followed routes such as this to take tourists up into the centre of the island and then off road, often to Roque Nublo, the spectacular basalt monolith that dominated so many views.

'Where are we going now?' Santiago demanded of the driver, tapping his shoulder this time. 'This is not the route to Playa del Inglès.'

'No, señora, you are correct,' the officer in the passenger seat said. He twisted around and looked at Santiago, smiling. 'It is a different route.'

'It is not even a route,' Santiago said.

'You are right.' Still smiling he drew his pistol from his holster and aimed it at Flynn's chest. To Santiago he said, 'Your weapon, señora.' He held out his left hand between the seats, palm upright. 'Or I will shoot Señor Flynn.'

'What?'

'Please . . . and then I will shoot you. Draw it out very carefully.'

'What is going on?' Santiago demanded.

'Give me your gun, now.' The officer's face was deadly serious.

113

Santiago glanced at Flynn, who sat tense and erect now. 'Better do what he says,' Flynn suggested.

'Sensible *hombre*,' the cop said.

Santiago moved her right hand slowly to the holster on her hip, flicked the catch with her thumb and then, with her finger and thumb on the grip of the weapon, a Glock 17, she withdrew it slowly and handed it over.

'Blasco,' she said, 'what are you doing?'

The officer said, 'Making up for lack of over-time,' as he took her gun, contorted around to drop it into the footwell in front of him. 'As is my friend, Officer Alvarez.' He jerked his head to indicate the driver.

Blasco remained facing the two passengers as Alvarez drove the car along the barranco, then pulled off the main road a couple of kilometres north of Arguineguín on to a rough track that descended towards a dry river bed. This was another location Flynn knew well because it was often used as a starting point for the safaris he guided, where he would meet up with other drivers and clients. Here they would start a convoy, and head up into the mountains after providing the tourists with a drink and some silly antics to get them all in good spirits.

The police car drew up behind a large mound of gravel and hard-core which was to be used for new road construction, supposedly. Flynn knew the mound – as big as a small hillock – had been there, virtually untouched, for four years now. It was beginning to grass over.

What it did, though, was provide cover from

the road so any passing motorists would be unable to see anything going on behind it.

Such as a cop car stopping with a prisoner in the back who was certain he did not have much longer to live. Particularly when Flynn saw that the other car parked here was a blue Rolls-Royce with two men lounging beside it. Aleksander Bashkim and the fruit of his loins, his son Pavli.

The police car stopped in a cloud of dust and grit and Flynn heard another car pull up behind. He glanced over his shoulder, not surprised to see Romero get out of the vehicle and walk towards them.

He stopped by the driver's window and tapped on it. The window slid down and Romero bent his knees and peered in, first at Flynn, smiling, and then at Santiago.

She asked angrily, '*Qué cojones?*'

In spite of having lived on the island for all those years, much to his embarrassment, Flynn's grasp of Spanish still remained tenuous. He understood and could respond to basic stuff – good morning, how are you, I'll have a beer, and the like – but more complex interaction still eluded him.

He did understand, however, what Santiago was getting at. 'What the fuck?' was pretty much the literal translation of what she had just said to Romero.

'You have big ears, Maria,' Romero said sadly. 'Pretty ones, but big ones. You should not have overheard my telephone call, otherwise I could have kept you away from this.'

She spat vehemently and swore in Spanish (and

Flynn knew enough of the language to know that she had basically called Romero a 'fucking cunt').

Romero laughed harshly. 'And I guess yours is a pretty one.' To the cops in the front of the car he said, 'Watch them.' He glanced warily at Flynn. 'Watch them carefully.' He pushed himself away from the car and went over to the men by the Rolls-Royce.

'Has this thing got child locks?' Flynn asked.

'*Sí*,' Santiago said ominously. 'We are trapped here.'

Flynn observed the meet-up between Romero and Bashkim though the front windscreen of the police car. They greeted each other like old friends, handshakes, smiles, much effusiveness. Flynn began to feel irate, now realizing that Romero's interview with him and his too-long incarceration at Puerto Rico had simply been delaying tactics so he could arrange a meeting here on the edge of the wilderness, where there were no witnesses other than buzzards hovering overhead. That was why he'd kept checking his watch.

Santiago flicked the door handle, confirming it was locked.

'Let me out,' she said.

Both officers in front had now turned in their seats and were looking back at the (now) two prisoners. Both had their pistols in hand, side by side like twins, pointing backwards.

Flynn was again weighing up his chances, which he calculated as slim.

'*Ahora sí que la hemos cagado*,' he said.

'*Sí* – deep shit,' Santiago confirmed.

116

The two cops laughed.

Flynn's eyes moved back to Romero and the Albanians by the Rolls.

This time he saw Aleksander pass an envelope to the Spaniard, who inspected the contents. Even from this distance Flynn could see that Romero's fat thumb was flicking across a very big wodge of notes.

'He's been paid to deliver us,' Flynn said.

'I see that. What are we going to do?'

'Die?' Flynn hazarded a guess.

There was much more shoulder slapping going on and the three men then turned towards the police car. Romero pointed, saying something. Bashkim senior nodded, laughed.

Pavli opened the back door of the Rolls, reached in and pulled something out. He stood upright with a pump-action sawn-off shotgun in his left hand. He held it vertically by the barrel and jerked it up and down quickly, racking the weapon – loading it by sliding the action and putting a cartridge in the breech. He swung it up, catching the stock in his right hand. With the weapon held diagonally across his chest he began to stride decisively towards the police car.

Flynn estimated twenty seconds tops before he reached it.

The two cops were still facing backwards, their guns pointed somewhere between him and Santiago, virtually side by side. He noticed that neither cop had his finger on the trigger and nor was either gun cocked and ready to fire.

He moved fast.

Ten years of having to deal with the thrashing

of dangerous sailfish had given him great skill in that respect.

His cuffed hands shot out and then upwards. The chain-link on the handcuffs meant that his wrists were perhaps three inches apart, a gap wide enough for him to grab the barrels of both guns and peel them out of the hands of their respective owners. He chucked them across to Santiago – she was as surprised as the two cops – and the guns clattered off her knees against her door. But Flynn did not stop there. He lurched forward, interlocking his fingers to form one huge, brick-like fist, which he jerked up between the two cops and with as much power as he could unleash in the confined space he did a kind of double-smash, one way, then the other, slamming the back of each hand into the face of each cop, connecting with their cheekbones before they knew what was happening.

With no backswing to add momentum to the blows he had to use all the power his muscles could provide to best effect, knowing that he had to smash them as hard as possible – which he did.

Each man slumped aside. Flynn hoped he had broken something in their faces and that they were experiencing searing pain, nausea and dizziness.

He could see that Pavli was still coming, now maybe thirteen seconds away.

He dropped back on his seat and twisted to Santiago, who was fumbling with the guns. Flynn grabbed the barrel of one, flipped it up into the air so it spun 180 degrees and caught it by the grip in his right hand.

'Cock it!' he screamed at Santiago; because of the handcuffs, this was not something he could do in a hurry.

She got the message as Flynn tilted the gun towards her and she pulled back the slide. A round slid into the breech. Flynn thumbed off the safety catch.

Flynn brought the weapon up between the two injured cops – inches away from their ears – and fired at Pavli through the windscreen. The used shell case flipped out the ejection port into the eyeball of one of the cops.

Pavli hurled himself sideways, reacting instantly, and as he moved brought the shotgun round and blasted the front of the police car. The windscreen shattered and the two injured officers were peppered with flying glass, while Flynn and Santiago cowered behind them for cover.

Flynn jerked to his right and fired two shots through the side window, reached through and used the barrel of the gun to pull up the outer door handle. He rolled out, putting another four rounds in Pavli's direction, noting that Bashkim and Romero were now huddled behind the Rolls-Royce, though Pavli was back on his feet, racking the shotgun again.

Flynn's shot had missed Pavli, and he fired two more at him. The gritty ground at his feet spat up tiny explosions of brown dirt, forcing Pavli to dive away again.

Looking back into the SEAT, Flynn saw Santiago still holding the other pistol but paralysed by terror.

The two cops in the front clutched their

bloodied, injured faces, stunned and made ineffective by the quick turn of events.

Flynn scrambled back behind the open door, knelt down and fired another two shots at Pavli through the V-shaped gap between the car and the door.

'Come on,' he screamed at Santiago.

Her mind seemed to click into gear. She threw herself across the back seat towards the open door. Flynn was trying to remember how many shots he had fired – one, two, four, two and two – eleven in total; assuming the magazine was full to start with and held fifteen rounds, he should have four remaining. He knew that these were assumptions which, if wrong, could have a fatal outcome.

He rose and fired another shot at Pavli as Santiago scrambled out behind him. He glimpsed Pavli rolling for cover behind a chunk of rock, then said to Santiago, 'Follow me.'

'Where to?'

'Fuck knows.'

He ran from the cover of the car at a crouch, keeping as low as he could across an open tract of ground, towards the actual dry river bed. He launched himself over the edge of the bank and skidded down the stony scree on his back, ripping his shirt and skin.

Santiago was right behind him, but she lost her footing and tumbled down the steep bank, ripping her trousers on a rocky outcrop, rolling to a stop beside Flynn, who was glad to see she still had the other pistol in her hand.

He pulled her to her feet and both of them sprinted across the flat of the river bed towards a jutting boulder on the opposite bank. They climbed up behind it, but Flynn's foot slipped and he rolled over on to his ankle, spraining it painfully. He fell to his knees and stabbed his left one on a sharp stone.

Looking back, Flynn saw Pavli appear at the top of the opposite bank, perhaps a hundred metres away, but it still did not deter the Albanian from aiming the sawn-off shotgun across the divide and blasting four consecutive shots that echoed around the valley.

They were all off target, just fired in anger.

Flynn got to his feet and steadied himself, then brought up the Glock and, using the boulder as a platform to steady his hands – still bound together – he took aim at Pavli, who saw what was happening, threw himself down and scampered away as Flynn squeezed off three rounds and missed with them all. Fifteen fired, and the slide clanked on empty: none left.

Santiago struggled to her feet and crouched by Flynn's side, both of them panting and both in shock at what had just happened. They stayed that way, covered by the boulder, until Pavli reappeared accompanied by Bashkim senior.

'Shit,' Flynn said, seeing what Bashkim handed to Pavli. He dragged Santiago down as Pavli opened fire with a Kalashnikov, which was effective over this range. He sprayed the weapon with as much gusto as he'd let rip with the shotgun, as though by yanking back hard he could make the bullets go further, be more effective. The slugs smacked into the rock, sharp splinters flying off dangerously, bullets skimming the top of the rock and whizzing by just above head height, until the magazine was empty, making the noise that Flynn recognized with relief – the snap of the firing pin clicking on an empty gun.

The sound of gunfire echoed and died away. Flynn dared to raise his eyes over the top of the boulder.

Pavli stood there with the Kalashnikov dangling loosely in his right hand, his chest heaving.

Bashkim stood next to him.

'Give me the gun,' Flynn said.

Santiago handed it to Flynn. He rose and took aim at Bashkim, who tipped his head back and roared with contemptuous laughter.

He made a megaphone by cupping his hands around his mouth.

'Flynn,' he bawled. 'Take your best shot. This will be the last chance you get.'

Sweat dribbled into Flynn's eyes. He had to towel it away by rubbing his forehead on his shoulder.

In spite of the distance he aimed carefully at Bashkim's body mass, the centre of his chest, adjusted his aim to allow for the bullet's trajectory over that distance, the fact that it would drop slightly, and his finger curled on the trigger

'Come on, shoot me,' Bashkim taunted, his arms wide open, presenting an open target.

It was as if Bashkim knew the exact moment that Flynn would pull the trigger because as Flynn squeezed, Bashkim's bravado deserted him and he threw himself sideways, as did Pavli.

Flynn missed. He probably would have done so anyway.

'Bastard,' he hissed as Bashkim got back to his feet, still laughing and brushing himself down.

'Mr Flynn,' he called, 'something for you to see.'

He beckoned to someone behind him and Romero came into view – dragging Karen with him. He had her in a wrestler's headlock under his right arm. She seemed slim and defenceless as the detective spun her around and threw her to the ground at Bashkim's feet. She hit the ground face first. Bashkim straddled her, grabbed a handful of her hair and pulled her up on to her knees.

Without warning, Pavli strode up to her, pivoted on his left foot and kicked her hard in the face.

Flynn lurched. Santiago laid a restraining hand on his arm.

Blood gushed from her broken nose now and Flynn could clearly see other facial injuries – black eyes, bleeding lips. Her T-shirt and shorts were ripped rags.

Fury almost overpowered Flynn. Santiago sensed this and gripped his arm tighter.

'Mr Flynn – we've had some fun, but this is no longer a game,' Bashkim called across the dry river. 'I am a flexible man and I have decided that I now require your services, as you are still alive. When you have provided them, I will release your girlfriend, but after that I will have to kill you because you murdered my son. An eye for an eye and all that. I will give you twenty-four hours to reach your decision, after which' – Flynn saw him shrug – 'she will be dead and probably so will you . . . but, just so you know

I'm not playing any more, a small demonstration of my commitment . . .'

Bashkim stood aside. The two cops who had been escorting Flynn came alongside him, their faces bleeding, the front of their uniforms blood red.

Bashkim turned to them. They looked at him fearfully. He patted one on the shoulder, then nodded at Pavli. In a brutal move, Pavli swung the Kalashnikov and smashed the barrel across the back of the head of the officer Bashkim had touched. The blow sent him down on to his hands and knees. His head lolled loosely between his shoulders.

Bashkim transferred the Kalashnikov into his left hand and held open his right, into which Romero placed a pistol, grip first.

Flynn thought: '*Santiago's gun!*'

Pavli stepped alongside the injured cop and pressed the muzzle of the gun against the back of the man's head at the point where skull met spine, so the gun was angled diagonally.

Flynn held his breath. Santiago whimpered.

Pavli pulled the trigger and the cop seemed to dive forward. His hands splayed out and the top of his head was removed by the exit of the nine mm slug.

'Fuck,' said Flynn, horrified by the execution.

'My God.' Santiago crossed herself.

'No games now,' Bashkim called. 'Twenty-four hours, after which I will be unable to control the wolves which will hunt you down.' He made the gesture of a telephone with his fingers and pointed at Romero with his other hand. 'Call us when you're ready.'

124

Nine

The irrigation channel was 200 years old, about a metre wide with stone sides and the clearest, coldest, purest mountain water from the ice caps at the centre of Gran Canaria flowing through it. It was a remnant of bygone times and the water was no longer used to irrigate farmland because that had long ceased to exist. The stone built channel ran through a deserted gorge close to the Degollada Ridge and it was one of the 'secret' places to which Flynn brought his safari clients towards the end of their dusty trek through the mountains, using tracks only a four-by-four vehicle plus an experienced driver/guide could negotiate. Here, they could drink or even bathe in the gushing, year round torrent. The manmade channel was just about wide enough for someone to sit or lie in, and made a welcome, refreshing halt.

After watching Bashkim, Pavli, Romero and the still-living cop leave, from the safety of their boulder, Flynn got Santiago to release him from his cuffs, then led her to this point, which was a tough three kilometre hike-and-scramble from that location. Flynn went ahead and no words passed between them at any time; both were immersed in dark thoughts.

When they descended into this tiny valley, picking their way through the ruins of an old farmhouse the irrigation channel once served, the sun had passed its peak heat of the day, though it was still strong, and both were thirsty, panting and sweating heavily. Santiago had her blazer thrown over her shoulder and her blouse pulled out of her slacks.

They fell on to their knees by the water channel, scooping up cupped handfuls of the beautiful liquid to drink greedily and throw over their heads.

Finally, drenched and sated, they fell on to their bottoms and collected their thoughts. Flynn leaned back on his hands, his face tilted towards the sun, feeling the water evaporating from his skin.

'I never knew this place existed,' Santiago admitted, appraising the little valley with wonder.

'I keep it close to my chest, so few people do. Not even other safari guides. I found it by accident and the tourists love it.' Flynn spoke keeping his eyes closed. 'I always fancied buying the old farmhouse and rebuilding it, maybe living here. Never happen,' he concluded, then fell silent. It seemed ridiculous discussing such trivialities in the circumstances, but it was probably human nature to do so, to lighten the most tragic of moments. Flynn had done it often in the marines and the police. He opened his eyes and looked at Santiago. 'How are you, detective?'

'I'm not sure, but I know I've witnessed something life-changing.' Her voice had a tremor in it.

He could tell she could not comprehend the enormity of it. She was controlling herself well, yet was also close to cracking, walking that fine line. He could see the strain in her face.

'What are you going to do?' she asked him. 'What are we going to do?'

'I'm not sure.'

'Helpful,' she muttered.

He sat up and knelt by the channel, emitting a groan of pain. He tugged the hem of his jeans up above his right ankle and inspected where he had hurt himself toppling over on the skid down the scree. The ankle was clearly swollen and was bleeding on the tip of the outer bone. He splashed cold water on it to ease the burning sensation.

'That looks very sore,' Santiago said.

'It is,' he confirmed.

'Let me look.' She crawled across to him, sat down beside him, her legs straight out in front of her. She took Flynn's leg and rested it carefully across her lap, pulled up his jeans a little further and ran her fingers softly over the swelling before removing his trainer in a curiously intimate gesture. 'I'm surprised you can walk.'

'I don't think it's broken,' he said, but winced when she touched him again. 'I don't think.' He rotated his ankle.

'Even so.' She looked at him, then reached into the channel, scooped up a handful of the pure liquid and sprinkled it on to the swelling.

He watched her carefully, liking what he saw.

She kept her eyes from catching his when she next spoke, almost dreamily, as she lightly massaged the cold water into the red swelling. 'What are you going to do?' she asked again.

Flynn exhaled until his lungs were empty, then said, 'Go to them. I have to. I have no choice.'

'They will kill you . . . I know men like that. You have killed that man's son and he wants his revenge.'

127

'I get that . . . but they've got Karen and if I don't . . . present myself . . . she'll be dead.'

'She's probably dead anyway.'

'At the moment she isn't. I have to assume she'll be kept alive until I meet with Bashkim, whenever that happens, and that at least gives us a chance, even if it is a fat one.'

'Uh? What do you mean?'

'Fat chance? No chance.'

Santiago grinned, dribbled more water on his ankle. 'What does he want from you?'

'I don't know. Something connected with *Faye*, my boat, I think.'

'Smuggling?'

'Highly possible – argh!' He had inadvertently moved his foot, sending a spike of pain up his leg.

'Know what I think?' Santiago said.

'No.'

'We should make our way to police headquarters in Las Palmas, speak to the chief of police.'

'Well, you would think that, wouldn't you?' He paused. 'Guess what?'

'What?'

'I don't think that's a good idea at all. Last time I called the cops, Romero turned up. That was a lesson harshly learned.'

'Not every police officer is corrupt,' she countered defensively.

'Maybe not . . . but if you want to spend the next thirty years in a Spanish jail, you go ahead, detective, because if there's one thing I've learned very quickly about Romero, it's that he's a master at fixing evidence.'

'How do you mean?'

128

'You were there,' Flynn said. 'He spun everything that happened today against me.'

'But you could prove him wrong – if it is wrong.'

'I was a cop once. I *know* how to fix evidence. It only takes a bit of imagination.'

'So how do you think he could fix the dead policeman? The murder we have both witnessed,' she challenged him.

Flynn grinned at her naivety – and also liked it. 'Let me think . . . first you have to remember we're dealing with dangerous, manipulative people, people who will lie to their back teeth, yeah? So . . . you and me – we're having an affair, we're lovers. How's that for starters?'

She blushed under her dark skin. Flynn gave her a meaningful look, then said, 'Let me see. It was all planned, my escape. You engineered to get into the car with me, as in, "Ooh, Detective Romero, I'll volunteer for this job" – and you bat your eyelashes at him.' He held up a hand to stifle her protestation. 'Then you stick your gun to the head of one of the cops driving us, make them change the route on to the five-oh-five and they tackle you, but you execute one of them, steal their guns. One of them escapes and will no doubt back up Romero's take on events.'

'But why did they kill him?' Tears formed in her eyes.

'Maybe he was unreliable, who knows? And your gun was the one used to commit that murder.'

'But . . .'

'See where I'm going with this?'

'But the forensic side of things?'

Flynn shrugged. 'As the cop in charge, Romero can manipulate anything . . . we've all done it.' Seeing her look of indignation he modified his assertion. 'Even just a teeny bit. Anyway, he could say we had help to escape . . . but the thing you can guarantee now is that you are one of the most wanted people on this island right now – me being the other, obviously, and,' Flynn added bleakly, 'I guarantee you won't be brought in alive. This is nasty, high level corruption, and a dead detective tells no tales.'

She stared numbly ahead, devastated, while her mind sifted through the scenario.

'You're innocent, he isn't. But he's on the payroll of some very bad men and he'll need to do two things: keep his name clean and stay alive to rake in as much money as he can from the baddies. He can't afford for you to go blabbing, just in case someone actually listens to you.'

A tear rolled down her cheek. She rubbed it away furiously.

'What exactly did you overhear?' Flynn asked softly.

'Romero talking on his phone . . . incriminating . . . he saw me and realized. I thought that if we got you as far as Playa del Inglès it would give me a chance to work things out, speak to the right people.'

'And we never got there. All that talk in the interview room . . . he was just killing time until Bashkim was ready for us.'

She grimaced. 'But why did they try to kill you if they need you for something? That does not make sense.'

130

'Ah well . . . Bashkim may not have wanted to kill me, but I fired first, if you recall, when the lovely Pavli was heading towards us. I initiated the fireworks, they responded. If I'm correct, they might just have been after you.'

She swallowed, then an expression of terror came over her face. She pushed Flynn's injured leg off her lap, causing him to yell in agony. She scrambled away on all fours and retched on the dry ground until, when she was empty, she sat back up and wiped her mouth. Then she came back to Flynn and sat next to him.

'Sorry about your leg,' she said.

'If it wasn't broken before, it is now.'

The remark drew a wan smile from her.

'My God, Señor Flynn, what do we do?'

'Find somewhere we can be safe for the night, then think it through, somehow come up with a plan to clear your name, although I don't know if we'll come up with any good answers.' He ran his hands over his face, stretching his features.

'I know of somewhere we could go, somewhere I think we would be safe,' Santiago said.

They threaded their way back to the GC-505. Flynn began to struggle as he negotiated the rocky pathways, now that the first flush of adrenalin, which had muted the pain of his ankle sprain and kept him going during that initial escape, had dissolved. Now his foot was hurting seriously and even though he was tough, hard and extremely fit, the searing pain was almost debilitating and was making him nauseous.

But he pushed on, taking extra care as to where he placed his feet. Santiago followed.

Finally they reached the road. Flynn put the time at about six p.m.

Here they would be exposed for about two kilometres while they walked north towards La Filipina, but at least the actual walking was less strenuous for Flynn on the shoulder of the tarmac road. At one point he had to sit and ease some pressure off his throbbing joint. He was not usually a man who allowed pain to control him, but at the moment it was slowly getting the better of him.

'Sorry,' he said to Santiago. She too had been bashed about during the escape. Her slacks were ripped and Flynn saw blood. Her blouse was also torn and there were bloodstains on her elbows.

At Flynn's suggestion she had dumped her police issue holster and the pistol was in a jacket pocket, out of sight. They looked an odd enough couple without a gun on display. Flynn had dismantled and ditched the other gun earlier.

'It's OK,' she said.

'Let's crack on.'

Flynn got gingerly to his feet. They took a moment to assess each other, but said nothing.

An old-fashioned flat back truck with wooden planks for sides was approaching from the south, one of many such vehicles on the island; they were used to transport crops, mainly bananas. A cloud of noxious fumes poured out of the exhaust, billowing behind the slow-moving truck.

Santiago stepped into the carriageway and flagged it down. Flynn thought the driver would just trundle past, but it stopped and he heard a quick conversation in Spanish between Santiago and the grizzled, crusty-looking old man at the wheel. She signalled to Flynn. 'We can hop in the back and he'll take us to La Filipina.'

Flynn looked suspiciously at the driver. He seemed innocent enough, but as they clambered in the man gestured Santiago back and said something urgently to her. Her shoulders dropped as she nodded, then returned, stone-faced.

'He says the police have a checkpoint set up three kilometres back, looking for a man and a woman who sound like us. They describe them as dangerous fugitives.'

'That'll be Romero covering his back, looking like he's doing something,' Flynn said. 'And what does he say?' He nodded at the driver.

'Fuck them.'

'Good man,' Flynn said, and acknowledged the old man, who was watching them in his cracked rear-view mirror. The man nodded.

They slid into the back of the truck and sat low, just behind the window in the driver's cab, using several bunches of bananas as cover. The truck began to roll with a crunch of gears, then kangarooed fifty metres before the driver got the hang of the clutch again.

'So they're after us,' Santiago said bleakly.

Flynn nodded. 'There's a dead cop in the mix and Romero needs suspects . . . lovers on the run . . . that's us.'

'Not so romantic as it sounds.'

'Especially as we're not lovers,' Flynn said. He pulled up his knees, aware Santiago was

133

scrutinizing him. He massaged his sprained ankle, glad of the relief.

'How can you take it all so calmly?' she said.

'Duck syndrome. Calm on top, paddling like fuck underneath.'

La Filipina was nothing more than a string of houses dotted along either side of the road. When the driver stopped, Flynn and Santiago slid off the back and the truck lurched away. The driver did not even check his mirror. Flynn did not blame him. Who would want to get involved?

They were on the correct side of the road to cut off on to a rough track leading towards the small reservoir of Excusabajara, maybe two kilometres north-east of the village. Well before they reached it, Santiago led Flynn into a long, steep driveway lined with pine trees that took them up to a restored and extended finca with south-facing views. A Range Rover and a Mercedes G-Wagen were parked on the gritty circular parking area at the front of the building. Flynn guessed the original finca could easily have been two centuries old, but it had been restored carefully and with love.

Santiago stopped Flynn. 'Wait here.'

They were by the side of the G-Wagen. Flynn leaned against it and got his first real view from the property. Despite his predicament, it took his breath away. From where he stood he could see through the magnificent valleys all the way south to Arguineguín and the shimmering waters of the Atlantic beyond.

Santiago left him and made her way alone to the front door, knocking softly. Flynn shrank on to his haunches, suddenly overwhelmingly hungry and thirsty and exhausted. For a moment his mind's eye flickered to Karen, Adam and Jose and he was almost consumed by grief. He beat off the sensation, boxed it away for later, but he knew it would come knocking.

He heard soft voices, recognizing Santiago's tones but not the other female voice. Even though they were speaking low there was an urgent tone to them, until finally the conversation was over and a few seconds later Santiago reappeared.

'It is all right. We can stay here for the night if we so wish.'

'Who is she?' Flynn was wary.

'An old friend. And, yes, we can trust her.'

'If you say so.'

Santiago offered Flynn her hand and helped him to his feet. They walked across to the front veranda of the finca where a woman of about the same age as Santiago was waiting for them.

'This is Flynn,' Santiago introduced him. 'Flynn, this is Jane.'

He bowed his head. 'Thank you for taking us in.'

'That's OK. Maria and I go way back.'

The northern English accent instantly jarred Flynn, but he could not be bothered to ask, just accepted it. He was too tired to speak.

'Come in.' She led them through a living room area, down a short hallway, and said, 'Two spare bedrooms here.' She pointed at two doors. 'They're connected by a bathroom, I'm afraid, but there are locking doors, if you see what I mean.' Then she glanced at Santiago and added, 'If that is necessary.'

135

'Thank you,' Flynn said.

'*Gracias*, Jane,' Santiago said and the two women embraced. When they separated, Jane said, 'There's a casserole on the range . . . it'll be ready in about twenty minutes. If you'd like to bathe and freshen up first, please do so. There is a lot of hot water.'

Flynn thanked her again.

With one last glance at them both, she turned and headed back to the main part of the house, leaving them standing in the hallway.

Flynn could hear Santiago in the connecting bath-room, the shower running, toilet flushing. He tried not to imagine too much as he sat on the edge of the metal-framed single bed in the room he was occupying. It was sparsely furnished, one bedside cabinet and a free-standing wardrobe. Nothing fancy, basic Spanish. But the bed felt springy and comfortable.

Eventually the sounds of ablution stopped in the bathroom. There was a pause, then a light knock on the door.

Flynn rose from the bed. He had been sitting on the edge of it, not daring to lie down because he knew he would have fallen asleep. He opened the door a crack. Santiago was on the other side with a huge fluffy bath towel wrapped around her. Her hair was wet and straggly and what had remained of make-up on her face after their flight was now gone. He saw she had smooth brown skin and wonderfully sculpted shoulders.

'Your turn,' she said. 'There's a towel in here.'

'Thank you.'

'How is your ankle?'

'Throbbing, stiff, sore.'

'There are some aspirin in here, too.'

'Great.'

'What about the cuts on your back? I noticed you'd cut yourself when you slid down into the river bed.'

'Sore, but I'll survive.'

'They'll need some kind of treatment. There is some antiseptic cream in here, also . . . but you won't be able to see or reach the cuts, I don't think.'

'You have cuts, too. On your legs and elbows.'

'I can reach them.'

Darn, he thought. 'I'll get a shower first and clean up, then take it from there.'

'Whatever you wish.'

She withdrew and Flynn watched her walk across the bathroom and out through the door into her bedroom.

Moments later he was standing underneath the hot, powerful jets of the shower fed from the water tank on the roof, heated by solar panels. He let the water dislodge the remnants of the terrible day. His mind was in turmoil, but he allowed his thoughts to roll and run and tried not to reach any conclusions or make plans because he realized he was at a low ebb and rash decisions were often made on an empty stomach and no sleep. He needed to fill one and catch up on the other.

It seemed such a long time since he had been pinned to a bed by a homicidal serial killer, and he chuckled at the thought. If he hadn't escaped from her none of what followed would have happened, and his liver would have been pan-fried and eaten by now.

He shampooed, soaped himself down, then finished showering, stepped out and towelled himself dry as he checked the wounds to his back. He looked as if he'd been mauled by a lion. There were a couple of deep gouges and a lot of scrapes and grazes, but nothing too serious. The problem was his foot.

He shoved four aspirin down his throat.

There was a knock on the door.

Flynn wrapped the towel around himself and answered it.

Santiago was now dressed in cropped chinos and a light blouse. Her hair was drawn back into a ponytail, accentuating the shape of her face and the largeness of her eyes. Flynn assumed the clothes had come courtesy of Jane.

'*Hola*,' she said.

'*Hola*.'

'Your back . . . let me see.'

Flynn revolved, showed her.

'Let me put some cream on the cuts. If they get infected . . .' She did not complete the sentence.

She shepherded him through to his bedroom and manoeuvred him on to the edge of the bed, then sat behind him and began to apply the cream carefully from a tube. It felt cool. Her fingertips felt cool.

A pair of three-quarter length cargo pants and a light blue T-shirt were laid out on the bed.

'These for me?' he asked unnecessarily.

'They are Jane's husband's. They should fit you.'

'He won't mind?'

'No he won't,' she said, and Flynn picked up something in her voice as she replied.

'That's very kind.'

'There – finished,' she declared, and wiped her fingertips on the edge of Flynn's towel.

'Thank you.'

'When you are dressed, go out on to the veranda at the back of the house. Jane's casserole will be waiting for us.'

'Brilliant.' Flynn seemed to have lost what little word power he possessed. He put it down to tiredness, being wanted for murder and the fact that he was sitting naked but for a towel wrapped around him with a beautiful Spanish lady behind him.

Santiago ran a fingertip across his shoulder, but then she was up and gone through the bathroom door, closing it softly behind her without a word or backward glance. Flynn could still feel the track of her finger, its sensation on his skin, could still feel it five minutes later when he sat down at the table on the veranda. On it was a terracotta casserole dish filled with steaming *sancocho*, a rustic Canarian stew consisting of chunks of salt fish, served with *papas arrugadas* and a *mojo* sauce, plus a home-made baguette still warm from the oven. A chilled bottle of Cruzcampo beer was also on the table, condensation dribbling down the bottle like beads of cold sweat.

Santiago and Jane came out. Santiago sat opposite Flynn with a large glass of red wine in one hand, the rest of the bottle in the other.

'I hope the food will be OK,' Jane said.

'It looks and smells delicious,' Flynn

139

complimented her. 'Thank you so much, Jane. Are you joining us?'

'No, I've already eaten . . . I'll be back in my study if you need me.'

She left with just a slight nod and a twinkle of her eyes at Santiago, who began to spoon out the meal while Flynn poured the beer, tore off some of the bread and dipped it in oil and balsamic vinegar.

When the bowls were full, Santiago said, 'Let's eat.'

They did. Both were ravenous and thirsty. Flynn ate heartily, dipping the bread into the stew which tasted of both the earth and the sea, a wicked combination. It was wonderful and he was drooling. Santiago ate well, too, and both had a second helping, finishing off the stew.

'I feel guilty about that,' Santiago said. 'Jane made the stew to freeze it.'

'Looks like we landed at just the right time, then.'

When it was over, Flynn exhaled and knew how a tiger must feel after devouring an antelope. 'Lovely,' he said, then, 'How are you feeling?'

'Like I'm on a date and all *that* was just a horrible nightmare. Don't people on the run live in holes in the ground?' She wilted, then refilled her glass of wine and took a long drink of it. 'I've tried to put it out of my mind for the time being because when I think about it, it overwhelms me and I want to scream.'

'We have to talk about it.'

'I know, but can't we leave it just a while? Maybe talk about something else?'

'OK,' Flynn said. He was relieved if he was honest with himself. 'Tell me about you and Jane. What's that all about? And tell me about you. How come you speak such flawless English?'

'I was born in Lancaster, England. I have dual nationality.'

Flynn blinked in surprise.

'My father is Spanish. He's a nuclear physicist and worked on the nuclear power stations in Heysham, near Morecambe on the Lancashire coast.'

Flynn sat back, amazed. Places he knew well, places he had policed.

'I spent my first five years as an English kid – speaking Spanish at home. We moved back to Madrid when my father got a lecturing post at a university.'

'And you became a cop?'

'Always wanted to be one . . . started off in Madrid. Only just transferred across here . . . six weeks ago.'

'Welcome to hell,' Flynn said.

'I thought it was paradise.' She screwed up her nose.

'It can be. Why the transfer?' Flynn probed.

'Personal reasons,' she said tightly. She touched her wedding ring finger involuntarily.

'OK . . . had enough of them in my time,' Flynn confessed. 'And Jane?'

'I went to York University. We met there, been friends ever since. She moved out here with her husband, say, six years ago? Unfortunately he died of a heart attack recently. Unexpected. He was a good man.'

141

'And she stayed on?'

'Yes . . . she loves it here and she's a writer. It suits her and with the internet, it's easy.'

Flynn took this all in – again, a normal conversation in extraordinary circumstances, between two people who, not many hours before, had not even known each other, who could have been dead and who might still be in the very near future. It was perhaps not as extreme, but he thought this must have been what it was like in the trenches in World War One . . . a bit.

'What about you?' she asked.

Flynn regarded her across the table. He rarely opened up to anyone. He had done to Karen and had got bitten for it, and he knew it was probably unwise to do so to Santiago, but he thought it was the right thing, so he did. He told her of his youth, the marines, the Falkland Islands followed by several tours of duty with the Special Boat Service in places with names he still dared not mention; then to the horrible firefight in Sierra Leone during which, as his colleagues fell around him on what was essentially a suicide mission, he vowed that if he lived he would get out at the earliest opportunity and do something with his life.

He lived, joined the cops.

He then told her how twenty years after that he had left under a cloud of false suspicion before coming to Gran Canaria, where he subsequently became a fishing boat skipper. He told her of the deceit surrounding his divorce, then falling in love with a woman who died because of him.

'Never gave my heart to anyone else until Karen came along. My body, yes, but not my heart,' he

142

concluded wistfully. Hearing himself talk, he knew that his second beer had gone straight to his head.

'Which brings us here,' she said.

He raised his beer. 'Aye, it does.'

Though he was exhausted, sleep would not come. At two a.m. he rose silently from his bed in his new pants and limped through the finca, finding a bottle of scotch and a glass and taking them out on to the veranda where he and Santiago had eaten. He arranged the chairs so he could put his foot up and slouch too, and rest a glass of whisky on his stomach.

It was then – and only then – that he allowed the door to open on his grief.

It gushed out of that compartment in his brain, flooding him.

Adam Castle and Jose, the two men who had saved his life and helped to make him what he had become now. Both dead in the most brutal of ways. It was possible Adam had been the author of his own misfortune, naively getting involved with violent criminals who thought nothing of murdering people standing in their way. That said, he had not deserved to die and nor had Jose, the completely innocent victim in all this. Flynn and the grumpy Spaniard had shared countless exciting moments on board, had brought in some stunning catches for the clients and had got drunk together on too many occasions to recall, other than that each one had been better than the last.

Flynn rubbed his eyes, then thought about Karen.

The prognosis was bleak, but he knew he had to present himself to Bashkim to see how it could all be played out and whether he could outmanoeuvre the gangster so at the very least Karen could walk free and alive, even if, ultimately, he himself had to face Bashkim's wrath.

Then there was Santiago. Another innocent sucked into something she did not deserve just because she had overheard one end of a telephone conversation. Flynn believed she was too dangerous to be allowed to live. If Romero was to survive intact, she had to be disposed of because if she was allowed her moment in court, as it were, someone might just believe her and start digging.

At least if she was dead, Romero could more easily pervert evidence to suit him. What better than a rogue cop shot down while trying to evade justice? Already Flynn could smell Romero emerging from the horseshit like a rose.

Ultimately, Flynn thought neither he nor Santiago could survive this.

And – bleakly – Karen could possibly be allowed to live, but Flynn had a horrible thought that if she did she would end up a prisoner in some squalid brothel, having been turned into a junkie and having twenty men forced on her every day until she became a useless husk; then her body would be disposed of, never found.

He knocked back a shot of the whisky – which deserved much better than to be guzzled – and he knew he was not alone.

He shot upright to see Santiago standing at the sliding doors. He gasped in relief.

144

'It's you . . . scared the crap out of me.' His eyes played over her. Once more, all she wore was a large fluffy bath towel.

'Sorry, I couldn't sleep.'

'Join the club.' He raised his glass. 'Detective Santiago.'

She padded out barefooted with an empty glass in her hand. She poured a large measure of the whisky in it, and filled his glass too. She stood next to him and both drank their spirits in one gulp. Then Santiago placed her glass on the table, took Flynn's out of his hand and put it alongside hers. She pulled him gently to his feet so he stood in front of her. He realized just how short and slim she was in comparison to his wide, six-two frame, and also just how beautiful she was with her black hair in disarray and tumbling across her face after being in bed, her eyes wide, lips soft and thick.

'I am very, very scared,' she whispered.

'Me too.'

She drew his hand towards her, gripping it tightly. They were standing only inches apart. Tilting her head slightly, she parted her lips and Flynn bent and kissed them, found them soft and delicious. Her tongue slithered into his mouth and a swell of something primal raced through his body. He slid a hand around her neck as she snaked her arms around his, went up on tiptoe, and they continued to kiss.

Flynn hardly remembered the next few moments. Almost inexplicably he found himself in Santiago's bedroom, on a bed twice the size of the one in his room – and she was naked, as was he, she

145

was straddling him, then he was slowly, deliciously, deep inside her as she arched her back, displaying her darkly nippled breasts. Flynn reached for them, caressing and rolling the hard nipples as she rose and dropped slowly and he could feel her heat and wetness as she ground her sex against him. She fell gently on him as their pace quickened, became urgent and intense. They held each other's faces as they came together in a wild, thrusting climax after which she collapsed on to him and they held each other tight, safe from the world for the moment.

Once he had spat her hair out of his mouth, he whispered in her ear. 'I can't keep calling you Detective Santiago, you know?'

Ten

It was a dark, dreamless four hour sleep. Flynn's eyes flickered open and he found himself lying on his back with his left arm trapped under Santiago's shoulders. She was deep asleep, breathing slowly. Flynn extracted himself gently. She rolled over with a murmur but did not wake. He grabbed his pants and T-shirt, went into the bathroom and swilled his face and mouth with fresh water. He ran a wet hand across his closely cropped head, then regarded his reflection in the mirror above the basin, wondering what the day would bring.

Santiago appeared naked at the door, looking

at Flynn through a mass of hair that reminded him of a thicket. He had to catch his breath. She looked amazing to him, smaller than she seemed when dressed, but conversely, her boobs seemed fuller when naked. He liked that dichotomy.

She said nothing but walked drowsily over to him, slid her arms around him and held him.

He could feel every soft or firm contour of her body pressed against him and despite himself felt a rush of blood.

She led him wordlessly back to bed, where they made love once more. This time it was with even greater tenderness as the spectre of the hours to come gathered darkly above them.

Flynn was on the back veranda. Jane had laid out freshly baked croissants and a large cafetière of rich, dark coffee that gave Flynn an instant jolt of energy. He was looking at Santiago's mobile phone – a smart phone – which had not been switched on since they'd got away from Bashkim and Romero. Flynn had told her to switch it off after she had told him that the police could track mobile phone signals on the islands just as efficiently as on the mainland. Her phone would also have been much easier to locate because Romero knew her number to start with. Flynn's own phone – that of the cracked screen – had been taken from him at the police station and not returned.

He toyed with the device, then slid it on the table and selected a warm croissant, which he laced with soft, gold butter.

When Santiago appeared, she was back to her

business-like self. She sat next to him, poured a coffee, took a roll.

'Are we OK?' she asked. 'No regrets?'

Flynn shook his head. 'None.'

'What about Karen? If this ends well . . .'

'If this ends well, we were finished before it began.'

Santiago nodded. 'So what's the plan?'

'Well, as I don't have Bashkim's number, I assume he expects us to make contact through Romero, though I'm reluctant to use your phone because of the tracing implications. I don't want the Spanish equivalent of SWAT descending on us before we finish breakfast. We need to have some advantage, however small. Maybe if we got down to Playa del Inglès we could buy a pay-as-you-go phone. I also want to know who I'm dealing with, so I need a phone to make some calls. Might help me. Either way, I end up meeting with Bashkim and you stay hidden.'

'I need to switch my phone on to get his number. I don't know it off by heart.'

'OK,' Flynn agreed. 'But do it quickly.' He was uncomfortable with this, but it needed to be done.

Santiago bit off a chunk of croissant. A crumb stuck to her lip. Flynn reached across and pushed it in for her. She smiled, then washed it down with a mouthful of coffee before rising from her seat, kissing him on the cheek and going inside. She returned a few minutes later with a mobile phone in one hand and a set of car keys in the other and placed both on the table with the smugness of a cat presenting a dead mouse to its owner.

'The phone belonged to Andrew, Jane's husband.

148

It's a pay-as-you-go; it's charged up and has about thirty euros' credit on it. He bought it just before he died. She doesn't want it back.'

'And the keys?'

'For the G-Wagen out front. Jane says we can use it. Again, it was Andrew's. It hasn't moved for weeks, but it should be OK.'

'I take it she wants that back?'

'When we've finished with it.'

'Your friend is a very nice person.'

'Yes, she is.'

Flynn took hold of Santiago's right wrist and checked her watch, which she wore on that side. 'It's just about the right time to annoy someone.'

'No, no, no.'

'Come on, mate,' Flynn pleaded.

He was standing at the far end of Jane's garden looking down the valley towards the coast. The sun had not risen fully yet, but its heat was spreading.

The man on the other end of the line was called Jerry Tope. He was detective constable in the Intelligence Unit based at Lancashire Constabulary's headquarters at Hutton, just to the south of Preston. Flynn and Tope had once been very good friends way back, and contemporaries. They had been such big mates that Flynn had once even told Tope's wife, the delectable Marina, a great big fat lie in order to cover up a huge, silly one night indiscretion of Tope's which could have resulted in a ruined marriage had Marina discovered the truth.

In short, Flynn had covered for a friend, taken

the blame for one night of drunken debauchery in Preston, one of those occasions which had, in those days, been affectionately and politically incorrectly called a 'Grab-a-Granny' night.

Tope had certainly grabbed a woman old enough to be his mother, and then gone into meltdown as his guilt almost made him blab the truth.

That had been many years ago. Even so, when Flynn had needed to uncover some delicate information that he had no right to have, he had phoned Tope – who, because of his role in intelligence, had instant access to such gems – and threatened to reveal all to Marina, who he knew would leave Tope bruised and penniless if she ever found out what happened that one sordid night all those years ago.

They had been desperate requests from Flynn and made with good reason, but even so he'd felt an odd pang of guilt about having to use his knowledge like the Sword of Damocles swinging over Tope's balding head.

In the background behind Tope Flynn could hear the noise of an office, the tap of keyboards, some conversations, so he knew he was speaking to Tope at work in the ground floor corner set of offices at headquarters that comprised the Intel Unit.

'I'm in a bit of a pickle and need some information, that's all,' Flynn said, deploying a huge understatement.

'I know,' Tope hissed.

Flynn went cold. 'You *know*?'

'Sort of.'

'How come?'

'Police in Gran Canaria made a formal request

150

for information about you . . . I just kinda overheard it, as I do.'

Flynn's jaw clenched as he ran this nugget of
information through his brain, recalling the file
that Romero had produced with all of Flynn's
background information. It hadn't occurred to
Flynn where he might have got it from – obviously from his personal file, which would be
archived at headquarters in Lancashire.

'They made an urgent request. Seems you've
been a busy boy . . . triple murder.'

'Who sanctioned the release of the information?
Was it that shit Henry Christie?'

'Henry? Why Henry?'

'Because he hates me?' Flynn answered,
phrasing it as a question.

'Nah, not Henry. He's retired now.'

'Oh.' This stumped Flynn for a moment. Henry
Christie was the name of the senior detective
who had essentially harassed Flynn out of the
cops over a false allegation that he had stolen a
huge amount of money from a big time drug
dealer. From then on Flynn's relationship with
Christie had been fractious, to say the least.

'Good. I'm glad he's gone. Who, then?'

'The chief constable. Just signed it off, simple.
One of the joys of being in the EU, a free flow
of information across borders.'

Flynn snorted at that, then said, 'So you believe
I killed three people, then?'

'I don't know what to think. All I did was see
a quick email.'

'Are you going to help me or what?' Flynn
asked. 'And whatever you say I won't tell Marina

151

that you slept with a woman twice your age in the nineteen eighties – she's probably in a care home now – or that I took you to the VD clinic.'

Tope took that on the chin and said, 'Actually, you sound tired.'

'Yeah. Tired and on the run, and I want to know who I'm up against, that's all.'

There was an uneasy silence.

'I'll see what I can do.'

Flynn ended the call with little feeling of hope, other than the tiny note of surprise in Jerry Tope's reaction to the name Aleksander Bashkim. It meant something to him but he remained tight-mouthed when Flynn pushed him. He did not want to commit to anything.

Flynn had made the call while walking slowly around Jane's large garden and as it concluded he had reached the back of the house, where Santiago was waiting for him.

'I've got Romero's number.' She waved a tiny piece of paper.

'Good. We need to get moving.'

'Was your phone call worth it?'

'Time will tell. Can we thank Jane and get out of her hair? Every extra minute we spend here is dangerous for her . . . if they're searching for us then they'll be knocking on her door sooner or later, and it'll be better for her if we're not here.'

'OK.'

Five minutes later, with Santiago at the wheel, they were on the road in the G-Wagen, Flynn slouched low, heading south towards Arguineguín. When they reached the coast road Flynn asked

152

her to turn towards Puerto Rico instead of to Playa del Inglès, much to her puzzlement.

'I need to get some money,' he explained.

'How do you intend to do that?'

'I need my debit card.'

'Wasn't it taken from you when you were arrested?'

Flynn smiled grimly and shook his head.

'I can get money,' Santiago offered.

'I'd rather not. They're likely to have accessed your bank details from your personal file and alerted your bank to inform them when you use an ATM. They'd be on to us too quickly.'

'What about your bank details?'

'Less likely they'll know them just yet. I do my banking online or use cash, so they won't have found any paperwork at my villa if they searched it, and they certainly won't have found my debit card – and I do all the online stuff from an internet caff in the commercial centre.'

'So where is your debit card, then?'

Flynn looked sideways at her. 'When I tell you this, I hope you'll tell me you're searching for a female serial killer who abducts men for sex and then cuts their cocks off.'

Jane Munro watched the G-Wagen pull out of her driveway and disappear, sighing with concern at her friend's predicament. She walked back into the house, gathered up her writing materials from her study – she always wrote first drafts with pen and paper – made fresh coffee, then settled on the rear veranda where she planned to spend the morning writing.

Since her husband died her life had been quite lonely. As a couple they had only just got accustomed to living on the island and when he died, Jane's first instinct was to race back to England, somewhere that was a comfort zone. Instead she made herself stay put and try to get through her grief in the place they both loved and had planned to grow old in.

It had been a tough, lonely few months and it had been her writing that held her together, spending time in the fantasy world she wrote about with lots of dungeons, knights and dragons. Her reconnection with Maria Santiago helped greatly. Her transfer to the island had been a godsend over the last few weeks and time spent with her had helped a little to heal the wound of Jane's husband's death.

So when Maria turned up desperate and bedraggled on the doorstep, asking for shelter, Jane could not even think about refusing to harbour her and the wonderful-looking man she had in tow.

Now they were gone and she was alone again, immersed in her fictional world.

She never heard anyone approach the house.

She just looked up, startled by the sudden appearance of three men, all carrying guns. One stepped up to her, smashed the side of his pistol across her head, sending her spinning off the chair on to the veranda.

He towered over her, the gun pointed at her head.

'Where are they?' he demanded.

* * *

154

Flynn gave Santiago directions to the apartment block he had woken up in the previous day, hog-tied to a bed, with his internal organs mapped out for him.

'You stay here. I won't be long,' he promised, then slid out of the car and ran up the steps leading to the swimming pool area at the front of the block. It was deserted. Sixty seconds later he was standing outside the door of the apartment that could have doubled as a slaughterhouse and his tomb if the cutlery in the kitchen drawer had been of better quality. He hovered there for a moment, took a pace back, then flat-footed the door. It clattered open on the first blow.

Instinct told him the apartment was empty – which was fine, as far as he was concerned. Assuming nothing, he entered vigilantly, still half-expecting a meat cleaver in the skull, but he had been correct. There was no serial killer at home and the place was exactly as he had left it, the bed broken and twisted, the bedding scattered, the zip-ties discarded. There was no trace of any of her belongings, though; she must have sneaked back at some stage to retrieve stuff. The carrier bag with the newly bought knives had also gone. She seemed to have done a bit of a clean-up.

This was good – but he hoped that the one thing he had neglected to pick up in his own haste to get out of the place, chasing the deranged lady, would still be there.

He recalled her sneeringly reading his name from it as she leaned on the bedroom door frame, then tossing it away with a flick of her wrist like a mini-Frisbee.

His debit card.

He hadn't seen exactly where it had skimmed to, but had a good idea. He went down on his hands and knees, then peered underneath the cheap dressing table pushed up against the wall opposite the bed.

It was still there. He could see a slight reflection off its surface and the raised contours of the embossed writing and numbers. His hand was too wide to slide under the dresser, so he attempted to slide the whole unit to one side but found it was screwed to the wall. He could, he supposed, have yanked it away from the fixings, but decided against it. Instead he found a thin slat of wood about ten inches long from the broken bed, went back on his hands and knees and used it carefully to ease out the card bit by bit, with a few dust bunnies and, grossly, a used condom.

He was about to pick the card up when he had a slight epiphany. He remembered that at the point when the woman was holding it she was not wearing gloves.

Carefully he picked the card up by its edges, tilted it slightly to the light and looked across it. He wasn't sure. He couldn't really see anything, but there was the possibility that the print of her thumb and forefinger could be on the surface – with his, obviously.

He was back with Santiago a minute later.

'Need to keep this safe somewhere,' he said, showing her the card. Santiago frowned – an expression Flynn was beginning to like a lot. 'Fingerprints at some stage, maybe DNA.'

'That is about number ten on our to-do list,' she said.

'You never know.' He placed the card on the dashboard. 'Let's go back to Playa. I'm less well known there.'

She slammed the G-Wagen into drive. Flynn sank low in his seat.

Playa del Inglès had woken up and was quite busy. Santiago left the G-Wagen in a town centre car park and the two of them walked swiftly through the ugly concrete sprawl of the resort and found a small shopping centre close to the beach. Still keeping his hands off the surface of the card, Flynn withdrew 500 euros from an ATM with no problem. Then he went into a small supermarket. On the kitchen goods aisle he discreetly opened a box containing zip-up freezer bags, stole one and slid the debit card into it to protect the surface. On the way out he bought a local English newspaper. There was nothing in it about the past day's events so he binned it and met up with Santiago, who was lounging in the shadows outside the shop. They found an elec-trical goods shop selling mobile phones and Flynn bought two cheap PAYG ones, already set up and charged, with twenty euros' credit on each.

After this they made their way down to the strip of shops and restaurants on either side of the long coastal promenade behind the beach. Away to their right were the huge sand dunes of Maspalomas and, to the left, the boardwalk to San Agustín. They found a quiet café, sat inside in the shadows, and Flynn switched on one of the new mobile phones and waited until it found a signal. He keyed in Romero's number, not bothering to withhold the number on the new phone.

A connection was made. It rang out.

Flynn and Santiago looked at each other.

'Here we go,' he said.

'Detective Romero,' came the curt answer.

'Puede ajudarme, por favor?' Flynn used his best Spanish accent to ask if the detective could help him.

'Sí, señor.' Another curt answer.

Flynn had pretty much used up his Spanish by then. He reverted to some basic English. 'Why don't you just fucking shoot yourself, then? That would help me a lot.'

Romero chuckled. 'Ah, Señor Flynn. Even now, you joke.'

'Yeah, I'm a real funny guy. Call me back on this number. I'm not wasting my credit on a cunt like you.'

Flynn cut the connection.

Santiago said, 'You have a way with words.'

'I'd like to have my way with his neck, if I could,' Flynn said. He was suddenly very angry, full of hatred for Romero.

The phone rang. Flynn touched the 'answer call' key, but did not speak.

'Señor Flynn?'

'Sí.'

'We need to speak face to face.'

'Just you and me? I'd like that.'

'No, afraid not.'

'Pity.'

Romero laughed.

'Somewhere public,' Flynn said.

'What difference would that make?'

'You'd be less trigger happy.'

'Not faced with a dangerous, desperate criminal like you. I would be more than willing to shoot you in the middle of a bull ring, surrounded by ten thousand people.'

'Where? When?' Flynn said.

'Mm . . . let me see . . . I am rather busy at the moment. You see, I'm at a crime scene. It seems that you and your lady friend have been extremely busy . . . you seem to leave dead bodies in your wake.'

'What does that mean?' Flynn swallowed drily, caught Santiago's eye, then looked away from her when she did that frown again. Flynn rotated his jaw.

'Well, we know you were here. It seems you have kept an innocent woman hostage overnight in order for you to get some sleep.'

Flynn's lips popped open, but he could not speak.

'Then you simply committed murder and moved on.'

Flynn shot to his feet, almost knocking the table over. Santiago drew back in surprise.

'What have you done?' Flynn growled.

'Well, it seems that Señora Santiago switched her mobile phone on this morning, and because we were constantly scanning the stratosphere we discovered the exact place that its signal pulsed from. A finca near to La Filipina. Of course, being efficient, I reacted instantly, but I was too late for the poor woman. You had already killed her and stolen one of her vehicles – for your

159

information, the details have been circulated to all police patrols. Being driven by a pair of ruthless, dangerous criminals . . . do not be surprised if you are shot on sight. Oh, and it would appear that the murder weapon in this case was the police-issued pistol belonging to Detective Santiago . . . the second person who has died by this weapon. But I'm only guessing at that.'

With the phone at his ear, Flynn stalked out of the café on to the boardwalk. 'If this is true, Romero, you're a dead man.'

The Spaniard laughed again. 'Midday at your boat, señor. Be there.'

The line went dead.

Flynn peeled the phone away from his ear, turned and saw Santiago was behind him.

'What is it, Flynn?'

He switched off the phone and removed the battery and SIM card, which he broke in two. He deposited the parts into a waste bin.

'What is it?' Santiago demanded again.

'How long did you have your phone switched on this morning?'

'What do you mean? Oh, just long enough for me to get Romero's number off my contacts list.'

'Just long enough for our location to be triangulated.'

Now it was Santiago's turn to register shock. 'He discovered where we were? It was on for less than a minute.'

'One pulse is all it takes.'

'Fuck,' she said despairingly. Then, 'We need to give ourselves up, take our chances. Drive to see the police chief in Las Palmas.'

Flynn shook his head. 'No.'

'What, then? We cannot outrun them, obviously.'

Flynn walked away from her on to the soft beach. She followed him, grabbed his arm and spun him around to face her. 'What, then?' she said again.

'I don't know . . . play the game . . . beat them at it . . . somehow.'

'How? We are alone in this, Steve. We're done.' She sank to her knees in the sand, all her strength deserting her as she began to sob. 'I've done nothing wrong. Why am I on the run?'

Flynn dropped to his knees, twisted around and sat next to her in the warm sand. His arm encircled her waist, feeling the sobs convulsing her body.

'Because you know something about a dangerous man who will do anything to feed – and also protect – his corruption.' He squeezed her tightly, his mouth a harsh line. 'I have to tell you something,' he said softly. 'Something that will make you realize once and for all what and who we are up against.'

Eleven

They huddled around the computer screen in one of the few remaining internet cafés in the Yumbo Centre in Playa del Inglés. Flynn had set up a new email account and they were waiting for the first message to arrive.

161

Santiago sat hunched stiffly, her hands clasped between her thighs as if she was cold.

Flynn glanced at her. 'You OK?'

She nodded without speaking, her eyes fixed on the computer screen.

Then she shook her head and the corners of her mouth turned down, but she held herself together. 'If it is true, she did not deserve that,' she said.

As gently as he could, but without mincing his words, Flynn had told her what Romero had said to him over the phone. At that moment there was no way of knowing if it was true, but in his heart Flynn knew it was. He and Santiago had been set up for another murder.

'Come on, mate,' he urged the computer as he impatiently awaited the first email from an actual human being, as opposed to the plethora of generated ones that had landed when he set up the account.

It came.

Flynn opened it and clicked on the first attachment.

It was a copy of one of Lancashire Constabulary's intelligence bulletins, several months old now. It gave details of a gang from Albania which was believed to have moved in and set up operations in the north-west of England, Lancashire in particular, and specifically the towns of Lancaster and Blackpool. The gang members were believed to be involved in a wide range of criminal activities – trafficking in drugs, arms and human beings and organs. They had also, it was believed, set up numerous brothels in these and other Lancashire towns, but the details were vague. An unknown female, aged around seventeen, had been found murdered in a park in Blackpool and was believed to have been trafficked from Syria by this gang.

Reading it, Flynn now felt a certain relief at having contacted and put a bit of pressure on Jerry Tope. Flynn had done a search for Albanian mafia gangs on his iPad the day before, sitting at the café in Puerto Rico, and noticed that Wikipedia made reference to them having set up in Lancaster, although there had been no more detail than that. It was this bit of information that had encouraged Flynn to phone Tope, who had now come up with some goods for him – although there were no actual names attached to the intel bulletin he was reading; it was just one of those general ones put out for information. Still interesting, though.

He closed the bulletin and opened the next attachment, which was also an intel bulletin.

This one had several grainy black and white photographs of a man, obviously culled from CCTV and surveillance cameras. They were quite blurred and the man's facial features were not too clear. He was hard to identify.

'Unless you know him.' Flynn muttered his thoughts aloud. 'Then it's obvious.' He turned to Santiago. 'Aleksander Bashkim,' he whispered. She nodded. He tabbed down the document. On top of the second page, Flynn's identification was confirmed. The supporting report went on to say that the Shkodra Clan – an Albanian mafia gang – headed by Aleksander Bashkim and his two sons, Pavli and Dardan (now RIP, Flynn thought), had set up operations in Lancashire. It went on to say this was only one of many outposts of the gang, which was known to operate in Albania itself, Italy, France, Spain and other parts of the UK. Bashkim was believed to have been heavily involved in the transportation of thousands of people across the Mediterranean from Libya to Italy, a journey on which many were known to have perished.

Flynn and Santiago read the document. Flynn skim-read, but Santiago read slowly and in detail. They saw that Bashkim senior was known as a *krye*, or boss, and his sons were *kryetars*, or underbosses. These three were the snake's head of that particular criminal clan.

Flynn sat back and let Santiago finish reading. His mouth pursed thoughtfully. It was clear that Bashkim was always expanding, looking for ways to earn more money from the enterprise, so it was no surprise that he was seeking opportunities in the Canary Islands, and Adam Castle's already established business was a good place to muscle in. The fact that the Canaries had become a staging post for migrants travelling from Africa to Europe would also be helpful to him. That line of business, Flynn knew, was ultra-lucrative and almost risk free.

Flynn wondered if this was the reason Bashkim wanted his fishing boat, although *Faye* was not remotely suited to carrying illegal immigrants, unless Bashkim wanted him to carry just four at a time – which he doubted.

He shrugged mentally.

Then the phone that Jane Munro had given him rang.

'Flynn.'

164

'It's me, Jerry. You get the email?'

'I did. Thanks.'

'Does it help?'

'Fills in a few blanks, helps me know what I'm going up against.'

'Up against?' Tope said. 'What is going on, Steve?'

'The less you know, the better. But do me a favour, find out what you can about these guys – y'know, the more off the record stuff.'

'Secret stuff?' Tope sighed. 'OK, but be careful, Steve. These people are mega-dangerous.'

'Tell me about it.'

'Oh, one thing I have learned . . . Bashkim is a money man.'

'What does that mean?'

'He's a banker. He looks after money. Launders it. He's known as a trusted hand and feeds dirty money back into the legitimate world. Don't know if that's any use to you?'

'Every little helps. Thanks . . . and by the way, don't use this number again. I'll have to destroy this phone now.'

'Jeez,' Tope said.

Flynn hung up, disassembled the phone, removed the battery and slid it behind the computer. Then he snapped the SIM card.

Santiago had been watching and listening.

'Time to move,' Flynn declared.

It was taking a chance, but Flynn decided to run the gauntlet of driving back from Playa del Inglès to Puerto Rico in Jane's G-Wagen. There was no time to hire a car and he didn't want to bother

165

stealing one or getting the bus; carjacking was an option, but he dismissed it.

He drove along the coast road with the beautiful glistening ocean over to his left, and they were not challenged at any point. As the road dipped into Puerto Rico, Flynn turned left on to the Puerto Base, the eastern section of the marina, out of sight of the opposite side where *Faye* was moored in the Puerto de Escala. He drove on to the wharf and stopped behind a row of sport-fishing boats. He knew the owner of every boat and though they were all in competition with each other for business, they were all friends.

'Let's go meet Tomas,' he said.

Santiago did not move.

'There's no point in both of us sticking our heads into the lion's mouth – not just yet, anyway – so, no, you can't come with me.'

Flynn saw her slim throat rise and fall as she swallowed. He leaned across and embraced her, feeling himself become far too emotional to keep a clear head, which was what he needed.

'About last night. Us,' she said. 'Did it mean anything?'

'Course it did.' He nodded. 'Either that or it was just two weak-willed individuals who saw a chance to fuck each other's brains out and went for it. I know which scenario I prefer.'

She emitted a short gasp of relief.

Flynn walked the short distance across to Puerto de Escala, still limping slightly from the ankle injury. It dawned on him for the first time that he was, appropriately enough, wearing dead

166

man's clothes. Trouble was he found them quite comfortable and maybe this was the outfit he was destined to wear to his grave.

He hoped not.

His problem as he strolled through the sunshine without – outwardly – a care in the world, was that he had no plan whatsoever. He was completely in someone else's hands, not even a trump card up his sleeve other than his own strength and cunning. He just knew he had to go into a situation to try and save someone he cared deeply about (he had stopped thinking he was in love with Karen); otherwise she would die.

And he also felt the weight of responsibility for the other person who had been dragged innocently into this situation.

He stopped at the back of the beach, next to the digital time, day, date and temperature display that hung from a lamppost on the promenade. It read '27 degrees' and '1156 hrs'.

Normally, he thought of himself as a brave man.

Today he wasn't feeling good about himself.

Today he would be fighting against the odds, walking into a set-up over which he had no control. He would have loved to have taken a gun with him, but that was out of the question. He just had to hope that Bashkim needed him for something that Flynn could use as a bargaining chip to his advantage.

Unfortunately he believed that Bashkim did not see anyone as indispensable. Quite the opposite, in fact, and if Flynn could not do what Bashkim wanted of him, then it was game over already.

He walked on, not into the lion's den he had mentioned, but into the lair of the wolf.

Looking across the marina he could see that *Faye* was still where he had left her, but that there were figures on deck and Bashkim's Rolls-Royce was parked on the quayside by the boat, together with a couple of other nondescript vehicles – a van and a car – that probably belonged to Romero and other lackeys. Bashkim now seemed to be authorized to drive on to the marina.

It was like walking to his own execution. Slow and unreal, like pushing through treacle.

Then he was there on the quay, looking across the extending gangplank on to *Faye*'s rear deck.

He had noticed, with a little tinge of satisfaction, two bullet holes in the front wing of the Rolls-Royce that must have been caused by his wayward shooting when he'd been taking pot shots at Bashkim and Pavli the day before.

And Bashkim was on deck, sitting in one of the side-benches; Romero lounged opposite while Pavli slouched in the fighting chair, facing away from Flynn towards the cabin. They were in discussion and for a brief moment did not see him. Flynn kicked himself – that was the first opportunity gone. If he'd had the pistol he could simply have walked up and taken all three out and then done a runner. But that boat sailed as Pavli spun on the chair, reacting to the startled looks of the other two men. Pavli slid off and stood up, as did Bashkim and Romero. Flynn saw Romero's right hand slide under his jacket.

Bashkim beckoned him. 'Come aboard, Mr Flynn.' All smiles and geniality.

Without having to be told, Flynn raised his hands and walked across the gangplank, stepping towards Pavli, who had a murderous expression on his face. Flynn stopped, maybe a metre away from him, fully expecting to be attacked.

'If you come for me, I'll kill you,' Flynn warned him – though in a friendly way.

Pavli's mouth warped into an amused grimace, but his eyes registered caution. That was good, Flynn thought, because if it came to it, Pavli would hesitate – and Flynn wouldn't.

Turning to Bashkim, Flynn said, 'Where is she? Where's Karen?'

Bashkim said, 'Close by . . . but you need to remember one thing, Flynn: I call the shots. I am in charge and you will follow my instructions and requests.'

Flynn nodded. 'OK, but I still need to see her. That's a given, otherwise I turn around now and walk away and if you want to shoot me in the back, so be it.'

He stepped past Pavli, who could not resist the opportunity. He swung and delivered a powerful blow into Flynn's guts, then with a double-fist he smashed him sideways across the head. Flynn had been tensing his stomach just as a precaution, though the impact still folded him over. He ducked under the second one and it missed by a centimetre. Flynn drew his fist back, about to smash it into Pavli's face.

'No,' Bashkim screamed.

Flynn stopped mid-delivery because out of the corner of his eye he had seen the gun in Romero's hand, pointed at him.

169

'No,' Bashkim said more softly, and called off his son.

Flynn now smiled at Pavli. He had expected him to have a pop, but it still hurt.

'Later,' Pavli said.

Romero moved forward. 'Turn around, arms out, let me search you.' He gestured with the gun.

Flynn raised his arms.

The detective ran his hands expertly over Flynn, quartering him as he pressed the muzzle of the gun under Flynn's ear. He was close enough for Flynn to be able to smell his aftershave, sweat, garlic and smoky breath. Flynn winced and glanced at the floor. Three cigarette stubs had been crushed out where Romero had been sitting and they had made ugly burn marks in the deck. Flynn's teeth ground at the disrespect, then he braced himself when Romero made a blade of his hand and jacked it up between Flynn's legs.

'Did you fuck her?' Romero breathed into Flynn's ear.

Flynn's eyes moved sideways. He gave the Spanish detective a look of weary contempt.

'If you didn't, you should have.' Romero grinned crookedly, then stood back and declared, 'He's clean.'

Bashkim said, 'Where is Santiago?'

'I don't know. She got frightened and ran.'

'I don't believe you.'

Flynn shrugged. 'Believe what you like. I don't know where she is.' He raised an eyebrow. 'Is that a worry?'

'Hardly.'

'More to the point, where is Karen?'

'Be my guest.' Bashkim gestured at the cabin door. 'She is here.'

'Hey – before you go,' Pavli called. He had backed off when his father interjected and was standing by the fighting chair. He had his cock out and was urinating heavily over the chair, drenching it in stinking piss. 'That is what I think of you.'

Flynn watched the arc of piss drenching a chair that had cost him over 2,000 euros – and that was cheap for a fighting chair. His only bit of satisfaction was to see that Pavli's cock was not much bigger than a button mushroom. Suddenly Pavli turned and aimed at Flynn, who sidestepped the green flow; instead it hit Romero, who glowered in disgust at Pavli.

'You are a fucking animal,' he roared.

Pavli roared back – but with laughter – as he tucked himself away, staining his tracksuit bottoms.

Of course, it was another plus for Flynn to see that there was no love lost between these men, their relationship fractious at best.

Only Bashkim remained unruffled. 'She's in the stateroom,' he told Flynn, then said to Pavli, 'Clean this up. You're no better than a dog.'

The son looked crestfallen and whined, 'But he murdered Dardan.'

'And for that I will take punitive action – when appropriate,' Bashkim replied softly, one eye on Flynn.

With foreboding, Flynn pushed open the door of the stateroom, but his relief at Karen's presence was instantly supplanted by horror and rage at

171

seeing her injuries close up, and the terror in her eyes.

She had been used as a punch bag, her face blackened and swollen; her left eye was cut and weeping pus, her cheek below it puffy, and it looked to Flynn as if her cheekbone was broken. Her lips were cut, bleeding, and her hair was matted with dried blood. Her shoulder was exposed and grazed and her clothing ripped. Flynn saw bloodstains all over it, possibly from the nose bleed she had obviously suffered. He also saw a weeping black and red cigar burn on her skin.

Nor did it calm Flynn down that she was standing up and a man was holding her from behind. Her arm was forced up her back and the blade of a huge knife had been laid across her throat.

Flynn stood there, immobile – then the man, someone Flynn had not seen before, withdrew the knife and shoved Karen across to him. She stumbled. Flynn swooped to catch her before she fell. He held her and manoeuvred her on to the edge of the bed, glaring at the man – probably one of Bashkim's heavies who usually lived underneath a rock.

Flynn sat next to her and held her, stroking her hair but not wanting to look at her wounds in case they drove him into a frenzy that would have been no good to anyone.

'Steve, you came,' she gasped. Her arms encircled him tightly.

'Yeah.' Her hair felt like rough wire. 'I came.'

'Thank God, thank you.'

'Who did this to you?' he whispered.

172

'The son . . . the son . . . he's evil, Steve. I . . .' She hesitated. 'He . . . raped me.'

Every single one of Flynn's muscles contracted.

'They're going to kill us, you know that, don't you? All because Adam wouldn't sign the business over to them.'

'How did they find you?'

'I hid in the pool house. It was easy enough, I suppose . . . I saw Adam die.' Her lips trembled. 'They shot him in the head. I'm sorry . . . I told them you were coming, and that Dardan waited for you.'

'Yeah, well, he should have gone when he had the chance.'

'Why?'

'I killed him.'

'Good . . . good.'

Bashkim appeared at the door. 'OK, enough,' he said.

Flynn disentangled himself. 'What now?'

'She goes, we talk.'

The man Flynn had not seen before hauled Karen off the boat and bundled her quickly and efficiently into the back of the van on the quayside, then drove away. Flynn watched it go, memorizing its make, colour and number. When it had gone out of sight he faced Bashkim, Pavli and Romero, hoping that he was doing a good job of hiding his murderous expression.

He wanted to kill each one, but the way Pavli was going to die would be particularly slow and brutal. That was the promise he made to himself. The other two could die quickly.

Bashkim had a half-grin on his face as if he

173

could read Flynn's mind and Flynn knew that, actually, the older man would be the hardest of the three to kill – the alpha dog.

'Let us retire to the cabin,' Bashkim said, as though they were going for aperitifs. They shuffled through and sat on the L-shaped sofa.

Romero lounged at the door and took out another cigarette. Behind him, Pavli placed a thick cigar into his mouth. Both lit up and as Pavli blew on the tip of the cigar, making it glow orange, he caught Flynn's eye. He then held the cigar between his thumb and forefinger and pretended to dab it on something, a gesture intended to arouse the ire in Flynn: he was pretending to burn Karen's flesh with it.

Flynn tore his eyes away, controlling his rage. To Bashkim he said, 'I'm not playing the tough guy here, but if either that cigarette or that cigar is put out on my deck, both of those guys are going overboard.'

Bashkim's eyes hooded over. 'I somehow do not think you are in any position to determine anything. That said, I agree.' He turned to his men. 'You both heard.'

Both scowled as if they'd been told off by a teacher.

'Now.' Bashkim's attention came back to Flynn. He leaned forward. 'You killed my son.'

'Either that, or he would've killed me. It was a no brainer.'

'I understand, but the fact remains that you have spilled the blood of my family. That means you will have to be dealt with . . . severely.'

'Tit for tat.'

Bashkim nodded. 'Dardan knew you were going to come to the villa and he wanted to deal with you himself. I was actually against it, but I allowed him his wishes . . .'

'You're such an indulgent dad.'

'I am a good father, actually.'

Flynn blinked at him. 'Nah . . . anyway, this isn't a counselling session. Why the bomb in the car?'

'That was Pavli's idea . . . fortunately you were not the one driving.'

'Why fortunately?'

'Because all along I've wanted you for something else. Like you say, I indulge my sons – a little too much sometimes – but you have survived, and now you can do something for me if you want to save the life of your girlfriend, though ultimately not your own. At the end of all this, you will die.'

'That's not very motivational.'

'Saving your girlfriend's life is, though.'

Flynn accepted that. 'OK, let's cut to the bone here.'

'You will do something for me and if you do it successfully, Miss Glass will be released unharmed though you will not . . . after all, I have a dead son to avenge . . . and if you are the man I think you are, you will do this thing for me.'

'How do I know you will keep your word?'

'You don't, but I promise you, you will watch Miss Glass walk away from this before I deal with you.'

Flynn knew that was as good as he was going to get.

'So what's this thing?'

175

'I want you to pick something up for me, then deliver it.'

Flynn chuckled grimly. 'That easy, eh?'

'How good are you with this boat?'

'The best.'

'And that is to the good, Mr Flynn.'

'Drugs, I assume,' Flynn ventured. 'You want me to run drugs.'

'Do I look like a drugs trafficker?' Bashkim said as if affronted.

'Yes.'

It was the Albanian's turn to chuckle grimly. 'Maybe, maybe so . . . however, the content of the package I wish you to pick up and deliver is not your concern. You will be the postman, that is all.' He looked at Romero, who drew in the last, long drag of his cigarette. He was about to drop it but caught Flynn's eye, thought better of it, stepped back out of the cabin and flicked it overboard.

Pavli was still smoking the huge cigar. His head was in a cloud of thick grey smoke and the end of the cigar glowed like a demon's eye in the middle.

Flynn twitched.

Romero re-entered the cabin with one of Flynn's sea charts, an old, well-folded map that Flynn had used for many years. In spite of all the new equipment on board that meant he could operate without such old-fashioned things, Flynn loved physical charts. They were things of beauty. A person could sail around the world without one – and some people did – but he liked the feel of it, the perspective and sense of place it gave him. He used new equipment, but his heart was still about thirty years out of date.

The detective opened the chart and laid it on the low table in the cabin. It showed the southern tip of Gran Canaria, west to the tiny island of El Hierro and a lot of the Atlantic Ocean beyond that. It was an area Flynn knew well, including the Sahara Seamounts – a range of mountains which did not rise above sea level anywhere to become land, and which provided rich game fishing grounds.

Bashkim placed a finger on El Hierro. 'You know this island?'

'Yes.'

He kept his finger on the map and dragged it to a point about seventy kilometres due west of the island. He looked at Flynn, who said nothing, but in his mind he guessed: a rendezvous – he had suspected something of this sort.

'If I give you a set of coordinates, could you sail to a location around here somewhere?'

Flynn hesitated. He didn't want it to seem too easy. He rubbed his chin. All he had to do was tap the bearings into his laptop and *Faye* would just take him there. It was that easy – in theory. 'Yes, I could.'

'So you could meet someone there?'

'Wherever you want.'

'You could pick up a package and then deliver it?'

'Depending on the size of the package, obviously. It would have to fit on the boat.'

Bashkim nodded thoughtfully.

Flynn said, 'With an early start, I could be there and back within a day, at a pinch, weather depending, then hand you your package.'

'No, no, you don't quite understand. I don't

want the package to come here. I need it to be delivered elsewhere.'

'Where would that be?'

Romero had obviously been riffling through Flynn's stack of neatly folded maps and charts, carefully stored on a shelf in the bridge. He had brought another one over which he opened up, wrestling with its size and creases and clearly having difficulty unfolding it successfully. Finally frustration overcame him and he bent and folded it in all directions until he found what he wanted. Flynn felt himself reddening and his breath became short as he watched Romero's tussle with the map; just another example of the disregard these people had for other people's property.

Romero dropped the map on to the table. It was actually an old Ordnance Survey map, one of many Flynn owned.

Bashkim gave Romero an irritated look, then leaned forward, adjusted the map and got his bearings before plonking the tip of his forefinger on it and saying, 'There.'

Flynn said, 'You're kidding.'

'I do not kid.'

'But that . . . that is a sea journey – a real sea journey.'

'Is this boat capable? Are you capable?'

'I could sail the southern oceans in this baby,' Flynn retorted proudly. 'Course I'm capable.'

'So the problem is?'

'You're talking about a journey of eighteen hundred miles. That is a long way.'

'How long would it take?'

Flynn ran it through his brain, calculating. 'Again, depending on the weather . . . ten days.'

'Does that include the original pick-up?'

'Twelve days, then,' he said. 'But it would need proper planning and preparation. You don't just set off on a trip like that and hope for the best.'

'What would you need?'

'Full fuel tanks. Spare tanks, also full. Food. Water. Supplies. An engine service beforehand – the boat is due one. A proper clean, too.'

'Don't you maintain it?'

'Yes . . . but an ocean journey is totally different to a day trip. I'd need to plan the journey, inform the authorities of the ports I would need to call at and refuel, restock.'

'No, you would not be allowed to do that. This has to be done as covertly as possible.'

Flynn made a helpless gesture. 'Can't do it, then.'

'You will have to.'

'Yes – I will have to stop on the way. It cannot be done otherwise – unless you provide me with a fuel tanker and a crew to accompany me.'

'Can you stop without drawing attention to yourself?'

Flynn nodded. 'Probably.'

'Then do it.'

'And it will cost money. Fuel is expensive, as is food; so is a service. Money I don't have.'

'How much?'

'Five thousand euros,' Flynn said blandly, expecting Bashkim to baulk at the figure, which he had plucked from the ether. Instead, he reached into his back pocket and withdrew a thick sheaf

179

of euro notes. He peeled off fifty one hundred euro notes and dropped them on to the table.

'I need you to meet with the package the day after tomorrow. How long will the boat take to prepare?'

'If I start now, I could have her fully prepared by tomorrow afternoon.' He had considered delaying tactics, but knew that could have been counterproductive. He had to go with the flow here, do things as quickly as possible for Karen's sake, all the while looking for a way out of this hell.

'Do it,' Bashkim said. 'Pavli will be with you from now on.'

'Marvellous,' Flynn said drily.

'You do anything . . . untoward . . . and Miss Glass will die. You do not contact anyone other than under Pavli's scrutiny, do you understand?'

'I will have to speak to people. I need my engineer for the service. I need to go shopping. I need to visit the chandlery. I need to eat, drink, sleep . . . refuel, all sorts of things.'

'Give me a list of the essentials and I will arrange to have them delivered to the boat. Do what you have to do, but do not try to shake Pavli off. He is not the brightest person, I know, but he is loyal, and if he thinks you are trying to be deceitful, he will kill you and I will think of another approach.'

Flynn inhaled a deep breath.

The game had begun, one with no rules but to survive.

Twelve

Although eminently capable of servicing his boat alone, Flynn did not necessarily want to admit that to Bashkim. So, with Pavli trailing behind him, he walked to the chandlery on the quayside. One of the partners who ran the business was also a service engineer Flynn used for any complex problems, though not usually for basic servicing. He wasn't available until next morning, so Flynn booked him and paid a deposit from Bashkim's wad.

After this, Flynn told Pavli he needed to eat. Despite the swearing and protestations, Flynn marched off with the Albanian grumbling in tow, up to the café he frequented on the first floor of the commercial centre by the marina.

He sat at a table overlooking the boats, and Pavli sat at another. It was rather like being stalked by an ape.

They ordered separately and Flynn was glad of this. Having to be in close proximity to Pavli would have been unbearable and he probably would not have been able to stop himself from tipping the bastard over the balcony rail.

Flynn had a sandwich, coffee and a bottle of water, again paid for with Bashkim's money. He decided he would use as much of it as possible, so he added a hefty tip.

He spun it out, sitting for a while with a second

181

coffee, his arm resting on the rail, aware of Pavli watching him from a couple of tables behind.

Flynn was lost in thoughts, mainly homicidal ones involving inserting a sizzling cigar butt into Pavli's actual butt-hole. He half-registered someone sitting down at a table a little further along from him – a slender woman dressed in baggy cargo pants, a military style shirt (rolled up at the front to display her midriff), large dark glasses and a baseball cap pulled down low. Tattoos emblazoned her forearms, and reappeared up the side of her neck like flames flickering up to and around her ears.

Flynn merely glanced in her direction, his mind still speculating on the intricacies of anal cigar butt insertion – until she removed her baseball cap to reveal a head shaved right down to the skull. It made him blink, but not really in surprise or horror. He had seen many ladies with such severe haircuts. Indeed, his own was not far from the bone. He also noticed the nose ring – which did slightly repel him – and the earrings and studs cascading around the edge of each ear.

Then his stomach tightened when the woman removed her large sunglasses as the waiter appeared with a menu for her. Speaking in Spanish, she ordered coffee and a churro.

Flynn almost choked on his coffee.

He glanced quickly around at Pavli, who seemed to have lost interest in him and was busy texting on his iPhone or possibly looking at pornography. Either way he was already distracted from his task of sticking close to Flynn.

As the new customer returned the menu to the

waiter, she caught Flynn's eye in the moment before putting her sunglasses back on.

And he could not help but grin.

There was nothing like hiding in plain sight.

The woman produced a paperback book from the pocket of her cargo pants and began to read.

Flynn threw back the last dregs of his coffee and stood up, folding a napkin into his pocket. He turned to Pavli and thought, 'I was right.' Pavli was rubbing a hand over his crotch, where his cock might – or might not – be. He looked up guiltily from his phone.

'I need to pee,' Flynn told him. 'You can come if you want.'

'You don' go nowhere without me.'

'I may need to shit as well.'

'Still applies.'

'In your dreams, Pavli. I go in the stall, you wait outside. I may be some time. It's a process I don't like to rush. Piles an' all that, you know.'

Flynn set off across the café and to the toilets at the back of the bar. Pavli scuttled after him.

The loo was only small: one cubicle, one urinal, a basin and a hand dryer. Very little space to manoeuvre. Flynn was about to set foot inside when Pavli grabbed his shoulder and stopped him.

'Let me check first.'

Flynn sighed. 'I get the impression you don't trust me.' He let Pavli pass, their faces only inches apart, and then he was inside the toilets – which was a mistake, because as the outer door hissed closed behind him on the pneumatic closer, Flynn quickly put his body weight on the door and flicked the butterfly lock.

Behind him, the newly cropped and decorated Santiago appeared from the café front.

'That is one severe haircut,' Flynn commented. He kissed her quickly, then grabbed a pen from the bar and scribbled on the napkin he had taken from his pocket. These were the rendezvous coordinates of the pick-up point in the Atlantic, which he had memorized.

'Don't you like it?' she asked, removing the cap. 'What about the tattoos?' She was trying to be light-hearted, but Flynn could see that her eyes were red from crying.

'In a dirty sort of way,' he admitted, and went on hurriedly, 'Look, I'm due here the day after tomorrow, but I'm not sure why as yet. To pick something up – probably from another boat. Then he wants me to sail to the UK. Karen is still alive, but they've hurt her.' He quickly scribbled another number on the napkin – the registered number of the van that had driven away with Karen in the back. 'A Peugeot van,' he said, and explained the significance of the number. 'I don't know if you can do anything with it.'

Pavli began to pound on the toilet door and shout obscenities.

'Go,' Flynn said, touching Santiago's arm.

'Jane really is dead,' she said.

'I guessed so.'

Pavli started to scream and kick the door now.

She put the glasses and hat back on. She darted into the ladies' loo.

Flynn turned his attention back to Pavli and said through the door, 'What's the matter?'

'Open fucking door,' Pavli said, and kicked it again.

Flynn flicked the lock and Pavli yanked it open, angry and suspicious.

'What you fucking up to?'

'Having fun with a big tough guy who likes hurting women.'

'Fuck you.'

'So, is the toilet clean?'

'No – I shat in it.'

'Good.'

Flynn eased past the muscled hulk and entered the toilet, closely followed by Pavli, who stepped into the cubicle behind him, preventing him from closing the door.

'Too intimate for me,' Flynn admitted.

Pavli shoved his sweating, round face into Flynn's. 'When you have done your job and it is time to die, I am going to tear your heart and lungs out and stuff your balls in your mouth.'

'Crikey!' Flynn said – then propelled Pavli backwards into the wall-mounted hand dryer, which started to blow out hot air. He slammed the cubicle door shut, then dropped his trousers, because he really did have to go.

Under Pavli's sullen, watchful scrutiny, Flynn worked hard for the rest of the day. He cleaned *Faye*, power washing the boat from stem to stern, including on and around the fighting chair where Pavli's urine had caked and dried. He checked all the equipment, from the electronic aids to basic safety equipment, including flares and fire extinguishers, all the lifejackets and flotation

185

suits, although he was pretty sure that if Pavli went overboard there wouldn't be a great deal of effort put into rescuing him.

During the afternoon a van arrived on the quayside carrying the food and drink supplies Flynn had listed, including a lot of energy bars, tins of beans and drinks. Flynn restocked the cupboards with it all.

By the end of the afternoon, as the sun began to drop low, he had completed this side of the preparations. He didn't refuel or fill up his spare tanks because it wasn't wise to have a boat moored up full to the brim with flammable fuel. That would have to wait until after the engine service in the morning, just before setting sail.

Pavli had opened the quayside sales kiosk to keep himself in the shade because Flynn had said that the on-board air conditioning unit was not working properly (a lie: he had just removed the fuse); he had also purposely harried him around the boat with the power washer and the vacuum cleaner, to the point where the gangster had flitted across to the less salubrious kiosk.

About six p.m., Flynn walked over to him.

'I'm done for the day. What happens now, o great one? Are we dining as a couple, then I woo you and we end up in bed together?'

'Maybe I will fuck you,' Pavli said. He squinted evilly at Flynn.

'That'd be nice. Anyway, I need a shower and a change of clothing and I'm going to my villa to do that. You can share a shower with me, if you like.'

Flynn flounced away with his best effeminate

186

walk, but found he could not sustain it for long. He wasn't built for being camp.

Pavli scurried after him.

Usually, Flynn's showers were short and practical. But knowing that his watcher was sitting out on the terrace sipping one of his beers, Flynn took his time over this one, which he guessed might be the last proper one he would be having for a while. Even though the shower on *Faye* was pretty good, he would have to conserve water on the journey. He also knew that lolling about in the shower would serve to irritate Pavli. He wanted to keep him in a continual state of irascibility.

He stepped out only when the water started to cool.

When he emerged after a change of clothing, Pavli said, 'I need shower, too.'

'Use mine,' Flynn offered, knowing the water would be freezing within about ten seconds.

'No. We go to my place.'

Flynn tried to look annoyed, but actually this pleased him. It would be good to know where Pavli crashed and if he was foolish enough to take Flynn there, then so be it.

After putting a few changes of underpants in a rucksack and locking the villa, Flynn was the one following Pavli up through the park, into the commercial centre. He led Flynn straight through and up into the streets behind, where there were many apartment blocks – close, in fact, to the apartment Flynn had been lured to by the lady killer.

Pavli's was a squalid, grim block. Flynn guessed it was an early Nineties build and there was little evidence of refurbishment since. Much of the concrete showed cracks, peeling paint and flaking.

Pavli waited for Flynn to catch up.

'I know I cannot be with you for every second of the day, and this is one of those occasions, but what you will do is wait outside my apartment for me to come back out. And that is that. You wait, OK? You do nothing, understand? I think you do something – she dies.'

'If you say so.'

Pavli jerked his head. Flynn followed him around to the stairs, then up on to a second floor walkway at the rear. Pavli stopped at an apartment door and unlocked it.

Before going in, he said, 'You remain here.'

Flynn nodded. He lounged on the wall and watched Pavli enter the apartment and close the door behind him. Flynn wondered what the living arrangements were for the Albanians. He guessed old man Bashkim would be holed up somewhere much more luxurious while his minions – his sons – would be left to fend for themselves in hovels like this. This was only guesswork because he still knew very little about the clan and the real reasons it had gravitated to the Canary Islands, although from what Jerry Tope had told him they had tentacles everywhere and the Canaries were probably a good draw for them. So maybe it was no surprise. Perhaps they'd latched on to Adam by luck and he had been stupid enough to be seduced by them until it was too late.

Then Flynn had to purge his mind of all thoughts of Adam because it made him grieve again.

Next to the apartment door was a high narrow

window which Flynn knew would be the shower/toilet.

He heard the toilet flush, then the pulsing of the shower and the sound of Pavli moving about.

Flynn tried the door, found it unlocked.

He stepped silently in.

It was basic. The shower room to the left, then along a short hallway which opened out into an open plan kitchen area and beyond that a space for a bed settee, with a small balcony further on. Just a studio apartment.

The place was as disgusting as Flynn expected it to be. It was a tip of discarded fast food wrappers, pizza boxes and bottles, and the reek of Pavli's cigars. Flynn's nose turned up as it was confirmed that Pavli was nothing more than a pig.

'Yuk,' he said.

He started to sift through Pavli's belongings. His wallet was on the bed. Flynn opened it and found it to be stuffed with cash – euros and sterling. He helped himself to a slim sheaf of both denominations, guessing Pavli would not have a clue how much he had. Next he bent down next to the unmade, grubby bed, where there was an open kit bag. Flynn looked into it and saw three handguns, all semi-automatic pistols of indeterminate make, most probably from former Russian states. They looked poorly maintained. There were half a dozen ammunition magazines for them, filled with nine mm bullets. Flynn dug a little deeper, hearing the shower still pounding.

A quick thought did cross his mind. If there was a good carving knife in one of the kitchen drawers, perhaps he should pay homage to classic cinema and recreate a famous shower stabbing scene – for real. It was just a passing fancy, because one day soon he and the psycho Pavli would probably act out a real life killing.

He separated a couple of items of clothing in the bag and saw two square blocks of something, each about six by three by two inches, wrapped in what looked like grease-proof paper, like huge slabs of soap or butter. Flynn lifted one out carefully and sniffed it.

Not the aroma of soap.

The aroma of linseed oil. The distinctive smell of plastic explosive, although Flynn could not determine exactly what. Possibly Semtex or C-4. He was not sure. What he did know was, this was the explosive used to blow up his car. He recalled smelling it at the scene. He had come across similar types of explosive after his stint in the Falklands – on a couple of tours of Northern Ireland; such substances were beloved of terrorists there back then.

He placed the block back where he had found it, then picked up several cigarette-like sticks he recognized as timers and detonators. He replaced these too, his face now a dark cloud of anger.

So Pavli was a bit of an explosives expert.

Not that it took major brainpower to use them. Any idiot could. Flynn could.

He rummaged a bit deeper and found more evidence of bomb making: two mercury tilt switches, crudely built mechanisms in which a blob of mercury would bring contacts together, complete a circuit and make a bomb explode.

He put them back.

The sound of the shower stopped.

Flynn stepped out of the apartment, closing the door behind him just a fraction of a second before Pavli emerged from the shower room.

With a bored expression, Flynn lounged against the wall. When Pavli came out clean-shaven, smelling of cheap aftershave and in a change of clothes, he eyed Flynn shiftily.

'I need to eat again,' Flynn told him.

Pavli nodded. Together they walked to the commercial centre, but Flynn pushed on because he wanted to eat on the beach.

Flynn decided it would be better to eat with Pavli that evening. When he settled at a table on the outside decking of one of the restaurants at the back of the beach, looking towards the marina, Pavli instinctively walked on, but Flynn called him back. They sat opposite each other, uncomfortable.

'This way you can get to know me better.' Flynn smiled.

Pavli simply shook his head.

Flynn ordered a Cruzcampo and when he gestured to Pavli he said he would have one too. Flynn then ordered pork chops, as did Pavli.

Then they sat waiting for the food and drink to arrive. Flynn leaned back and looked over his companion's shoulder out to sea.

'So what are we after? What or who are we picking up?'

'Wait, see,' Pavli said. 'Just do your job. No more questions.'

The beer arrived. Flynn sipped his. Pavli downed his in one and immediately ordered another before the waitress even got a chance to turn away from the table.

'I need to pee,' Flynn said.

'You piss and shit a lot.'

'English bladder and bowels.' He pushed himself up.

'Don't do anything silly,' Pavli warned him, and obviously could not be bothered to follow Flynn this time.

Flynn shot him an exaggerated withering look and set off for the men's toilets.

She was good, he had to admit.

He had not seen her on any part of the journey up to and back from Pavli's apartment, but she was behind him as he entered the gents'. They embraced and danced into a cubicle, kissing passionately in the very unhygienic environment. Flynn's hands cupped her shaved head. For some reason the emery board texture sent a shiver down his spine. It was curiously arousing.

They separated, gasping.

'Did you follow us up to Pavli's apartment?'

She nodded.

'Good.' Flynn hurriedly gave her some instructions, whispering them into her earringed lobe. Then he said, 'Where did you get the tatts?'

'Woman I know in the centre, usually does henna. Just temporary.'

'Do they go all the way down?'

'I hope you'll find out one day soon.' She gave him one more kiss, biting and twisting his bottom lip, then spun out of the cubicle and was gone, like a spirit.

Flynn found he had a little difficulty in peeing.

Before returning to the table, he spoke briefly to a waiter he knew.

'You took your time.' Pavli was agitated.

'Prostate. Sometimes there's a wait involved.'

Pavli nodded. His second beer was in front of him, two-thirds consumed.

'You want me to check yours for you?' Flynn offered. 'I could do it with a beer bottle, say.'

The food arrived, halting any further conversation, which was probably just as well.

The pork chops were huge, tender and moist and Flynn ate a splendid meal in silence, ordering another beer for himself and one more for Pavli, who had finished his second and was eating his food like an ogre. When the beer arrived, Pavli immediately necked a third of his, then set about devouring his second chop, picking it up and ripping the meat off the bone with his teeth.

Their conversation remained stilted even though Pavli drank far in excess of Flynn, not realizing that his drink had been spiked, and when they moved casually on to spirits, he drank four whiskies in quick succession in the time it took Flynn to drink one.

Eventually Pavli slumped in his chair, staring wetly at Flynn, very drunk.

'We're sleeping on the boat, you know,' he slurred.

'I know.'

'So you don' do somethink stupid.'

'Don't worry, I won't. But what about you?'

'Me?'

'You might do something stupid.'

193

'I won't . . . I gots my eyes on you, you cunts.' His words slurred and his English got worse at the same time.

Flynn signalled the waiter. 'Another drink and *la cuenta, por favor.*'

He paid the bill with the money he'd extracted from Pavli's wallet, then stood up to leave after Pavli had downed another neat vodka and Flynn had discreetly poured his into the sand.

Pavli pushed himself to his feet, leaned on the table and lost his balance, overturning it, sending glasses crashing on to the decking. Flynn caught him by his bicep before he pitched headlong in the sand. As he wrestled him upright, Pavli glared into Flynn's eyes in a moment of clarity.

'You bastard. I'm drunk.'

'Yep.' Flynn rotated him and dipped his hand into his back pocket, fishing out Pavli's wallet. He took out 300 euros and handed it to the waiter for the damage caused (which would probably cost about five euros in total). Flynn believed in giving good tips, especially with other people's money.

He steered the Albanian off the decking and up to the promenade, then stood aside smirking as he staggered from side to side, sometimes backwards, but generally in the direction of the marina until they arrived back at *Faye*.

The gangplank was extended and proved to be a great challenge for Pavli, who just about made it across on to the deck. There he stumbled, caught himself on the fighting chair and tried to catch it to keep upright, but it swivelled and essentially threw him on to the deck.

He picked himself up, mumbling incoherently

194

– in his mother tongue, Flynn assumed – and staggered into the cabin, where Flynn had left out bottles of whisky and vodka on the sideboard. They attracted Pavli like a beacon. He grabbed the vodka, whirled over to the settee and fell on to it. He unscrewed the bottle and took a long pull of the clear, sometimes deadly, liquid.

Flynn sat opposite sipping a whisky and water and watched Pavli drink himself into oblivion.

It took about an hour before he was completely insensible. He then fell into a deep sleep with the bottle of vodka perched on his chest. Flynn eased it gently from his grasp, then heaved him to his feet with Pavli murmuring into Flynn's ear as he manoeuvred him through the cabin, down the steps into the stateroom. Here he just pushed him face first on to the bed, splayed out like a starfish. Flynn drew the line at undressing him but said, 'Good night, you vicious bastard,' softly into his ear, switched off the light and closed the door.

Back on deck he doused all the lights other than the safety ones, then sat in the dark for half an hour in the shadows at the back of the cabin to try and work out if anyone was keeping him under surveillance. He didn't know if anyone was watching him, but had to assume they were.

He hated not being in control of any of these events. He knew that if there was to be any hope of seeing Karen alive again he had to go with the flow, but that he must also watch for and then leap on any opportunities that might arise – whatever they might be – while at the same time trying to put in place anything that might be useful if things did not turn out how he would like.

195

The quayside was deserted now. He was as sure as he could be that no one else was keeping an eye on him.

He could hear the occasional waft and beat of music from the commercial centre, but mainly the gentle lapping of water around the boats and the clank of rigging against the masts of the yachts moored close by. He checked his watch. Time to make a move. Before doing so he checked on Pavli, who was snoring deeply and dribbling on to the duvet.

Flynn moved quickly off the boat and into the deep shadow under the sea wall. Crouching, he made his way around the marina until forced to emerge into the street lights. He went past the restaurants which at that point were still busy. Then he ran up the steps behind the commercial centre to his favourite café, the one where he and Pavli had eaten earlier in the day and somehow the Albanian had ended up locked in the toilet.

There were few customers now, a couple playing pool. Flynn acknowledged the owner, then ducked into the ladies' toilets, which were not in use.

As in the men's there was just the one stall. Flynn entered it, locked the door and lifted the top off the toilet cistern. He peered in. Other than the flushing mechanism and water, there was nothing else in it. He replaced the lid, cursing, then backed out of the cubicle – where he reversed into Santiago.

'This what you're looking for?' She held up a plastic carrier bag.

'Probably. Has it got everything in it?'

'*Sí.*'

'Then we probably need to get out of here . . . I know a dark alley,' he grinned wolfishly.

'Do you mean somewhere we can meet up and have cheap sex?'

'Absolutely.'

They exited the toilet, then the café, and descended a set of steps leading to a passageway between two buildings. It was unlit and as dark as Flynn had promised and out of sight of the road. Santiago grabbed him, pulled him towards her, kissing him fiercely with a raw passion that shocked him. But then he got over that and responded just as urgently, unable to keep his hands off her sandpaper head – and her backside.

'We can't do it here,' he breathed into her ear.

'You're a strong guy, aren't you?'

'Yuh.'

'Then we can.' She backed him into a recessed doorway which was the fire exit for the ground floor shop next to them.

And they did.

Afterwards they clung to each other, breathless, until their heartbeats subsided. Only then did they speak.

'How will this end?' she asked.

'I don't know,' Flynn admitted.

'I have found something out. The van they took Karen away in . . . the Peugeot?'

'Go on.'

'It was found abandoned at Las Palmas airport. It had been stolen.'

'How do you know this? Who have you spoken to?'

'Just a friend, someone I know at Las Palmas.'

'A cop?'

'No, a civilian worker . . . a computer operator in admin.'

'You need to be careful who you speak to,' Flynn warned.

'I can trust her.'

'Maybe . . . but you're wanted for murder and you can't believe anyone is your friend. Even if they are, Romero might be watching and they could suffer.'

'OK, OK, I get it.'

'Good.' Flynn kissed her forehead and said, 'So what does that mean, the airport?'

'I don't know.'

'I need to get back to the boat and you need to get back into hiding, at least for the time being. Have you found somewhere?'

'Tomas is letting me sleep on his boat. I should be safe enough there.'

'OK, you should be.' Flynn took out his wallet and generously pushed 1,000 euros of Bashkim's money into her fist. 'That should help. Somehow we need to sort out Romero, but I think I need to get this part out of the way first.'

They embraced strongly, broke apart and then quickly went their own ways.

He arrived back at *Faye* a few minutes later with the carrier bag and boarded silently. Pavli had rolled on to his back and was still splayed out, snoring heavily and surrounded by a pall of body odours. Flynn said a prayer in which he hoped Pavli would swallow his tongue, then went back on deck. He opened the engine hatch and reached in to stow the plastic bag on a hook before settling on one of the cabin sofas, pulling a sleeping bag over him and trying to get some sleep, which he knew he would need.

Sleep was fitful, but he thought he eventually managed a solid chunk of about four hours. The remainder was horrible tossing and turning, mind-spinning stuff. He wondered if the abandoned car at the airport meant anything and he constantly re-juggled all the angles, but still feeling helpless and out of control did not make it any easier.

He was awake when the sun rose in the east over Africa, drinking coffee on the deck while sitting in the fighting chair.

He had been down in the engine compartment before the engineer arrived from the chandlery and started the service. Flynn asked him to make as much noise as possible and eventually Pavli came out, roused by the clanking of spanners on the engine block.

He looked dreadful, standing there swaying with an evil expression. Sometime during the night he had ripped off his shirt and was naked from the waist up, displaying his bulk and muscles and tattoos to great effect.

He really was a monster fuelled by steroids.

Flynn's mouth twitched with a grin, which broadened as Pavli suddenly lurched across to the rail, heaved noisily and was violently sick over the side, starting an instant feeding frenzy amongst the tiny fish in the water.

'You bastard,' Pavli snarled, seeing Flynn's face. 'You got me drunk on purpose.'

Flynn gave him a wink, then handed a spanner down to the engineer.

After a visit to the refuelling point, where he filled *Faye*'s tanks to the maximum and loaded up with all the extra cans, Flynn edged the boat out of the marina into the open ocean.

As he ran parallel with the Muelle Deportivo, the long strip of quayside that acted as a barrier for Puerto Base, Flynn spotted a lone, slim figure on the sea wall watching his departure.

He did not wave to the person, but did wonder if he would ever see her again.

Thirteen

A series of underwater mountains known as the Saharan Seamounts lies south-west of the Canary Islands. Flynn knew of them because every March, for the last three years, he had taken a group of marine biologists to dive around the slopes and also to send submersible cameras deep down to record the unusual marine life at depths of up to 600 metres. He had seen some of the video results, which included rare forms of coral and anemone and rare fish such as the rosy dory and, Flynn's own favourite, the bluntnose sixgill shark.

The coordinates for his secret rendezvous placed Flynn and his boat somewhere between Papa and Echo Seamounts and he was required to be in position at noon the day after leaving Gran

Canaria. He had taken his time over the journey, spending the night at anchor off the island of El Hierro before continuing to the destination.

It had been an uneventful journey, weather- and Pavli-wise.

Faye had easily ploughed through a wind speed hovering between forces three and four, which meant fairly gentle to moderate breezes, with large wavelets becoming much longer waves and crests breaking into white horses. It had been a pleasure to be at the helm of a boat he had personally selected (then bought with Adam Castle's money) and he felt as if he had nurtured their relationship – because that was what it was. A relationship, each knowing and compensating for the other's weaknesses, foibles, strengths and good habits. About the only time Flynn liked to use that dreaded word 'relationship'. He hoped it was a relationship that did not have to end any day soon.

As regards Pavli, he had spent the first afternoon at sea alternating between being copiously sick and recovering in the stateroom, occasionally surfacing to peer across to the horizon as though he knew what he was looking for. Flynn was glad to see this, since Pavli hadn't been sick the first time he'd taken him out, when he'd ended up shooting at dolphins. Flynn knew that an ocean journey was a very different proposition to a day trip. Pavli wore his lifejacket fastidiously, muttered every time he saw Flynn and constantly checked what, to Flynn, looked like a hand-held GPS.

They said little of any consequence to each other.

Flynn concentrated on his job and blacked out

all murderous or despairing thoughts. He had a task to achieve before he could move forward.

The night at anchor by El Hierro could have been pleasant with the right company. Flynn heated up a ready meal of chilli con carne, accompanied by water, no alcohol.

Pavli took his portion and retired to the stateroom to eat alone and swig from a new bottle of vodka that had been in Flynn's store. He obviously didn't really need much encouragement to drink. He fell asleep early, slept long and by the time he woke Flynn was at sea again, having eaten his own breakfast before Pavli reappeared bleary-eyed but in a better state than the morning before. He fried himself some bacon and made a sandwich with it, then stole some of Flynn's coffee.

Later that morning, Flynn was holding *Faye* steady at the meeting point. The sea rolled pleasantly enough and the boat was easy to keep on station.

There were no other vessels visible.

Just before noon Pavli came on deck and stood next to Flynn on the bridge, checking his GPS in one hand, with a smart phone in the other.

'We are here, ya?' he asked Flynn. He showed the GPS to Flynn.

'Ya,' he confirmed. He put his powerful binoculars to his eyes and scanned the horizon. There was a large cruise ship out there, gliding regally south towards Cape Verde, but nothing else as he swept a full three-sixty, then checked his radar screen as it picked up a new, tiny dot.

'It's here,' Pavli confirmed, pointing across the bows.

Flynn picked up the binos again and homed in on the dot, which began to grow very slowly. Eventually he saw it was a container ship, stacked high and very long, sailing slowly.

'What the hell's that?' he asked.

Pavli did not respond.

Flynn kept *Faye* steady, supressing the urge to go and meet up. He kept watching the vessel grow in the binoculars until maybe a mile separated them and he could appreciate the immense size of it.

He scoured the bows for a name and country of origin. There was neither.

Pavli stepped out of the bridge on to the rear deck, clutching his phone to his ear, speaking quietly and urgently.

Flynn watched the ship, knowing it would not be able to stop. It was an ancient ocean-going monster, he guessed probably over forty years old. It was essentially a rust bucket, flying no flag, with no identity, no home. With the binoculars he saw figures moving on the deck and watched as a hoist swung out and lowered a rigid inflatable boat (RIB) on to the water with four people on board and what looked like three large crates – and Flynn was thinking drugs again.

'Shit,' he thought. 'I used to catch drug couriers.'

The RIB angled away from the ship and the man at the wheel applied power. Its nose lifted and it skimmed across the whitecaps towards *Faye*. It was decelerating only moments later to come alongside. One of the men on board threw a rope across which Flynn caught and secured, and he got his first proper look into the RIB.

Four people on board, three crates and two big holdalls. Three of the men looked as though they were crew members; the fourth, obviously the passenger, was a small dark-skinned man, moustached and wiry, clad in warm clothing. He waved at Pavli as the two boats came side to side.

Using the hoisting pole, and directed by Pavli, Flynn winched the three crates on board and manoeuvred them on to the deck.

All that remained was to get the man aboard.

'You get back into the bridge, keep the boat steady,' Pavli ordered Flynn.

He did not argue, but going on to the bridge didn't prevent him from witnessing the horror of what happened next.

The passenger turned to the three men and shook their hands, evidently a gesture to ensure they dropped their guard. Then he drew a pistol from his waistband and, with a smoothness and lack of hesitation that said this man was no stranger to terrible violence, he shot each of them in the head with clinical precision. One went over the side of the RIB, the other two crumpled where they were shot.

Pavli then helped the man aboard *Faye*, at the same time unfastening the rope and allowing the RIB to bob away.

'I want those crates stored in the stateroom,' Pavli said to Flynn, as he and the man walked past carrying the holdalls.

The man glanced sideways at Flynn with fierce black eyes, then he was gone below.

Numb with shock at the brutal act of murder he had just seen, Flynn dragged the crates below, keeping his head down, not looking at the man, and when he had done the task he sat at the helm, blinking with fear, his mouth dry.

By this time the RIB had drifted out of sight and the container ship was a dot on the eastern horizon.

Pavli popped his head up from below and said, 'Coffee, food – and head north.' He jerked his thumb southwards, showing his non-existent sense of direction.

The weather remained kind all the way back to the Canary Islands but, following Pavli's instructions, Flynn circumnavigated Gran Canaria and ploughed towards Lanzarote, where they arrived late in the day.

Flynn wanted to go into Puerto Calero on the eastern coast, where he knew he could probably get away without having too many officials nosing around. When he mentioned it to Pavli, who was scuttling back and forth from the state-room to the galley and back, looking after his guest – Flynn was told no. He had to carry on and find a sheltered bay on the Isla de Alegranza, the most northerly island in the Canary chain.

Flynn did not know it well except that it was, like all the other islands, a volcano sticking up out of the water. It was actually privately owned by a Spanish family.

'No,' he protested, 'there is nowhere safe for the night.'

Faye was just rounding the southern tip of Lanzarote and Puerto Calero was perhaps twenty minutes distant.

'You do as I say,' Pavli bridled.

Flynn looked blandly at him. 'We need fresh water, we need to refuel . . . that's one thing about being at sea, you can't just pop into Aldi or a petrol station, because they don't exist here.'

Suddenly Flynn was looking into the muzzle of a nine mm semi-automatic pistol.

'You do as I say,' Pavli said.

'If I do,' Flynn said softly, 'we will all die of thirst, run out of fuel and then, shit-a-doodle, we might get rescued by the coastguard, who will search the boat – because they're like that – and all this will be for nothing.'

'Is there a problem?'

The voice was the passenger's. This was the first time since boarding in those auspicious circumstances that he had put his head out of the stateroom.

'No problem, just an asshole,' Pavli said. He jerked the gun at Flynn's face.

'Problem – we need fuel and water,' Flynn explained. 'Puerto Calero has what we need, Alegranza doesn't.' He leaned towards Pavli to make the point. 'It's not hard.'

'Can we use the port without drawing attention to ourselves?' the passenger asked.

Flynn nodded. 'Easily.'

'Then I would like to do so,' the man said. Flynn wasn't certain whether the accent was Spanish or Mexican – there was a difference – but it was clearly one or the other. Flynn assumed the latter. The man turned to Pavli. 'I wish to go ashore. I have been holed up in a dirty shithole of a stinking boat for almost two weeks. I want to find a shower, long and hot, then I want a change of clothing and to eat somewhere nice. I presume those things will be possible?'

Pavli shrugged.

The man looked at Flynn, who said, 'They are possible.'

'In that case—'

'What about him?' Pavli demanded, suddenly agitated. 'I don't trust him.'

The man regarded Pavli, then Flynn again – and Flynn saw the look of a killer, someone used to having his own way. 'You realize the cost of doing something you may regret?'

'I've been made aware.'

'In that case, you are going to ensure you do not do anything to jeopardize your position.'

'I won't,' Flynn said, failing to add, *Unless I get the chance.*

The man nodded. He reached out with a dry, smooth hand to shake Flynn's. 'You may call me Carlos.'

'I'll stay as Flynn.'

'As you like . . . now I suggest you take on fuel and water first, then if there is space for us in port, Pavli and I will go ashore and you will remain on board. You will guard but not examine the cargo I brought on board. Do you understand?'

'If you do, I'll kill you,' Pavli added. Flynn nodded. Pavli tapped Flynn's face patronizingly. 'We may bring you back a pizza.'

'Seafood, please,' Flynn said.

Refuelled and re-watered, Flynn edged *Faye* into a berth after contacting the port office by radio and being given the nod to slide in. The two men then left him to his own devices while they went to the office to 'deal' with their arrival and overnight stay.

Flynn read into that that silver was going to cross palms.

He had a shower and rinsed his clothes through, sitting on the rear deck in his skivvies, curiosity burning a hole in his brain.

They were ashore; he was on board.

On balance, he thought, is it worth checking what has been brought on while there is the chance to do so?

Of course it is, he answered himself.

They had been gone half an hour and Flynn hoped they had found a shower in the hotel by the marina. Even if they hadn't, he was going to look.

He went down to the stateroom. There was nowhere big enough to hide what had been brought on board, no large cupboards or hidden compartments, so the holdalls and crates were stacked in the space either side of the stateroom berth. Flynn paused, wondering if he was putting Karen in more jeopardy.

Just a peek, he thought.

The holdalls were simple enough, just zipped, not padlocked. They were one on top of the other. Flynn stepped across and unzipped the top one, exposing the contents. It was packed full of sealed, watertight slabs, wrapped in parcel tape. He did not have to be told he was looking at a multi-million pound consignment of cocaine.

He pulled back the zip.

The crates were different, made of wood, the slats tightly abutted to each other so it was impossible to see what was inside them without jemmying the lids off, something that would be noticed.

He was intrigued but thought that they were probably packed with drugs as well.

There was an awful lot of money in that stateroom, the kind of seizure that would make the career of a drug squad cop, as he had once been. Tens of millions of dollars/euros/sterling.

He backed out of the stateroom and returned to the deck, then pulled himself up the ladder to the flying bridge where he sat, still in his underwear, and tried to enjoy the evening as much as possible.

His passengers returned an hour later, clean, fed, in new clothes and relaxed. Pavli carried a huge pizza box, the sight of which made Flynn slaver like one of Pavlov's dogs. He slid back down the ladder and Pavli shoved the box into his hands. Flynn backed away with it, protective like a beast on a kill. He opened it and saw and smelled the fine aroma of a huge seafood pizza.

'Jeez,' he said, voraciously tearing off a slice and folding it into his mouth.

The man called Carlos walked past and patted him on the back. 'Enjoy, *amigo*,' he said, and ducked down the steps.

Pavli paused and grinned as Flynn swallowed, then selected another triangular portion stacked with prawns and tuna.

'Enjoy,' Pavli sneered. 'I have spat on it.'

Flynn ran his tongue over his teeth and looked

down his nose at Pavli. 'I don't care.' He tipped his head back and lowered the pointed end into the yawning cavern that was his mouth.

At six next morning, Flynn nosed *Faye* out of her overnight mooring. He was at the helm with a mug of coffee and a slice of toast clamped between his teeth. *Faye* was an easy boat to handle at any speed, always graceful and responsive. He knew he had struck lucky when he had found her for sale in the marina in Ibiza Town almost five years before.

They were in the open sea moments later, the breeze strong and fresh, the weather forecast good, ploughing north along the Lanzarote coastline with a fine dawn view of that stunning island's volcanic profile. Flynn had decided to get going on the next leg of the journey which would take them to Madeira, where he would refuel, water, not dawdle, then find a safe cove for the night. He wanted to move on as quickly as possible now, although he drew the line at night running. Not because he didn't feel safe doing it – he had spent many dark hours fishing in very dangerous waters – but because of coastguard and naval activity, folk who were always interested in small boats moving during darkness. Flynn wanted to hide in plain sight, draw no untoward attention to himself. He knew if *Faye* was boarded and searched, even routinely, it would be the end of Karen. He had to complete this task successfully if there was to be any chance of rescuing her and saving himself.

His two guests were more than happy with the

plan. They spent the majority of their time either asleep or in the cabin – and that suited Flynn.

He found shelter on Madeira's western edge where he dropped anchor and, after a meal of beans on toast, which tasted amazing, he stretched out on deck and slept. Carlos had taken over the main stateroom and Pavli the second stateroom, much smaller with a bunk bed.

The morning after found them travelling in a north-easterly direction towards the southern tip of Portugal, the Algarve, close to places from which Magellan and Vasco da Gama had set sail on their historic voyages of discovery (and plunder) hundreds of years before. Flynn then essentially coast-hopped until, after an overnight stop in La Coruña, he began the long haul across the Bay of Biscay, where many a ship had been caught out in ferocious storms and many a sailor had lost his life.

Flynn remained tense as, once again, he travelled north-east across the bay, but he had great faith in *Faye*. The weather did take a turn for the worse, becoming a force seven, a wind speed of twenty-eight to thirty-three knots and wave heights somewhere in the region of four metres. The sea heaped up as the wind speed increased and white foam blew in ghostly streaks off the wave tops.

Faye seemed to revel in the contest. All Flynn needed to do was pick the right course, make tiny adjustments and allow her to deal with what was thrown at her.

It continued for four solid hours, by which time Flynn was happy to see the back of it and was proud to bursting of his gal.

211

He was also exhausted himself.

He set her on automatic pilot and swung down from the bridge into the cabin, expecting to find Pavli and Carlos sitting there, continuing to be no use whatsoever to him, but there was no sign of them. He frowned and, unannounced, went to the stateroom, where he found them. Carlos was on the bed, stretched out. Pavli sat on the corner of it and it was apparent that Flynn had caught them in the act – their heads turned guiltily.

But the act was nothing sexual.

The lid of one of the crates had been prised off, exposing the contents.

Pavli shot to his feet. He was holding a clear plastic package of a similar size to those Flynn had seen in the holdalls. But this one – a vacuum package – did not contain cocaine. Flynn glimpsed that it had been torn open and was crammed with one hundred dollar bills. He further glimpsed that the crate was stacked and packed tight with similar sealed packets.

Pavli quickly hid the one in his hand behind his back and stepped smartly in front of the open crate, obscuring Flynn's view. Carlos sat bolt upright.

'Fuck do you want?' Pavli said.

'Sorry, guys, have I interrupted something?'

'I said what do you want?'

Flynn tried to keep his eyes off the open crate. 'I'd hoped to make further progress, but the storm has slowed us right down – and I'm knackered. We're about forty miles from La Rochelle. I intend to head there, restock and get some sleep.'

'Do it,' Carlos said.

'Now fuck off out,' Pavli added.

Flynn grinned, took another glance at the crate and reversed out of the stateroom. He returned to the bridge, where he was unable to keep his mind from mental calculations. It wasn't beyond the realms of possibility that each package contained a quarter of a million dollars, which equated to two and a half thousand vacuum-packed hundred dollar bills. It was a thick package that Pavli had in his mitt. Four packs equalled a million dollars. Ten packs, two and a half million. Flynn thought each case could possibly hold one hundred packs. So, three cases, three hundred packs, with a quarter of a million in each.

Flynn began to sweat coldly.

$75,000,000.

But, he had to admit, it was an uneducated guess.

Could be more, could be less. And he did fail his CSE in maths.

So he had now become a drug runner and a money launderer, because he had no doubt that the cash on board was going to be found a new home in Europe, somewhere.

My, he thought. How times change . . . and on that note, he steered for La Rochelle.

The night in La Rochelle was uneventful. His guests stayed on board while he was sent to fetch in food, because they now no longer trusted him now that he knew what treasure lay below decks. They all ate on the rear deck and neither of his passengers said anything to him about the money, no warnings or anything.

He would have preferred to have had the hard

word from Pavli, but it never came. Flynn easily worked out why the men were not bothered by what he knew.

At the end of it all, he was going to die. They could tell him all their secrets and they would go to the grave with him.

Not that he expected to end up in a grave anything deeper than a scrape in the ground.

'So, what lies ahead?' Carlos asked eventually – a leading question.

'Just a hop across the English Channel now, depending on the weather,' Flynn said. 'Then we'll be in British waters.' He looked at Pavli. 'And I'll need to be told exactly where I'm headed.'

'In good time, in good time,' Pavli said.

Next day was great boating weather as Flynn manoeuvred out of La Rochelle and turned north-west. The sea was calm, hardly any wind – ideal for a boat with an engine, not so good if sail dependent.

Flynn enjoyed this section of the journey.

As they rounded the Île d'Ouessant Pavli joined him at the bridge. Flynn gave him a short glance.

'You saw the money,' Pavli accused him.

'I have eyes.'

'Can you add up?'

'Two and two usually make four.'

'How much would you say?'

'A million?' Flynn lied.

Pavli threw his head back and laughed. 'Each package contains a quarter of a million dollars,' he boasted. 'Vacuum-packed, so air is sucked out. You know?'

Flynn nodded. 'I know how that feels.'

Pavli's laugh stopped abruptly. He glowered at Flynn, then said, 'Yes, fair. But no, not a million or even two.'

'Three, then,' he guessed.

'More,' Pavli egged him on.

'Four . . . I give up.'

'Seventy-five. Million. Dollars.'

Flynn's insides did a somersault, then a back-flip. His adding up was better than he thought. Hence the covering of tracks, he thought. And killing the witnesses in the RIB. It was a sum worth killing for. And the reason that he, Flynn, would not be alive much longer. The trail was being ruthlessly wiped out.

'Seventy-five million dollars,' Pavli reiterated.

'I heard. Good for you. Crikey.'

'Crikey? What does that mean?'

'Wow, then.' *I'm dead*, Flynn thought. 'I take it he's stolen the money and he's on the run?' he punted off the top of his head. 'What did he do? Screw over a cartel?'

Pavli's mouth went tight, redness seeped up around his neck and Flynn knew he was in the right ball park. 'You just sail this boat up towards Irish Sea.'

Flynn aimed between Land's End and the Isles of Scilly, heading due north from that point. Here the weather was heavy again, the going slow and treacherous, requiring all his concentration in a very dangerous stretch of water. Eventually he made the decision to find shelter and cut across to St Brides Bay, just north of Milford

215

Haven in South Wales. He waited here until the weather evened out before setting north again around the tip of St David's Head into St George's Channel, between Wexford in Ireland and Dyfed in Wales, then more or less following the coast of Cardigan Bay, cutting out again to pass the tip of the Lleyn Peninsula, where the weather turned perfect.

He was up on the flying bridge, steering the boat from there, taking in views of the Welsh mountains.

Pavli and Carlos had made one of their brief forays on deck and were standing side by side at the back of the boat, chatting.

Flynn half-watched them, cynically. He was surprised when they both threw their heads back and roared with laughter at some shared joke.

Pavli's left arm went around Carlos's shoulder. A friendly gesture.

Flynn looked away in disgust.

Then he heard something in the wind.

A cry.

He spun back. The cry had come from Carlos's lips. He had been forced down to his knees by Pavli, who had quickly stepped behind him. His muscled left arm was hooked around his neck, while the palm of his right hand was spread across the right side of Carlos's face.

Flynn started to shout, but the words stuck in his throat.

All of Pavli's muscles, his arms, shoulders and neck tensed like steel cable as he took a killing grip on the Mexican's head and twisted it as though he was opening a huge screw top bottle.

Carlos's head jerked around through 180 degrees and he was looking up at Flynn.

Flynn was almost certain he heard a nauseous snap as the neck broke, at which moment Carlos's wide eyes were connected to Flynn's in a nano-second of imploration. But it was too late for him. Pavli had broken his neck easily in a move-ment that was well-practised and precise.

He let the body slither down.

There was no post-death twitching. Carlos was simply and instantly dead.

Pavli stood back and looked up to Flynn, giving him a mock salute as if he'd just spotted him down a shopping aisle. Then he bent over and pulled open the tuna door on the rear of the boat, dragged Carlos over to it. Pavli pulled out a pair of pliers from his back pocket. Flynn watched, mesmerized with horror, as Pavli pinched off each of the Mexican's fingertips, tossing each one into the wake behind the boat. The gulls that had been lazily following the boat now shrieked with delight and dive-bombed the water for the morsels.

After this, Pavli flipped Carlos on to his back and began to stomp his right heel into his face, smashing the bone structure and, more impor-tantly, dislodging the teeth, which he then picked out and tossed overboard, like little white cubes of sugar.

Finally, Pavli folded Carlos through the tuna door, stood back and watched the body float away, only to be dive-bombed by the gulls. He rubbed his hands together and, looking back up at Flynn, cupped them around his mouth to make a megaphone.

'Señor Carlos appears to have fallen overboard. He swims with the fishes,' he called. 'And now, my friend, I need to shit.' He laughed uproariously, then went into the cabin.

Flynn turned away, stunned . . . *covering tracks*, he thought.

Fourteen

Pavli reappeared from below decks with an Admiralty chart in his hands, folded open roughly. He plonked it down in front of Flynn who was at the wheel, jabbed his fat forefinger on to the chart and said, 'Destination.'

Flynn looked down.

Pavli's finger was on the tiny port of Glasson Dock on the north coast of Lancashire.

'You sail into the dock, then up through the lock into the yacht basin. We berth at the marina there. All paperwork is taken care of.'

'OK, then what?'

'Then that is it, my friend. Your job is done and you have saved your girlfriend's life, but not, maybe, your own.' Pavli shrugged and his eyes held the promise of murder. 'You have done well. Maybe my father will be merciful.'

Flynn glanced up at the sky, checking for a flying pig.

'He will be there, then?' Flynn asked. Pavli nodded. 'And Karen?'

Pavli remained noncommittal on that point.

They were just north-east of Anglesey with about sixty miles still to travel across the Irish Sea. Flynn edged the throttle up a notch and *Faye* raised her skirt slightly, 'just showing her calf muscles', Flynn called it.

The weather worsened as they passed Blackpool. Flynn was able to spot the Tower for a few brief moments before a low cloud base engulfed the structure.

It was a familiar landmark to him, the place where he had begun and more or less ended his police career in Lancashire Constabulary. It was also the place where his first and only marriage up to this juncture began and ended. It was a bitter-sweet place for him, stacked with memories – as was Lancashire itself, the place where he grew up. And because of that, he knew Glasson Dock very well. When he was a kid he and his parents sometimes ventured there on hot summer days to eat fish and chips on the quayside and stroll up the canal and along the old railway line.

He often wondered if this was the place that ignited his passion for boats and the sea. He'd always found the sound of rigging clanking against masts a magical noise and loved the look of boats of all shapes, sizes and conditions.

This was also the place where he had once caught a very big time drug dealer, a certain Jack Boone, now deceased. Boone had been running RIBs into Glasson under cover of darkness, stacked with drugs for distribution through a country-wide network that spider-webbed out from Lancashire.

Maybe Bashkim had also seen Glasson as a

soft touch. People like him were always scouting for such places. A small port, on the southern tip of the River Lune estuary, with very little officialdom and close links to the M6 motorway; Manchester was just an hour away, and Glasgow could be reached in two. Road infrastructure was just as important to drug barons and people traffickers as it was to legit businesses. And often the illegitimate ones piggy-backed the legit ones.

So, used carefully, Glasson could be a good spot.

Flynn stayed just ahead of the bad weather but as he reached the Point of Lune – the place where the river officially ended and joined the sea – and positioned *Faye* between marker buoys on the Shoulder of Lune in order to pick up the river channel, the rain hit hard, pelting the windows like pebble dashing.

He powered back. Although the tide was high, there was always the chance of grounding boats on the unpredictable and changing sand banks of the estuary. He managed it safely, turning in through the dock gates into safe harbour.

It was almost eight p.m.

His hands at the wheel and throttle were now dithery and his heart was beginning to pick up a pace. The gates to the inner lock were already open; he chugged carefully in and they closed behind him. The water began to rise as the lock filled steadily. Less than ten minutes later the top gates were opened by the lock-keeper and he motored slowly into the yacht basin, the marina diagonally across to the right. He steered *Faye* over and even in the darkening light and heavy rain he could see figures waiting on the jetty.

Three men. One waved frantically and beckoned Flynn into the narrow gap between two piers, then indicated the spot where he should moor. They were dark, sullen figures.

'Our reception committee?' Flynn asked Pavli.

'You could say that.'

Flynn did all the work as Pavli watched. He threw the mooring ropes over to the men and they dropped the nooses over two capstans until finally *Faye* was settled and in place. Flynn cut the engines and patted her dashboard, whispering, 'Well done, babe.' Then he walked out of the bridge to the rear deck as Pavli fed out the extending electronic gangplank across to the jetty for Bashkim senior (one of the three men) to cross. He dropped light-footed on to the deck.

Flynn stood back, tense. He watched Bashkim and Pavli have a whispered conversation which ended with laughter. The men then stood apart.

Bashkim approached Flynn. 'You have done well. I salute you. Who could have known it would be so easy to bring such an amount of money and drugs into a country unchallenged?'

'It's always easy until you get caught.'

'True – and we haven't been caught, have we?'

'Not yet.' Flynn could feel himself starting to simmer, hating this pseudo-friendliness with a killer and his killer son.

'You'll be wondering where your girlfriend is?'

Flynn remained silent. He glanced at the other two men, still on the quayside, watching. The rain began to fall harder.

'I believe this is an area you know well?' Bashkim said.

'Your research is amazing.'

'In that case – there is a car park about a mile away from here on foot, where the old railway track begins. Over the bridge.'

Flynn did know it. He had pulled a dead woman out of the river near there a few years before.

'OK,' he said.

'There is an old van parked there, close to the picnic site. She is in it. As a treat, we brought her to meet you.'

Hence the Peugeot van at Las Palmas airport, Flynn thought. Somehow they had managed to smuggle Karen out of Gran Canaria.

Bashkim flicked his fingers. 'Away you go.'

Flynn knew it would not be that easy, but he did not have time to waste or argue. He grabbed his rucksack, jumped on to the gangplank, crossed it and shoved his way between the two heavies, who blocked his way and jostled him just for fun. He started to run, expecting a bullet in the back – which did not come.

The rain drenched him almost immediately as he picked up speed and hurtled through the boat yard to Tithebarn Hill, veered left, then left again over the narrow road bridge spanning the Lancaster Canal. On the other side he ran across the main road and over to the old railway track which was now a footpath and cycle way. He ran over the next bridge across the tiny River Conder and into the car park, which at first appeared to be deserted. Beyond a toilet block he caught sight of the nose of a van, and further up another vehicle. He ran to the first one, which was an old Citroën Berlingo.

222

He ripped open the driver's door, but the cab was empty. He could not see into the rear because of the partition panel behind the seats, so slamming the door he sprinted around the back and yanked the doors open.

His groan was like that of a wounded beast.

The dim and flickering interior light showed him Karen's body. She was lying in a foetal position, her ankles trussed together with parcel tape and her hands bound in front of her.

There was enough light for Flynn to see the horrible, ugly gunshot wound to the back of her head. Her mouth lolled open, oozing blood, which was pooling under her head and shoulders on the metal floor of the van.

She was naked and dead.

Flynn stood between the open van doors, transfixed by this sight and the numb sensation of utter failure within him.

His knees sagged.

A tiny portion of his mind was dimly aware of two figures walking towards him, two men who had climbed out of the vehicle parked further down the car park.

But now all time was standing still for him as the rain crashed on to him, pouring from his head, drenching him.

His mind clicked back into action, but he remained standing between the doors as the men came closer.

Even then, he knew they were here to kill him and complete his failure.

He could not see their features, just their size – both big enough – and the black shape of the gun hanging in the hand of the man on the right. The other had a mobile phone up to his ear.

When Flynn stepped backwards away from the van they stopped, maybe four metres away from him, cautious. Perhaps they had been warned about him. The one with the gun brought it up and aimed, holding it sideways, parallel to the ground like gangsters in films – *not* the way to hold a handgun.

The one with the phone said, 'This is for you.'

He held out the phone.

'Come for it, take it, then get down on your knees.'

Flynn edged away from the van. 'You do this?' he asked the man, jerking his head towards the inside of the van.

'Business,' the one with the phone said, and urged Flynn to take it from him. 'Mr Bashkim wants to speak to you.'

Flynn took it, put it to his ear. 'Yes.'

'Ahh, Mr Flynn . . . great job, well done . . . just unfortunate the woman had to die. She had seen too much for me to find it comfortable with her alive. As for you . . . ultimately you murdered my son. I cannot forgive this. May I suggest you simply kneel down now and it will be over quickly, unlike the death of Dardan, who must have bled out slowly in front of your eyes with a knife in his throat. These two men are professional killers. They will dispatch you instantly.'

Flynn said nothing.

He took the phone from his ear, handed it back to the man.

'Sorry mate, just a job,' the guy said.

'I get it,' Flynn said.

224

The man pocketed the phone, then withdrew a snub-nosed revolver from his jacket pocket, a .38. Two guns were now pointed at Flynn.

'Knees, please,' the phone guy said.

They were standing three metres away from him now and both knew they were dealing with a man who was devastated by what he had just discovered. He would be easy and pliable.

Flynn started to bend his knees. His right hand came up to his forehead – a gesture associated with disbelief and grief. He shook his head.

'Please, guys . . . one minute with her . . . all I ask,' he begged.

The phone guy made a gesture of impatience, opening his arms, dropping his shoulders and tutting, raising his eyes towards the black sky. He was about to say, *For fuck's sake . . .*

Guy number two kept his gun aimed steadily at Flynn, standing a metre to the left of phone-guy. He too shook his head with annoyance . . . the things hit men had to do, the compassion they had to show . . .

'One minute. All I ask,' Flynn said again.

The killers exchanged a glance . . .

. . . Except they didn't get a chance to exchange a glance, if that meant they looked at each other and then looked back. A movement of two parts. Turn and look; look back.

They completed the first part of it – managed to look at each other to check that both agreed to this last request made by the condemned man.

Then Flynn exploded with savagery.

As phone-guy's head swivelled sideways and, for the tiniest of moments, he was not looking

225

at Flynn, Flynn moved, covering the gap between them in an instant.

It was a blur in the rain and darkness, although Flynn himself saw it all in slow motion.

He sidestepped and pivoted around phone-guy's right arm, which he grabbed as the man shouted – but by the time the noise came out of his mouth, Flynn had taken hold of phone-guy's gun hand in his own right hand. Flynn's bigger, stronger hand encompassed it and effectively took charge of the weapon. As he did this he also moved in tightly behind phone-guy's body and slid his left arm around the man's neck. From there, Flynn twisted the whole of phone-guy's body around so he faced gunman-guy, who still had not quite worked out what was happening.

Suddenly the proposed victim had taken control of his mate.

Flynn jerked phone-guy around so he was like a shield in front of him, brought the gun up so it was aimed at gunman-guy, forced his own forefinger into the trigger guard over phone-guy's finger and yanked the trigger back twice.

They were never going to be perfect shots.

Too much going on.

The snub-nosed revolver fired, jerking all over the place with phone-guy's struggle and the recoil, but the bullets had the desired effect as far as Flynn was concerned.

The first bullet slammed into gunman-guy's lower gut, the second into his left thigh.

Gunman-guy doubled over with the impact, clutching his stomach as if he had been gut-punched by a cheating boxer.

226

Flynn knew the man wasn't mortally wounded and that if he kept his head he could still be a problem, which meant that Flynn now had to deal efficiently and effectively – and fast – with phone-guy.

But he had started to struggle violently, back-jabbing his left elbow into Flynn's ribcage while also trying to contort savagely out of his grip and stamp on his feet. He managed to wrench his gun hand free and stumbled away from him like some deformed ballet dancer.

Flynn had been in many street fights, but although he was still fit and fast the instinct in him was lazy and he had to force himself to keep up with developments.

Phone-guy came around too quickly, the gun still in his hand, and arced towards Flynn. Flynn stepped inside the sweep of the arm, got in close and quickly and ferociously head-butted phone-guy – which was about the best option at that intimate distance.

It wasn't the best of blows, but it had the desired effect as Flynn's hard forehead slammed down on to the bridge of the man's nose without having the benefit of the space to rear back his head before striking. He'd had to rely simply on his neck muscles for power and momentum. Phone-guy's septum crumbled under the brick that was Flynn's skull. It broke too easily, Flynn thought in parallel. Even in the moment he guessed the man was probably a coke addict and the gristle that separated his nostrils had already disinte-grated from overuse of the white powder.

Phone-guy fell like a plant pot dropped from

a high building. The blow unlocked his knees and next thing he was on all fours, with blood gushing from a flattened face. The gun had dropped from his hand. Flynn swooped and picked it up, swivelling then to turn his attention to gunman-guy, still on his knees, clutching the wound to his lower stomach with his hands crossed over his belly, the gun still in his hand.

Flynn guessed that just at that moment the feeling the guy was experiencing would be similar to having been kicked in the stomach by a rugby player, along with a sensation of creeping numbness.

Flynn knew exactly how that felt – because that was how he was feeling too.

The man raised his face to Flynn and tried to bring up the gun, but his hand dithered weakly.

Flynn did another sidestep, but the gun did not follow him. In fact, gunman-guy slumped forward, groaned and dropped the weapon on the wet ground.

Flynn gave both men the consideration they were, apparently, going to show him.

He scooped up gunman-guy's pistol, stepped up and placed the muzzle hard against the man's temple and shot him twice in the head. He toppled over and blood spurted out of the wounds like a fountain.

Flynn turned back to phone-guy, who was still on all fours, jerking his head and causing his blood to spray out, like a wet dog shaking itself. He was in a swirling, disoriented world following the head butt. Flynn placed the muzzle of the pistol against the back of his skull and pulled the trigger. Phone-guy shot forward headlong like a diver doing a belly flop.

Flynn stood over them for a moment, breathing heavily, then went through their pockets and found their mobile phones.

On gunman-guy's phone he tapped in a memorized number but did not press the call button.

On phone-guy's mobile he went to the last call made and pressed redial.

The rain continued to drench him as he waited for the connection. He walked towards the car park entrance from where he could just see the north-facing harbour wall of the yacht basin across at Glasson Dock. Across to the left of this, though Flynn could not see it, was the marina where he had just moored *Faye*, about half a mile directly distant. In daylight he could possibly have seen the masts of the yachts, but in the ever deepening gloom and heavy rain of this particular night, there was nothing.

The call was answered.

Flynn recognized Bashkim's voice: 'Is it done?'

'It's done,' Flynn said.

There was a pause. Flynn imagined Bashkim's face screwed up and frowning.

He glanced at the screen of the phone in his left hand, the one with the number on it ready to call.

'That is you, Mr Flynn?'

'It is.'

Bashkim laughed, but there was a false bravado to it. 'You are very dangerous . . . I compliment you . . . but first . . . how was it, seeing your dead woman?'

Flynn's face was murderous.

Somewhere in the background, behind Bashkim, Flynn heard Pavli's voice shout, 'Be careful with those crates.'

Bashkim spoke again. 'Second, I will still come for you. I still require . . . what is it you touchy-feely westerners say? Closure.'

'But I'm coming for you now,' Flynn said.

Bashkim laughed. 'Better you run, my friend.'

'I don't think so. You'll be dead before you know it.'

'I don't think so,' he said with confidence.

'Think again.'

With a heavy heart, Flynn pressed the call icon on the other phone, then brought it up to his other ear so there was a phone on each side of his head.

It was a simple bomb. A slab of Pavli's plastic explosive. One of Pavli's own detonators pressed into it, wired up to the mobile phone that Flynn had asked Santiago to buy and register, but never use.

It was taped under the deck in *Faye*'s engine compartment, in the centre of the boat, just below the bridge. The phone had been on constant charge, plugged into the boat's electrical system so it would not run down during the long sea voyage.

The phone call activated the detonator.

The bomb exploded.

Simple.

Although Flynn could not actually see *Faye* from where he stood, he did see the huge blue and gold flame of the explosion that erupted

230

against the black evening sky. A moment later he heard the 'whump' of the blast itself as the sound hit him, followed almost immediately by the blast of wind that struck his face.

Flynn's tears flowed and mixed with the rainwater that drenched his upturned face.

Fifteen

After abandoning phone-guy's car on Blackpool Road in the Lea area of Preston, Flynn jogged up Lea Road and on to the housing estate that branched out from Summer Trees Avenue. Finally, exhausted, drenched, a shivering wreck, he arrived at a small semi-detached house, where he hesitated for just a moment at the garden gate before going to the front door and banging on it.

It was almost ten p.m. Lights were on in the house, people were in.

He knocked again, saw movement through the frosted glass panel in the uPVC front door.

A face pressed up to it, distorted by the cut of the glass. It reminded Flynn of a Picasso, one eye below the other, the mouth disjointed, the nose seemingly broken but yet still recognizable: Jerry Tope.

Flynn heard a groan as Tope also recognized him, but the door was unlocked and opened to the width allowed by the security chain.

Tope blasphemed, then said, 'What the hell are you doing here?'

'Can I come in?'

'You look like shite. Is that blood on you?' He was speaking through the gap. 'You look like a wild man.'

'I'm gonna get really wild unless you open up. I need somewhere to crash.'

'You look like you've already crashed.' Jerry Tope sighed with defeat. His jaw sagged as he worked through the pros and cons of allowing this man into his house in this state, but he closed the door, unlatched the chain and opened up, looking with horror at Flynn in all his glory.

'Thank you,' Flynn said genuinely.

'Kitchen, not front room.' Tope pointed down the hall.

'Is Marina in?'

'No – I just don't want your crap in the lounge.'

'She not here?'

'Didn't I just say that? No! She's at her mum's in London for the week.'

For the first time Flynn actually took in his old comrade's appearance. He wasn't in lounging-about gear but smart casuals, and Flynn caught a vague whiff of aftershave.

'You sly old dog. The cat's away and you're going out to play.'

Tope's wide nostrils flared and his head seemed to contract into his shoulders in an example of body language that screamed 'guilty'.

'Just out for a pint,' he said.

They had reached the kitchen and under the glare of the spots it was Tope's turn really to take on board Flynn's appearance which, on a continuum, was about as far away from his own as could be. He swore at the sight of the blood-stains on Flynn's chest and up his arms, his dirty, dishevelled clothing, his saturation, several days' growth on his face and a very haunted look.

'And I say again – what the hell are you doing here?'

Tope's mobile phone started to ring.

'Hang on, let me get this.'

He picked the phone up from a kitchen worktop, glanced at the caller ID and mouthed 'Work' to Flynn before stepping back into the hallway and answering, 'DC Tope . . .' He walked into the living room and Flynn could only hear the low murmur of his voice until the door opened again and he concluded the call by saying, 'I'll be there in about half an hour.'

He came back into the kitchen, holding his phone and looking thoughtfully at Flynn. 'They want me to turn out . . . apparently there's been a big incident up at Glasson Dock, five dead . . .' His voice trailed off to nothingness as a terrible realization came to him. 'Tell me it's not you.'

Flynn licked his lips and maintained eye contact with Tope, letting him come to his own conclusion.

Once again, Tope blasphemed.

Steve Flynn decided he needed to have a bath, to submerse in hot water and let it cover him and work through to his cold bones. He went up to Tope's bathroom and filled the bath with water so hot he had trouble easing himself into it. Finally he did; he exhaled long and hard and lay there covered in Radox bubbles, staring blankly at the ceiling as he worked back through the events of the past few days. In particular he thought of that evening, from the point just north of Anglesey when Pavli murdered a man in cold blood and threw him to the fishes until he found Karen's poor body in the back of a van, murdered so brutally – an image he could not erase from his mind.

Finally he lifted himself out and dried off before finding a pair of Tope's tracksuit bottoms and an old T-shirt. Then he went down to the kitchen and found a bottle of whisky at the back of a cupboard – a cheap supermarket brand – and poured himself half a tumbler full, drank it, then refilled the glass and went into the lounge to wait.

Before Tope had turned out he had found an old PAYG mobile phone for Flynn from a stack of used ones, all since updated, in a kitchen drawer. He promised Flynn it would work once charged up and there was still a bit of credit in it.

Flynn turned the phone in his hand. The corners of his mouth drooped and a wave of grief shrouded him darkly as he visualized himself walking back to the Berlingo where Karen's body lay. He had clambered in next to her, lifted her lifeless body up and held her tightly, rocking her gently as he cried for her, her brother and himself. Her blood had soaked on to his clothes. He wasn't sure how long it was before he had laid her gently down and walked away.

He had helped himself to the contents of phone-guy and gunman-guy's wallets – a couple of hundred pounds – and then stolen their van.

He had nowhere else to go but to Jerry Tope's house and now here he was, waiting and seeing.

He put the phone down, picked up the whisky

234

and drank the whole lot. It seared down his throat, bringing more tears to his eyes.

The thud of the front door closing woke him. He was still on the settee, knees drawn up with a throw pulled over him. He sat up, rubbing his eyes against the streaming sunlight cutting through the gap in the front room curtains. The clock on the mantelpiece told him he had slept for almost ten hours, which also meant that Jerry Tope had spent that length of time at work after the call-out.

Tope walked through to the kitchen. Flynn heard mugs rattling, the sound of the kettle being filled.

A couple of minutes later he came into the lounge, handing Flynn a mug of coffee and looking disdainfully at the empty bottle of whisky. He sat on an armchair, leaned forward with his hands wrapped around his mug.

'Four men and one woman dead,' he stated. 'One boat blown to smithereens. Millions of dollars floating through the air like confetti and millions of pounds of cocaine floating through the air like snow.'

Flynn swallowed drily and took a sip of the coffee. His throat had closed tight. He looked at Tope who, although dressed in last night's 'going out' attire, now looked worn and shabby, as did his clothing.

'I have to set up an intelligence cell for what looks like being one of Lancashire Constabulary's biggest ever criminal investigations since the handless corpse murder back in seventy-nine.

One which will cost thousands of man hours and will probably go on for years. But yet, yet, yet . . .' – he sucked his teeth – 'I have the feeling that if I march you into a police station, we could probably have a result right now. What do you say to that, Steve?' He waited, immobile, for the answer.

'Was the boat a mess?'

'Yes. The hull was split in two and basically now lies under the water of the yacht marina at Glasson Dock.'

Flynn felt sick. Then he said, 'Four dead? Plus the . . .' – he could hardly bring himself to say it – 'woman?'

Tope nodded.

'Who are they?'

'Well, two men found dead with their brains blown out were cheapo contract killers for hire. Brothers. Lee and Andy Benson. Manchester hoods, associated' – and here Tope raised his bushy eyebrows – 'with the Albanian mafia, would you believe?' His voice mocked Flynn. 'The very people you were asking me about just the other day.'

'OK.'

'BIG coincidence.'

'Admittedly.'

'The woman we don't know as yet . . . and the other two dead guys were caught in the blast on the boat. They are in several pieces, like some macabre jigsaw. Horrible.'

'Who are they?'

Tope shrugged. 'Oddly enough, not identified at the moment.'

'I need to see them,' Flynn blurted.

Tope sneered. 'As if – and which bit of them?'

'I might be able to ID them for you – on the QT.'

'Oh, so now you know something? You didn't when I left.'

'I've slept since then.'

'We haven't got all their bits yet. Bits of dead bodies have rained down over Glasson like some terrible biblical storm. Someone found an arm in the sea lock. One big fucking bomb.'

'Let me see what you have,' Flynn insisted.

'Like I can waltz you into the mortuary at Lancaster.'

'You could if you wanted.'

'No, I couldn't.' Tope picked up a signal in Flynn's face. 'And I'll tell you what, Steve,' he said assertively, 'if you want to tell Marina that I slept with a slapper granny twenty years ago, then do it, because as far as I'm concerned, I'm not being held to ransom by you any more. That boat has sailed, as it were.'

'OK.' Flynn rubbed his eyes with his knuckles, blinked. His eyes were like grit.

'So?' Tope offered.

'I'll give you a lead – how about that?'

'Right, OK.' He was very unimpressed by the situation.

'Go on the internet: the FBI website, the DEA website, whatever, NBC, BBC, I don't know.'

'What am I looking for?'

'A Mexican cartel guy called Carlos.'

'They're all called fucking Carlos! And what has this to do—'

Flynn held up a finger. 'Yeah, but they haven't all just disappeared with millions of dollars in vacuum packs and a few million dollars' worth of cocaine . . . and probably left a trail of bodies behind.'

'That's it?'

'You're a hacker – get hacking.'

'And this all has some connection with the exploding boat?'

'Yes.' Flynn was hoping that it would be best to feed something to Tope under the circumstances, something that was the truth, and set him off in a direction that would satisfy him, keep him onside and keep the cops off his backside. 'Supposing all this is just a big underworld fallout over money and coke – usual shit. That's a good hypothesis, isn't it?'

'Steve,' Tope whined, 'this is very big shit.'

'I know . . . and by the way, just so you don't have to pretend to phone me . . . just for your information, I lost my boat about two weeks ago in a poker game – don't recall the guy's name.'

Tope stared at him, totally bemused.

And Flynn was thinking, *If they can twist things, so can I.*

Somewhere in the house a mobile phone rang out.

'Not mine,' Tope said.

Flynn looked at the one Tope had supplied to him – and it wasn't that one either. Flynn jumped to his feet and ran upstairs to the bathroom where his bloodstained clothes were piled up next to his rucksack. In the pocket of his jeans was the mobile phone belonging to phone-guy, the one

Flynn had used to call Bashkim from the car park. He scrabbled for it, pressed answer but said nothing, just listened.

Then, ashen-faced, he took the phone away from his ear and leaned on the wash basin, looking at himself in the mirror hanging above it.

He spoke to himself.

Three words.

'I have failed.'

In fury he hurled the phone against the tiled wall and it smashed to pieces.

Sixteen

Jerry Tope didn't particularly like computers but he understood them, knew how to access them, how to travel through the cyber world, how to hack secret databases. It was a skill he used to good effect in his work as an intelligence analyst in the police, though not one that ever got him promotion. But he loved digging. That was his *raison d'être* – to go to places no one had any right to go to. He also enjoyed a cyber-chase. If he was discovered 'burgling' and was pursued, he loved outmanoeuvring the chaser, leading them up blind alleys and sometimes stopping to challenge them, then sticking his middle cyber-finger up and running off again like a naughty boy in the orchard. He had once been caught by the FBI, but never since. And that capture only resulted in a wrist-slap – and a job offer that he refused.

To find the information Steve Flynn wanted was therefore relatively easy, something anyone with a bit of know-how could do – at least initially. Searching news reports and crime bulletins was straightforward enough until he found what he was looking for.

What most people could not do was dig deeper.

So when he found reports about a Mexican drug smuggler who had escaped from police custody in Chicago and then reappeared in Mexico, and who was then suspected of destroying the home and murdering the family of the man he believed had informed on him to the DEA, Tope was certain he had found the full name of the man Flynn knew as Carlos.

'Carlos Esposito.' Tope sat back. Smug.

He and Flynn were in the small back bedroom of Tope's house that he used as his study and brewing room.

It could be expected that someone like Tope, regarded by most as a computer geek, might have a bank of devices, stacks on stacks, wall-mounted monitors around the room. As it was he had just the two laptops side by side on his desk. The rest of the room was crammed with equipment for the real love of his life, home brewing. Bottles of beer and wine, vats of cider, bubbled away, fermenting around the room as if he was sitting in a tiny one-man brewery. It was his ambition when he retired from the police to do just that – start up a microbrewery and maybe run a pub.

Flynn was in an office chair behind Tope, peering over his shoulder.

'Leader of a drug cartel . . . responsible for

many gruesome murders – including that of an undercover FBI agent . . . blah, blah, blah,' Tope was saying. 'Arrested in Chicago, escapes while in transit from one prison to another . . . big breakout, three guards and another FBI agent murdered. Then, obviously he skedaddles back to Mexico,' – he pronounced it 'Meh-thee-co', much to Flynn's annoyance – 'does the deed with the guy who grassed him up, steals a ton of his money, so intel says, and hasn't been seen for six months . . . no intelligence on him whatsoever.'

'Until he gets picked up mid-Atlantic with cash and drugs on him. Seems he was running to Bashkim.'

'And how would you know that?' Tope asked sharply.

Flynn held up his hands. 'Just guessing . . . but don't be surprised if a body washes up in Beaumaris with no fingertips and a smashed-in jaw.'

'Shit,' Tope said. 'I am going to get in so much trouble.'

'Just look on me as a nameless informant,' Flynn suggested.

'Informants have to be registered.'

'Not in my day.'

'Shit,' Tope said again. He leaned forward, urgently tapped a few keys and found a BBC report of a body being caught in a fishing net off Conwy, North Wales, unidentified as yet. He glanced at Flynn, who said, 'Don't ask.'

Tope shook his head despairingly.

'And that should be enough for you to be going on with, mate . . . looks like Glasson was just a big fallout between gangsters.'

'Don't fucking "mate" me. You're putting me in a horrendous position here,' Tope whined.

'You wanna be in my position,' Flynn retorted dourly.

Flynn persuaded Tope to drop him off at Sainsbury's superstore in Fulwood. He handed Tope a small package with instructions and then Tope went in to work, while Flynn went into the store and exchanged 500 of Bashkim's euros for sterling at the money desk. Then he went shopping and bought himself two new sets of clothes, and two more PAYG mobile phones from the technology department. Neither phone was charged so he made his way to a Starbucks café near Preston North End's football ground, Deepdale, where he found a socket and a signal, bought a large, wet latte, extra hot, a breakfast panini and a cinnamon swirl. At his table he picked up one of the phones, went through the rigmarole of signing up – giving false details – and made a call.

It seemed to take a very long time for the person to answer.

Then it was there. Timid, afraid maybe, all in the one word, '*Sí?*'

'Is that Maria Santiago?'

'Oh God, Flynn, it's you!'

'*Sí, sí*, it is . . . *cómo estás?*'

'Horrible, horrible . . . how are you? Oh, God, I've been so worried . . . Flynn, Flynn . . . to hear your voice again . . . oh, God!'

'It's good to hear you, too. Are you all right?'

'Yes, *sí*, I am.'

'Where are you?'

'Tenerife . . . it's a good place to hide. Tomas brought me on his boat . . . I have a friend . . .'

'Have you got another phone you can use? One you haven't used yet?'

'Yes.'

'Give me the number and I'll call that . . . we still need to keep a step ahead.'

'OK, OK.' She reeled off another number.

'How's your skinhead?' Flynn asked, imagining his hands touching it.

'To the skull,' she laughed.

'Good. Look, I'll call you on the other phone.'

'Flynn, Flynn,' she said before he could hang up.

'What?'

'Karen.'

Suddenly Flynn could not talk, but after taking a deep breath and bracing himself, he said, 'She's dead.'

When he phoned back he took the chance of having a longer conversation but still kept it quite brief. He told her what had happened to him: his journey, Carlos, finding Karen's body, the bomb he had set on *Faye* as his little insurance policy.

Santiago listened in silence, though Flynn could hear her gasp and sob at various points until finally she said, 'But you didn't kill them?'

'No. Somehow Bashkim and Pavli escaped the blast. I don't know if they're injured or not, I just know when the cops and ambulance arrived, they weren't there.'

Bashkim's taunting voice played in his brain – the phone call he'd listened to in Tope's bathroom, made to the mobile Flynn had taken from phone-guy, the call with Bashkim at the other end.

'*A good try, Mr Flynn, but you missed me and my son.*'

'And you have been to the police?' Santiago interrupted his thoughts. 'Told them your story?'

'That,' Flynn declared, 'would be much too complicated.' He didn't tell her about Tope. 'But as far as I can make out, they're putting it down to a gangland fallout at the moment. Although the presence of Karen's body, as yet unidentified, is a mystery to them.'

'Are you going to tell them who she is?'

'I'll set them on a course,' he said. Having to leave her body behind was weighing heavily on him, but he'd made the decision because it would have made it almost impossible to carry on and do what he needed to do. He also knew that she would be cared for in death by the police until she was returned to her family, together with Adam. There would be some terrible outpourings of grief, which he had to avoid for the time being, but he knew that sometime in the not too distant future he would visit the parents and tell them some of the truth, with omissions. 'It's not good, I know,' he admitted to Santiago, 'and I'm not proud of leaving her.'

'I think I understand,' she said gently. 'And your poor boat . . .'

'Don't go there,' Flynn said heavily, then, 'Hey – and you, Tenerife.'

'Yes . . . Tomas brought me here on his boat. I've been lying low in Playa de Las Américas

244

ever since, waiting to hear from you. My friend is a holiday courier and I'm at her place.'

'How about Romero?'

'Well,' she admitted, 'I have spoken to my friend in the admin department in Las Palmas – I know, I've told her to be careful,' she said, before Flynn could interrupt. 'She says it is rumoured that Romero is seen every night in and around Adam's clubs in Puerto Rico, lording it like he owns them. Otherwise, she doesn't know what's happening, but the TV bulletins with my face on are not as frequent . . . and anyway, they all show my official photograph with my beautiful long hair, which I miss so much. How long will this go on?'

Flynn went silent, then said, 'Because these guys are still alive, I think that clearing your name is the first thing we need to do.'

'But how? And your name, too.'

'I did stick a knife in Dardan's throat, I guess.'

'Self-defence.'

'I know that, but I'm not sure the Spanish justice system will agree.'

'If I can clear my name, I can prove you are not guilty of murder,' she said, full of confidence.

'Maybe . . .'

'For certain, Steve Flynn.'

'Maybe,' he sighed.

'But where do we go from here?' she asked. 'I can't live like this. One day soon I will be arrested and Romero will twist everything and I will be convicted of murdering another police officer and a woman who was my friend, as well as aiding

245

and abetting your escape – none of which I did! And they will still be hunting you, Steve.'

He caught a bus back from Deepdale to Lea, noticing that the car he had used to get him away from Glasson Dock was still parked up where he had left it. From the bus stop he walked back to Tope's house and let himself in with the spare key he had managed to wheedle out of his old friend who, strangely, was not warming to his presence.

Flynn decided to treat Tope, so from ingredients bought in Sainsbury's he made a chicken casserole, which he cooked slowly and which would be ready for consumption whenever Tope landed.

Like a date.

It was just after eight p.m. when he arrived, drained.

Flynn did not push him on anything because he could sense that Tope's blue touchpaper wouldn't need much lighting. Without questions, he let Tope go and have a long hot shower, then reappear looking almost human, dressed in what Flynn guessed was called loungewear – slobbing gear.

He heaped out the casserole with baby new potatoes and tinned carrots, and sat in a fairly strained silence as they ate the feast.

'That was good, actually,' Tope conceded, emptying his plate.

'Good. Now – what have you got for me?'

'In terms of the explosion . . . still very little. Lots of body parts still being collected – a severed foot off a nearby church roof, for example. The army bomb guys have been up and they say that whoever made and planted the bomb knew what they were doing.'

Flynn blushed modestly.

'But no ID yet of the dead bodies, although we do now have a lead on the dead lady . . . apparently Colne police station received an anonymous phone call suggesting a name, would you believe?' He gave Flynn a pissed-off expression.

'Well I never,' Flynn said primly, then closed his eyes as the memory of Karen shrouded him again. When he opened them, he said, 'Jerry, I know this isn't in your remit, but can you try to ensure her body is treated with dignity . . . the post-mortem and all that?'

Tope frowned, not getting it.

'If I say I don't give a fuck what you do with the other bodies, does that make it clearer for you?'

Tope's eyes narrowed, amazed that Flynn's hard man mask had slipped, something he had not witnessed in a long time. 'Maybe you should just tell me everything.'

'Screw that.' Flynn's mask was firmly back in place.

'As regards the bomb, it is in fragments, obviously. It was a mobile phone wired to a detonator and it looks possible that one of the dead guys from the car park – you know, one that was shot – used a phone from that location to blow it.'

'Oh, right. Anything else?'

Tope sighed. He went out to bring his briefcase into the kitchen. He put it on to the table and opened it, took out an envelope which he slid over to Flynn. 'I have no idea what this is about.'

Flynn opened the envelope, slid out the contents

247

– a small plastic bag containing his debit card and a folded sheet of A4 paper. The debit card was what Flynn had forced on to Tope earlier, before being dropped off at Sainsbury's, to see if there was anything he could get from it. The paper was a result from the national fingerprint database, plus a summary of previous convictions – in this case just the one.

'Who is she?' Tope asked. 'Other than someone convicted of a minor assault three years ago.'

Flynn did not answer.

His mind was – at last – starting to function again, but just to irk Tope he said, 'It says here she's called—'

'I know what it says there,' Tope grumbled.

Flynn looked at the details, trying desperately to formulate something he had been very short of recently: a plan. His eyebrows rose as he regarded Tope staring expectantly at him, urging a response – but Flynn's thinking flicked off in another direction.

'Let me ask you something.'

Tope's features turned sour. 'What?'

'When a cop's on the take, how careful do you think they are? Hypothetically speaking.'

Tope shrugged irritably. 'Sly and surreptitious, but maybe not as careful as they could be. That's why they usually get caught.'

'Hidden bank accounts, d'you reckon? Stuff like that?'

'Possibly.'

'Thing is, you see,' – Flynn sat forward, making Tope jump – 'cops on the take are sly and under-hand, but the thing about cops is that, usually

248

– and there are exceptions – they're really only one per cent smarter than most crims. That's why crims get caught – because they're just one per cent dumber than the fuzz.'

'You're going round in circles.'

'I know. My head's a shed – but I think I'm pulling the walls back up a bit.'

'Get on with it.'

'The thing about bent cops is that they think they can outsmart everyone else. They think they can influence and twist stuff – evidence, people, other cops – even when they've been blown.'

'I still have no idea what you're talking about.'

'Are you any good at accessing bank files, accounts and such like?'

'Me?'

'No, your freaking dog. Yes, you.'

'If I have a starting point, I can access anything.' It was a matter-of-fact statement.

'A Spanish bank. Would that be a problem?'

'The language of the cyber community is the same the world over.'

'Is that a yes?' Flynn said impatiently.

Tope nodded. 'But it can take time.'

'When are you back at work?'

'Eight tomorrow.'

'Then we have all night.' Flynn waved the fingerprint result. 'But first, can you find out as much about this person as possible? I need to know how to pin her down.'

'Why? What is she to you?'

'An asset, I hope. While you're doing that for me, I need to make a call and get some details for you as a starting point.'

'All night, you say?'

'Unless you get some quick results . . . which include the present locations of Pavli and Aleksander Bashkim.'

One hour later, Flynn sat down behind Tope in the study/brewing room. Tope lifted a sheet of paper from the printer and gave it to him.

'The details you wanted.'

Flynn ran his eyes across the sheet. 'Brilliant.'

'Now I'm into Santander's customer database, just following some trails.'

'Thanks, mate, I appreciate this.'

'Stop calling me mate.' Tope turned his attention back to his laptops.

It was three a.m.

Flynn was stretched out on Tope's settee, unable to sleep, his eyes clamped firmly on the ceiling.

He heard the sound of Tope's footfalls on the stairs and sat up as the living room door opened and the man himself entered, carrying a folder. He looked exhausted. Bags under his eyes, which themselves were red raw from too much screen glaring and knuckle rubbing. His hair was in disarray from having ruffled it in frustration over the last few hours.

He tossed the file to Flynn, gave him a lazy wave, then disappeared back upstairs, where he threw himself on his bed and went instantly to sleep.

There were only a few sheets of paper in the file, but there was enough information on them. Flynn read them several times so he fully understood what he was looking at, then picked up a

250

fresh mobile phone and dialled yet another number for Santiago. She answered instantly.

With a lot of mumbling and grumbling, Tope reluctantly drove Flynn to Liverpool John Lennon Airport next evening. He was booked on a flight to Las Palmas. He knew he was maybe taking a chance by using his own passport but there was no time to try and get a false ID (although he knew a man who did a very lucrative line in false passports). He trusted to luck that no one was expecting him to return to Gran Canaria so openly and under his own name.

Tope pulled up at the drop-off zone with yet more grumbles that even this had to be paid for – the privilege of dropping off passengers who would then spend more money at the airport.

On the journey he had brought Flynn up to date with what he knew of the police investigation of the bombing and deaths in Glasson Dock, a story that had hit the media big style.

The two people killed by the bomb still had to be identified, but there was a growing belief amongst the senior detectives running the show that they were from overseas. The young woman who had been shot in the back of the van had now been formally identified and enquiries had commenced to follow up her story.

'And they know that the boat belonged to you,' Tope revealed with a 'clang'. 'They don't know where you are and are liaising with the cops in Gran Canaria about you.'

Flynn bit his inner cheek, feeling a bit like a fish in a trawl net which was tightening slowly.

'Like I said . . . lost it in a poker game.'

'You might need to come up with a better answer than that,' Tope suggested.

'I'll worry about it when the cops knock on my door . . . just so long as it's not a certain detective from Gran Canaria. Any rumours I'm actually involved in any of this, though?'

Tope shrugged. 'I'm just an intel bod.'

'Find out . . . any news on the whereabouts of Bashkim and his boy?'

'No. I've looked at some stuff but they're not in the frame for anything.' Tope's eyebrows knitted together. 'I take it they were there, at the scene of the explosion? I mean, you haven't told me as such . . . that said, you haven't *actually* told me if you were there either.'

'Let's keep it that way, eh?'

'Yeah, great . . . keep me in the dark, feed me on shit . . . yet expect me to do all these things for you.'

'A friend in need—'

'Is a twat,' Tope said. 'I don't like any of this, Steve. Actually, I am doing this because you are my friend, sadly – but if it all goes tits up for you . . .'

'I know, don't even mention your name. I get it. I'm out of your hair now, so just forget every-thing, pretend you haven't seen me and make sure your cyber footprints are covered, yeah?'

Outside the airport Tope said sincerely, 'Be careful, Steve. I don't know the whole of what you're involved in but I can fill in some of the blanks, even though you've told me fuck all . . . watch yourself and, hey, don't come back to my doorstep.'

'I won't – and thanks.' Flynn proffered his right hand and they shook.

He drew away as Flynn walked into the terminal building with his rucksack slung over his shoulder.

Flynn tensed as his passport was zipped through the customs computer – but no bells or whistles sounded, and the official handed it back and waved him through.

As all flights should be, it was uneventful. Flynn settled himself as comfortably as he could with a frame as broad and long as his in the confined space of the plane's seats, which had hardly any legroom. He pulled down the peak of his new baseball cap (from Sainsbury's) to keep his face in the shadows. He munched a sandwich he'd bought before boarding and sipped a bottle of water. He did succumb to a mug of tea when the drinks came round, keeping his face hidden. He dozed for about an hour on the four and a half hour flight and did not speak to or acknowledge the woman sitting next to him, but was aware of her sidelong glances.

He was awake for landing and had to admit that it was good to be coming back to what was his home, though he wasn't sure what awaited him and whether or not he would be able to get back any of his old life eventually.

But that was his ultimate goal, one way or another.

The first part of the plan began as soon as he disembarked from the plane.

Customs and immigration officers were as uninterested as usual, the guy in the glass booth waving him through without even a cursory glance at his passport – which was good. He had no luggage, so a couple of minutes later he was in the arrivals hall where, his cap again down over his eyes, never once raising his face to be caught by CCTV, he lounged by a wall to watch the other passengers file out.

Those without hold luggage were the first to emerge.

He waited, firing up yet another mobile phone as he did and sending a short text message, which was acknowledged. He exhaled with relief at that one.

Some lucky passengers with cases started to appear and Flynn panicked just a tad, wondering if he was in the wrong place.

Then the crew of the aircraft came out. Pilot, co-pilot, chief steward and the rest of the cabin crew, two women, one man. They all looked smart but weary, tugging their small wheeled suitcases behind them like pets.

Flynn's eyes focused on one of the steward-esses. He pushed himself away from the wall and followed the group on to the concourse outside the terminal building.

Including the stewardess, they formed a gaggle, chatting amiably amongst themselves. From information provided by Jerry Tope, Flynn already knew they were on a two night stopover and were due to staff a flight to Sofia, Bulgaria the day after tomorrow.

The pilot and co-pilot broke away and hailed a taxi from the front of the rank.

That left the chief steward and three cabin crew.

Flynn saw the one who interested him shake her head at the others. She was going her own way, which was good because the remaining three gestured for another cab and piled into it, laughing.

Leaving the one woman behind.

Flynn moved in so he was a couple of metres behind her.

She glanced around, saw him, but again his cap was low over his eyes and she showed no sign of recognition, just as she had not recognized him on the plane as she did her job, up and down the aisle.

She hailed the next taxi – but before the driver could react, another cab shot past the line of taxis and screeched in to the kerb, causing a sudden burst of angry horns from behind. The driver reached over and opened the back door. At the same time, Flynn wrenched the woman's suitcase out of her grip and said, 'Here, let me help you.'

He flung it in the taxi and bundled the woman in after it, his right hand splayed on her skull and pushing down her head so she would not bang it. As Flynn jumped in and slammed the door, the taxi lurched away.

Flynn did not want to give the woman any time to struggle, even though she had started to do so.

He simply smashed his right fist into the side of her head with a blow that stunned her into insensibility. She withered in his arms, her eyes rolling like a doll's. Flynn eased her into the seat, reached for the seatbelt and fastened it so she would not slither off.

He sat back.

The taxi driver adjusted the rear-view mirror.

'Hello there,' he said, looking at the two dark beautiful eyes reflected in it.

'*Hola*,' Santiago replied.

Seventeen

Flynn stood on the balcony of the two bedroomed apartment set in a slightly elevated position over the concrete sprawl of Playa del Inglès, the haphazard, unplanned resort just a few miles south of the airport. Flynn had never warmed to the place, a hastily assembled concrete mass of identical streets and identical hotels. It completely lacked any charm. Although Puerto Rico was no picture postcard, its geography kept it in check and it had some heart, probably because of the town park and marina.

Playa, though, was a place in which a person could remain anonymous.

He drank water, wanting to keep his head clear from now on.

Turning at the sound of bare feet coming up behind him, he smiled at Santiago – the cop on the run turned taxi thief and driver. She was dressed in a grey military style top and baggy camouflage trousers and, Flynn noticed – in spite of his predicament – no bra. She sidled up to him, held him tight. He kissed her softly.

'It's so good to see you,' she said, when they separated. 'I thought I would never see you again.'

'I thought the same.'

'I am so sorry about Karen.'

'Yeah.' He raised his eyes, could just about see the ocean between the high-rises. His jawline hardened. Santiago reached up and touched his cheek.

'These men kill people we love. They have no conscience,' she said. 'They do not keep their word and can never, ever be trusted.'

'And that is why I must take the fight to them,' he said. He spoke quietly, without emotion. He actually thought that what he said was corny, but knew no other way of expressing it. 'We won't be safe until they have been dealt with – wouldn't be even if we had the help of the police, who do not have the resources to protect us.' He looked seriously at her. 'I want to kill them. I want to see them dead at my feet.' He visualized it. 'I don't want them to go to jail. I don't want them to sneer across a court room. I don't want expensive lawyers to get them off on a technicality. I want to kill them. You have to know that.'

The words frightened him and terrified her.

But what terrified her even more was her own response.

'So do I,' she whispered. 'I've thought of nothing else since I last saw you. For once I do not believe in the law, and that scares me.'

They looked into each other's eyes for a very long time before kissing, long and hard and with passion.

Gasping, they drew away from each other. Flynn smiled grimly as he said, 'It's a damn shame we've kidnapped a serial killer and tied her to the bed in there, otherwise I'd be very tempted to—'

257

Santiago placed a forefinger over his lips before he could speak his wish.

'Shh. Once this is over, we will fuck until the cows come home, as the British say.'

'Remember me?'

She was conscious now, the side of her face red and slightly swollen where Flynn had delivered his perfectly weighted blow in the taxi. She was also fastened to the bed in the same way in which she had secured him on their previous encounter in a bedroom. She was not naked, however, but still dressed in the uniform of the budget airline for which she worked, although her pencil skirt had ridden up her thighs, exposing the top of her stockings. A strip of duct tape was covering her mouth.

She glared at Flynn and said something from behind the tape; the words were muffled, but their meaning was clear enough to Flynn. She writhed in an attempt to struggle free, but this bed was much sturdier than the one she'd attached Flynn to.

He bounced down on to his haunches, bringing his eyes to her level.

'You won't get free,' he said.

She had another writhing fit, then gave up, defeated.

'Happy?'

Another muffled curse.

'Good,' Flynn said. 'Now then, you need to listen to me and we need to have a little conversation. I'm going to remove your muzzle but if you scream or shout when I do it'll go back on,

258

and later tonight you'll find yourself weighed down with concrete slabs on the bottom of the Atlantic Ocean. Do you understand?'

She nodded suspiciously.

'Good – because, you see, I don't have much time.'

He reached over, tore the strip from her mouth.

'Bastard, bastard, bastard – what the fuck do you think you're doing? Once I get out of here I'm going to the cops . . .'

Flynn chortled and jerked his thumb behind him to where Santiago stood with her head tilted, aiming a semi-automatic pistol at the woman's head. 'We are the cops . . . sort of.'

He sat on the edge of the bed. She squirmed away from him as though he was diseased.

'Don't you dare touch me,' she warned.

'I've had my fill of touching you. Far too dangerous.'

'What d'you want, what d'you want from me?' She started to cry. 'Sex? Rape? If so, just get it over with.'

Flynn shook his head, then unfolded several sheets of paper which had travelled with him from the UK. He read: 'Tracey Jayne Martin?' He arched his eyebrows at her. 'Currently employed as cabin crew by a very budget airline.'

She stopped crying and kept two very malevolent eyes fixed on him. 'And?'

'And? The murderer of at least fourteen men across Europe in the last four years, from Prague to Pisa, Malaga to Malta – but, I note with interest, none in Britain. Very clever. Don't shit on your own doorstep. Very wise. All destinations

259

of that airline, I might add. Modus operandi – lure unsuspecting males from a nightclub or bar into a rented apartment, screw them, drug them . . . butcher them.'

Flynn watched her expression change to a snarl as he spoke.

'You've got the wrong person. I don't even know you.'

'Well, I might say something different.'

'Look, what're you on about? I'm a fuckin' air stewardess. I don't kill men.'

'Some might say different, if they could. You cut out their hearts, lungs, livers and guts and cut off their dicks.'

'Not me.'

'Look, I haven't got time to arse about, Tracey.' He held up the clear food bag he had stolen from a shop in Playa which still contained his debit card, now with a film of fingerprint powder across it. 'You had your fingers all over this before you threw it away.' Flynn smiled. 'I assumed you had a bit of a panic on when you discovered I'd managed to get free. Unfortunately for you, your fingerprints are on record in the UK.'

The realization slowly dawned on her face.

'You are a very bad girl,' he said, 'and you've just had some bad luck. Me.'

'They were all bastards – including you,' she said. 'So what's this all about? You obviously don't want to give me to the cops . . . the real cops.'

'Actually, I do. In my heart of hearts, I do. You're a sick, perverted psycho who ensnared unsuspecting men to suffer brutal deaths which none of them deserved.'

'Every one of them did,' she said with total belief.

'No they didn't,' Flynn said softly. 'And you are a sly, intelligent person too. Not one of your murder scenes leaves a trace of you . . . very forensically aware . . . except in my case.'

'I should've checked the cutlery drawer first.'

'A rule of thumb for a serial killer – always check the cutlery, I would have thought . . . but it's the little things that come back to haunt you—'

'Flynn – get on with it,' Santiago snapped impatiently.

'OK.' He smiled at Tracey; a more genteel-looking woman he could not imagine. But it did not matter what she looked like; it was what went on inside a person's head that was the problem, and could drive someone hovering on the far edge of the mental stability continuum right off the brink. Even though he had been outwitted by this woman, tied up for slaughter, he still did have a problem imagining her plunging a knife into his heart – and yet he knew she would have done. Fourteen murdered and disembowelled men were proof of that pudding. 'I want to give you a chance, Tracey, the only one you will ever be given, so do not misunderstand this.'

'You don't know fuck all,' she said harshly. 'You can't prove fuck all!'

Flynn held up a sheet of paper. 'On here are the dates of every single murder you have committed.' He took out another sheet. 'On this is your flying schedule for the last four years, ever since you first killed. The dates tie in nicely with every single killing.' He read: 'Prague, eighth July 2013 – one man mutilated, his corpse

261

and its contents scattered across the city. You land the day before, take off the day after.'

'Where did you get that information? I have rights. You're not allowed to—'

Flynn shook his head. 'To what? Do a bit of computer hacking? Look at your flight schedule? But you're allowed to slice off a man's genitals? Yin and yang out of kilter on that one, *love*.' He knew the final word would annoy her. It did.

'See – there you fucking go. "*Love*"! You patronizing male shit-head. I wish I'd run you down on the quayside!'

He ignored the outburst and went on, 'Mm, not quick enough there, were you? Valletta, Malta, twenty-seventh July 2013. One man murdered in Sliema, mutilated. You arrive the day before, leave the day after. I mean, sort of slots into place, doesn't it?'

'You can't prove a thing. Coincidence doesn't mean guilt.'

'I agree . . . but let me see . . . where do you live?' He checked another sheet of paper. 'St Helens, Merseyside. Ideal for Liverpool airport.'

'Yeah, my job.'

Conversationally he said, 'Thing about serial killers is they often take a memento, a keepsake of their . . . conquests.'

A dark shadow crossed her face.

'You see, as well as accessing all these databases – which will be done legally if you don't agree to what I want – I've also looked at detailed police reports of the crime scenes. As well as having mutilation, disembowelment and so on in common, there is also another thing that links the killings,

262

something the cops have never revealed to the press. And you know what that is, don't you?'

From her facial reaction and the blinking of her eyes it was obvious that she did. 'No,' she said stubbornly.

Flynn read out her address in St Helens, a town just to the north of Liverpool, and he gave her an exaggerated wink.

Before being dropped off at Liverpool airport Flynn had begged one last favour from Jerry Tope, who had looked as though he would rather have committed suicide than help.

But help he did and instead of driving straight to the airport, Flynn got him to drive to St Helens and park up close to the terraced street on which Tracey Jayne Martin lived. Under sufferance Tope walked past her house to try and work out if she was still at home. He could not be certain on the first walk-past, but as he sauntered back to the car he almost bumped into her coming out of the house in her full cabin crew uniform. She slammed the front door shut and heaved her pull-along suitcase into a taxi that had just pulled up.

Tope dropped back into his car as the taxi carrying Tracey drove past, and Flynn sank low in his seat.

'Ten minutes,' Flynn said, 'just in case she's forgotten something.'

'Then what?'

Flynn did not reply. The minutes passed with agonizing slowness and silence until Flynn said, 'Stay here. If I'm not back in fifteen minutes, call the cops. Just kidding.'

As he got out and slammed the door, he heard Tope mutter 'Wanker' under his breath.

Flynn looked back through the window and said, 'I heard that.' Then he set off and made his way to the back alley behind the row of terraced houses in which Tracey lived, one of many similar rows in St Helens, a fairly typical northern town still displaying many reminders of its industrial heritage. The alley was quiet, deserted. Flynn counted his way down until he came to Tracey's high-walled back yard. The door to it was locked. Flynn put his shoulder to it, but it held firmly.

Knowing he did not have a great deal of time to play with – because he wanted to be on the same plane as her – he simply stepped back, then flat-footed the door. It crashed open. He ducked into her back yard. It was quite small but with room enough for a small garden shed, probably used for storage, Flynn guessed.

He crouched low to keep out of sight of neighbours' houses and went to the back door, noticing that, as at the front of the house, there was no burglar alarm on the wall, which was good. The rear room was all kitchen, Flynn saw as he peered through the window, shading his eyes; it was a basic but modern room and the window he was looking through was a double-glazed uPVC unit. The back door, however, wasn't. It was made of wood and had a single-glazed window, making his task much more straightforward.

He jabbed his elbow through the glass, which broke easily. He picked out some broken pieces still in the frame, placed them carefully down and inspected what he had done. It had been all very well to break the window, but the door was still secured by a mortise lock and key, and the window wasn't quite big enough for him to climb through even if he removed all the broken glass from it.

And the key wasn't in the door.

Slowly, so as not to slice his jugular, he poked his head through to see if the key was on a hook near the door. Not a terribly security conscious thing to do, but something people did – left keys hanging within reaching distance of the door.

He smiled.

Two keys on a fob hung on a hook by the door.

Seconds later Flynn entered the house of a serial killer.

It was a very normal-looking house, owned by a single lady. Basic, clean, functional, one or two nice pieces of pottery, some family photos.

Just normal. No sign of gimp masks or torture chambers and very hard to believe that someone who had killed over a dozen times lived here.

Flynn was mildly disappointed.

He was also miffed that he could not find what he had hoped to find.

At least not initially.

His search took him through the two bedrooms upstairs; one was clearly the main one with a double bed, teddy bears and other cuddly toys, the second a guest room. He searched all the drawers and cupboards but found nothing of interest.

Downstairs there was quite a large lounge at the front of the house, plus the kitchen and a loo, but again, nothing to excite him.

Deflated, he went to the back door and saw the two keys on the fob, one in the back door, the other hanging down. His eyes rose through the broken window towards the shed in the back yard, standing maybe two metres away from the back of the house, secured by a very basic mortise. He drew the back door key out, crossed to the shed and inserted the second key into the door. It unlocked it.

It was a six by six foot construction, no windows, a shelf on the left of the door and a series of shelves on the back wall.

'Shit.' Flynn's insides contracted.

On the top shelf were fourteen jam jars, each with a label on.

He stepped in and peered at the labels. Each had a day, date, location and name written on it.

Flynn swallowed as he looked at what made this ordinary house in the fairly ordinary town of St Helens very extraordinary.

The keepsakes of a serial killer.

He swallowed back something very nasty in his throat, then went back into the kitchen and looked through the cupboards, finding exactly what he needed. Back in the shed, he selected one of the jam jars at random.

It was dated fourteenth February – ironic, he thought – 2014. The name was Karamov, the location Berlin.

Flynn decanted the contents, almost retching as he did. Then he locked the shed and back door behind him, tossed the keys far into the kitchen and a few moments later was sitting alongside Tope, being driven to Liverpool John Lennon Airport.

* * *

'No?' Flynn asked. 'You sure?'

He reached down to the floor and picked up a 150 ml plastic pot made by a company called Sistema. It was made of clear, hard plastic with a screw top, designed for people who want to take yogurt in packed lunches. He had carried it through customs and immigration at Liverpool and it had been in his pocket as he stepped through the metal detector which, mercifully, did not beep. Had he been stopped and searched, and had the yogurt pot been found, he would have had some explaining to do.

He held up the pot for Tracey to see.

'Isaac Karamov, murdered fourteenth February 2014 in Berlin,' he said. He gave the pot a little shake, the contents slurping sickeningly, making him a tad nauseous. 'Keepsake?' he prompted her. 'Memento? The left eyeball, gouged out of the skull and eye socket of each of your victims, now all proudly on display in the shed in your back yard, like specimens in a natural history museum. Now why do you do that, Tracey?'

'A man once winked at me.'

'You really do have some personal issues to address.'

Flynn placed the yogurt pot on the floor.

'What do you want?' she asked, resigned to fate.

'This is the deal, Tracey . . . and you either take it, or I'll shove you through the door of a cop shop with a note pinned to you saying "I'm a serial killer". Or I'll do what I said before – and drown you.'

'Like I said, what do you want?'

'We want you to catch a man for us.'

267

Eighteen

Santiago replaced the receiver on the public phone box near the mouth of the subway, close to the steps leading up to the commercial centre in Puerto Rico.

Flynn was standing by a concrete wall next to the steps, trying to stay in shadow and keep incognito – though being six-two with shoulders as broad as a surfboard it wasn't easy.

Santiago walked across to him, still in her baggy cargo pants and a basketball vest under a denim jacket, a look which, Flynn had to admit, suited her in a very alluring way. That and the skinhead, the temporary tattoos, the earrings and the nose and lip rings, which seemed to have multiplied since she had first adopted the look. She looked like a stereotypical drug user – which showed Flynn, again, what stereotyping did. She fitted her baseball cap as she approached him.

It was a good disguise, Flynn thought.

He did hope, though, that it wouldn't be long before she could return to normal.

'And?' he asked. She had been on the phone to her friend who worked at Las Palmas police station, getting an update on Romero.

'The talk is, he is running a half-baked investigation, although he seems to be bullshitting everyone up the chain. Rumour is he should have caught me – and you – by now.'

'You can't catch folk who aren't there.'

'I agree . . . but, to be honest, she doesn't know a lot – she's only a typist.' She sidled up to Flynn and slid her arms around him. He shivered internally at the contours of her body pressed up close. 'And every night he's here, in and around the pubs and clubs that Adam owned. She doesn't know what he's doing.'

'He could be running them for Bashkim in his absence.'

'And he's got a couple of off-duty cops in tow, ones who are not the best, if you know what I mean. Knuckle-heads.'

'Dirty?'

'Possibly.'

'Bodyguards?'

'Possibly.'

'So prising him away from them could be problematic?'

'Possibly.'

Flynn looked down at her. 'A lot of possibles in this equation.'

'*Sí*. What do you think about our serial killer lady?'

Flynn shrugged. 'Who knows? She'll either flee or go for it. If she runs, then we'll have to have another look at a way of getting Romero off the street without causing a kerfuffle. Thing is, if she does what we ask, then she gets a chance to disappear. If she legs it, then I'll make sure she's in custody within a day . . . I think she'll do it. Crazy plan, but could work.'

'"Crazy" being the operative word,' Santiago said.

'Not too certain about the word "plan", either.'

* * *

She identified her next victim easily.

He was in the bar of O'Castle's Irish Pub in the commercial centre, drinking spirits. She did not like the look of him. An overweight, podgy Spaniard at least twenty years older than herself and not typical of the men she liked to kill, even though killing a man like this would also be a pleasure if she got the chance.

He was leering at young girls from his position at the bar and when one walked past within groping distance he made no secret of grabbing her bottom. She spun ferociously and tried to smack him but he dragged her roughly towards him, a dirty, contemptuous look on his sweating face.

'My fucking bar,' he said. 'I do what I fucking like.' He flicked her away. 'Dirty bitch.'

'Fuck you,' she said bravely, ready to have another pop at him, but her two friends intervened and hauled her away. They drank up and left.

Romero spun back to the bar, seeing that the bartender was staring at him with horror.

Romero pointed at him. 'What is your problem, *amigo*? You want to keep your job? You keep your shitty looks off your face . . . I'm the boss here, now . . . this bar is under new management – *comprende*?'

'Yeah, yeah,' the young lad said meekly.

Romero slid off his bar stool, jerked his head at the two young men sitting in the far corner of the bar. They downed their drinks, followed him out.

Tracey had been wrong about Romero.

He was exactly the kind of man she would like to kill.

* * *

270

Romero spent some time in Adam Castle's other bar, The English, before moving at midnight into the Electron nightclub, another of Castle's businesses. He took up regal residence in a roped-off seating area by the bar overlooking the dance floor, which was packed with gyrating, air-fisting bodies, dancing to the pounding beats.

Romero sat with his two tame cops, waited on by glum-looking staff, before mooching around the club with the cops at his heels and then going to the front door, where he chatted to the new bouncers.

Flynn and Santiago were skulking in the shadows across the concourse. They saw him come out and talk with the doormen. Flynn – who had occasionally acted in that capacity for Castle when he was short-staffed – had never seen these guys on the door. He assumed they were Bashkim's men. It was an old adage but still held true – control the doors, you control the drugs – and replacing Adam's employees, who were rigorously vetted, was obviously Bashkim's first step in that process. Castle had a strong anti-drug policy and his two clubs in the town were often cited as examples of how such places should be run. A reputation about to be smashed to smithereens, Flynn thought glumly. Once Bashkim had set up shop properly here, the illegal substances would start to flow and there would be police protection.

'Crying shame,' Flynn muttered.

He watched Romero carefully, and his two cops-cum-heavies.

When they turned to go back inside he glimpsed

271

the handgun tucked into the back waistband of one of the cops as the guy adjusted his jacket.

'One's armed,' he said.

'Which means both could be,' Santiago said. She had spotted the gun too.

'Or all three, which could be a problem.'

They strutted cockily back to their seats where a bottle of champagne awaited them.

As Romero sipped his drink he noticed Tracey for the first time. She was moving alone on the edge of the dance floor, sinuously, sexily, her eye-line occasionally crossing his. Accidentally, it seemed. Romero became mesmerized by her gyrations, his mouth curling into a dirty grin as he watched her body move underneath the skimpy dress she wore. On one 'accidental' eye-line cross she smiled at him, then stopped dancing and mimed that she needed a drink.

He beckoned her over.

She made a coy *Who, me?* gesture.

He nodded and said something to one of his men, who stood up and brought her to sit next to him as he poured her a glass of the champagne.

They clinked glasses and she surveyed him across the rim of hers.

'You're Spanish,' she said.

'*Sí,*' he said deeply, 'and you are very beautiful.'

She batted her eyelashes and crossed her long legs, making it very clear she was not wearing underwear.

* * *

272

'Shit,' Flynn said.

It was an hour later. He and Santiago were still in the shadows opposite the club when Romero and Tracey stumbled out drunkenly, arms interlinked like lovers. That bit was going to plan, but not the next: the two cop bodyguards slotted in behind the happy couple and began to follow.

'He's taking his new found position seriously,' Flynn said. 'Either that or he's shit scared of meeting either you or me in a dark alley. You, probably.'

With hatred burning in her eyes, Santiago watched Romero's progress up the next set of concrete steps.

'You know, Steve Flynn, I honestly never believed I would want to kill someone – but I do. I cannot believe how much I despise that man.' Santiago's voice was bleak and sad.

'A corrupt cop, someone who's twisted evidence to turn you into a murderer on the run and who killed a close friend of yours . . . what's not to like? I love the guy.'

She pounded him on the arm. Hard.

Rubbing his bicep he said, 'We need to think about those two guys; they could be a problem.'

The concourse was crowded with late night/ early morning revellers, loud drunks, groups of singing males and females, stag and hen parties, ultra-loud music booming from the bars and clubs. It was therefore easy for Flynn and Santiago to follow without being made. Not that Romero or his two goons were even looking around. Romero was too busy trying to get his hand on Tracey's fanny and boobs and the two cops were listless and bored, and had drunk too much to be

273

effective bodyguards. Which was good as far as Flynn was concerned, but they were in the way.

At least they were all heading in the right direction, up to an apartment just behind the Avenida de Gran Canaria that Santiago had rented for cash (giving no name) for a week.

Flynn was getting frustrated.

He upped his pace a little, threading through a group of girls; they wolf-whistled him and scowled at Santiago, who jerked them the finger.

One of the bodyguards spoke into the other's ear, then cut away to the right where there was an underpass leading to the road running along the outer perimeter of the commercial centre.

The other man gave a gesture of impatience and kept going behind Romero, shaking his head.

Flynn started to jog. He veered into the underpass and stopped dead, cursing because he could not see where the cop had gone. He slowed to a walk, checking doorways until he heard a gasp and then the unmistakable sound of a man having a long, well-deserved, satisfying piss.

He found him down a short alleyway behind a shop. He was facing a wall but standing back a metre, gleefully spraying and arcing a stream of urine over it, making shapes with it. Occasionally it glittered in the light available. He groaned with pleasure and relief.

Flynn stepped into a shadow waiting for the torrent to abate because, as much as it would have given him a massive advantage to go for the man while he was still in the act, it might also have led Flynn to being covered in it.

Finally it subsided. Flynn was quite impressed

by the power of the man's bladder and prostate.

Humming happily, the man tucked himself away, zipped up his jeans with a jaunty flick of his right leg, turned away from the wall and started to walk back in Flynn's direction. Although not hiding in complete darkness Flynn was not easy to spot pressed up against the wall.

At the last possible moment, he stepped out.

'Hey, fuck you!' the cop said, annoyed at having his path blocked. 'Out of my way, big boy.'

He tried to shoulder past Flynn, who laid his hand on the centre of the man's chest and pushed him backwards, drawing the expected response.

He swung a punch at Flynn.

It was a drunken punch. Flynn caught it easily. His big right palm closed over the cop's fist, then screwed the whole arm around and instantly, through the application of pain, forced him down to his knees. Flynn twisted further, not allowing the man to bend his arm at the elbow and bringing a scream from the cop, then even more until the arm popped out of the shoulder socket with a disgusting crack.

Flynn kept on, mercilessly forcing the man to the ground until he could slam his foot into the side of his face, knocking him unconscious, then lowering him down and laying him out, allowing the loose arm to fall at an unnatural angle.

The whole encounter, from the first touch, lasted maybe fifteen seconds.

Flynn quickly went through the cop's pockets and rooted out his mobile phone, which he tossed up on to the roof of the building they were next to. He did not find a gun.

He was back with Santiago a minute later. She was still behind the other cop, who was now caught between the devil and the deep blue sea. Romero and his catch for the night were well ahead, but his buddy seemed to have disappeared into the darkness. He stood with his hands on his hips, weighing up the situation.

Beyond him, Romero could not care. He and Tracey were almost at the north exit of the centre, entwined and with eyes only for each other.

The bodyguard was in a quandary.

He called to Romero in Spanish. 'Boss . . . Geraldo has gone to piss. He's not back. You need to wait for us.'

Romero stopped and turned angrily. 'Go – find him.'

'You wait here, boss . . . don't go on.'

'OK, OK,' Romero assured him, but the bait that Tracey was playing out was very strong indeed and it did not help Romero's resolve when she grasped the front of his trousers and pulled him along. Sometimes a man has to be led. He gave one last look to see where his bodyguard had gone, then caved in and went with Tracey's infinitely more interesting promise. She was now twerking him, gyrating her bottom against his groin. He made a lecherous grab for her, but she skipped out of reach and he chased after her like a bull elephant on heat.

The second cop jogged back to the underpass, straight past Flynn and Santiago, not even glancing at them. Flynn followed.

He was back less than a minute later with a mobile phone in his hand that he dismantled and dropped into three separate bins, and a gun tucked into his waistband.

Ahead, Tracey and Romero had exited the commercial centre and were going up steps towards the rented apartment.

She led Romero tantalizingly up the steps and on to the second floor walkway.

Flynn and Santiago held back and watched Tracey coax the detective to the door of the apartment. She placed the key in the door – at which moment, Romero's mobile phone rang. He took it out, peered at the caller display and fended off Tracey's less than subtle tugs and pouts, saying, 'I must answer this.'

Flynn swore under his breath, hoping it wasn't either of the bodyguards using a spare phone or calling from a public phone box, though he doubted it. So far their absence at his heels had not perturbed Romero. The prospect of getting laid was much more exciting than the whereabouts of a couple of second class minders who couldn't keep their concentration up. But if this was one of them calling, the little scam here could suddenly become a little more difficult to implement.

'I'm sure I hit them hard enough,' Flynn whispered, voicing his own thoughts. 'And I broke one arm each.'

'You broke their arms?' Santiago hissed.

'Uh – yeah, well, sort of.'

Romero looked away from Tracey and answered the phone. 'Romero . . . Bashkim? Yes, yes, it is me, Romero . . .'

'Bashkim,' Flynn whispered.

Santiago gave him a deadpan look and said, 'I know, I'm standing next to you. I have ears.'

'Sorry.'

'No . . . no,' Romero was saying. 'No, I haven't seen or heard anything about him . . . I don't know if he's back. I'll try to check flights . . . how come you didn't just kill him? I thought that was the plan.'

'See – even they had a plan,' Flynn said into Santiago's ear.

Romero leaned on the rail of the walkway at the back of the apartment block. 'No, I haven't killed that bitch either, because I haven't caught her . . . but I will . . . matter of time . . . yes, I'll watch out for him . . . *sí*, all good here.' He looked at Tracey. She had framed herself seductively in the door, pouting with sexuality. 'Yes, I am looking after your new businesses . . . soon, I promise . . . and I will . . .' He hung up and advanced on Tracey, who beckoned him inside.

Flynn and Santiago sat on the top step. He placed his arm around her shoulders and hugged her.

Now it was a waiting game.

Tracey came out twenty minutes later with a flimsy dressing gown wrapped tightly around her and motioned for Flynn and Santiago to join her in the apartment. She stood aside and let them filter in ahead of her, her eyes watching Flynn distrustfully.

Romero was splayed out naked on the double bed, drugged, grunting in his sleep.

Both Flynn and Santiago said, 'Eww,' simultaneously. He was not a pretty sight.

'How long will he be out?' Flynn asked Tracey. 'You being the Rohypnol expert.'

'Maximum four hours; probably start coming round slowly after three and a bit.'

'OK.'

'Can I get dressed now?'

Flynn said, 'Yes – go.'

They watched him come back to life as the drug wore off. It took time. His eyes blinked open, closed again – then reality hit him, they sprang open and he started to buck like a bronco as he attempted to free his wrists and ankles from the zip-ties that attached him to the sturdy bed, his shouts muffled and terrified behind the tape over his mouth.

It was like having a pit bull terrier in a noose, but Flynn knew he would not escape in the same way as he himself had managed.

Eventually, sweating, exhausted, he stopped.

Santiago walked across to him.

She – like Flynn – was now dressed from head to foot in a protective forensic suit, covering her head, face, body, legs and feet. Her hands were in surgeon's gloves, a surgical face mask over the lower part of her face, just her eyes showing.

Romero watched as she walked around the bed.

'Have you quite finished now?' she asked him, seeing the dawn of realization in his eyes. She stood over him. 'Yes, it is me,' she said and tugged down the elasticated mask, revealing her face.

He shouted something – a curse or obscenity – from behind the tape and started to thrash against his bindings, but to no effect.

279

Again, eventually, he gave up. His chest heaved with the effort.

Flynn joined Santiago. He pulled down his mask. 'I'm here, too.'

He had the second bodyguard's Glock in his hand. He leaned over and placed the muzzle in the centre of Romero's forehead, forcing the man to emit a mournful wail from somewhere deep down in his throat and attempt to cower away. His breathing came in desperate bursts through his nose and his big round face turned from brown to red as his blood pressure rose to a dangerous high.

Flynn kept the gun to his head and thumbed back the trigger.

'Keep still,' he said. Romero ceased moving. 'Good,' Flynn said. 'I am now going to take the tape off your mouth, detective. If you shout or do anything ridiculous, I will simply kill you . . . nod if you understand.'

Romero nodded gladly.

Flynn peeled the tape away, enjoying ripping it off with a few moustache hairs. Except for a squeak of pain, Romero stayed quiet.

'Good,' Flynn said again. 'Now then . . .'

Romero sat at the small dining table in the apartment. He was naked. Santiago sat opposite. Flynn stood to one side behind her, the Glock hanging loosely by his side. Romero was, so far, being very compliant, though Flynn guessed this was more to save his soul, work out a way to escape and try to gain an advantage than for any other reason. He was devious and Flynn was not going to forget that.

280

The drug had now worn off and he had been provided with coffee and a bottle of water.

'What do you want from me?' he asked Santiago in English. He had begun to talk in Spanish, but had been told to speak English at all times. He looked at their forensic suits and was *compos mentis* enough to realize this was not a good omen.

'A full confession of your wrongdoings,' Santiago said.

Romero snorted.

'That is the only possible way in which you will walk out of here alive,' she told him, and reiterated, 'the only way.'

'So why are you both dressed like that?' He gestured at the suits – which Santiago had bought from a wholesaler in Las Palmas. 'I know about forensics and contamination . . . I am no fool. You will kill me anyway.'

'We will not kill you,' she said.

Romero raised his eyebrows and looked at Flynn. 'You are a dead man, you know that, don't you, Señor Flynn?'

Under the surgeon's mask, Flynn smiled.

Romero turned back to Santiago, challenging her. 'You and he are both murderers and you will face justice, one way or another.'

On the table in front of Santiago was a slim brown file which she opened, but did not refer to. She glanced at Flynn, who stepped over to a small camcorder on a tripod. He switched it on and pointed it at Romero, but did not press record.

Santiago said, 'Tell me what your relationship is with the Bashkim crime family from Albania.'

'I have never heard of the Bashkim crime family.'

'Have you ever received any payments from the Bashkim crime family?'

'No. I do not know of the Bashkim crime family.'

'But yet they pay you two thousand euros each month. Am I correct?'

'I do not know what you are talking about.' Romero's eyes dropped to the folder between him and Santiago.

'Do you receive your police salary from the Canary Island Police Force, and is it paid into your Santander current account?'

'Yes. What is that about? I am a cop. I get paid. It is my salary.'

'You have other bank accounts?'

'I have a savings account. What is unusual about that?'

'You have other accounts—'

Romero started to say something – a denial – then checked himself and glanced at the file again.

Santiago still did not refer to the papers in front of her. 'How is your mother?'

'What?'

'It is a simple question.'

'What has my mother got to do with this?'

'She is now an old lady – am I correct? And your father is dead.'

'Yes – so fucking what?'

'Is she proud of you? A senior detective?'

'Yes.'

'She won't be after this.' Santiago slid a sheet of paper over to him. 'This is a list of bank accounts in your name – your current account, your savings account and three more accounts, in which are payments from another source besides the government.'

'Where did you get—?' he stammered.

'There are payments into these accounts – two thousand euros each month for the last eighteen months, some thirty-six thousand euros, plus two single payments, one of eight thousand euros and one of eleven thousand euros—'

'Fuck you,' Romero cut in.

'Now if you hadn't been silly enough to transfer funds from one of these accounts into your normal account and also into your mother's account, we would never have discovered their existence or their link to the Bashkim crime clan, because, you see, all this extra money came from them.'

Romero ran a hand across his features.

'You are a corrupt cop,' Santiago said flatly. 'And evil, too.'

Flynn watched him, almost saw the cogs rotating in the man's brain, as he weighed this up.

'What do you want?'

'A full and frank admission of your guilt, your complicity with the Bashkims and what you have been doing for the last month – including killing my friend.'

'My name is Ramos Francisco Romero. I am a detective with the Gran Canarian Police Department.' He looked unemotionally into the lens of the camcorder on the tripod, behind which stood Flynn and Santiago. 'I make this statement of my own free will. I wish to admit my guilt and corruption. First, I have been on the payroll

283

of the Bashkim crime family for the last three years, ever since they began operating on the Canary Islands. I began this association with them because I was in debt through gambling, and they cleared this debt for me.' He shrugged. 'Simple as that. They pay me two thousand euros each month and occasionally I receive a bonus.

'I became aware that Adam Castle, a businessman on Gran Canaria, had run into debt, and I engineered a meeting between him and Aleksander Bashkim, the head of the crime family. But I know that Castle had second thoughts about dealing with them and wished to back out. Bashkim's son, Dardan, killed him because of this. I know that Steve Flynn stumbled on the murder of Adam Castle and had to kill Dardan Bashkim in self-defence. I manipulated evidence so it would appear that Flynn murdered both Dardan and Adam Castle. As Flynn was being transported to Playa del Inglès police station for questioning, with Detective Santiago as his escort, they were ambushed and a police officer was killed by Pavli, Bashkim's other son. Flynn and Santiago fled the scene and I subsequently accused them of murdering the police officer, which was untrue. They did not kill him. Pavli did. I know this because I witnessed this murder.

'Also, Jose Galvez, Mr Flynn's crew member, was murdered by Pavli who fixed a bomb to Flynn's car, hoping to kill Flynn. He killed Galvez by mistake. I know he put the bomb on the car because I was there when he did it. I also intended to manipulate those circumstances to make it appear that Flynn had killed Galvez. He didn't.'

Romero took a breath, then eyed Santiago hesitantly before saying, 'When the manhunt was on for Flynn and Detective Santiago, I learned they were staying at a finca owned by Santiago's friend, Jane Munro. By the time I reached the address they had gone but Señora Munro was there. I beat her to death while questioning her. It was my intention to blame Flynn and Santiago for this murder, but they are innocent.

'That is my confession, made freely.'

Flynn switched off the camcorder and dismantled the tripod.

He then sat opposite Romero and opened an envelope, extracting several gloss photographs which he laid out carefully in front of Romero.

They were crime scene photographs, fourteen of them, from the murders committed across Europe by Tracey Jayne Martin.

'The lady you met last night? Her handiwork,' Flynn said.

Romero looked at the gruesome killings of men. Some photos were of men still tied to beds; others were of beds with almost empty cadavers on them, hearts, lungs and other organs having been dug out; others were of organs in bins. Jerry Tope had acquired them for Flynn from various police databases.

'Holy Jesus,' Romero said.

'Now you have a choice, my friend,' Flynn explained. 'Either we let this lady loose on you – she's sitting in the bedroom now, scalpel sharpened and ready to rock – or I can put one bullet in your gun and you can put it to your head and take your own life in shameful remorse.' Flynn sat back. 'Your choice, *amigo*.' He gave him a symbolic wink.

'That wasn't the deal.'

'No,' Flynn said, 'it wasn't. But the problem is that you are a sneaky, underhand fucker and if we take you to a police station together with this video you will start to lie and cheat your way out of the situation. Be a cry-baby, boo-hoo, say you were under duress—'

'I was.'

'I know you were . . . but if you're dead you won't be able to claim that, will you? Y'see,' – Flynn leaned forward, his eyes ablaze – 'I know people like you.'

'I won't. I won't do either of those things. Take me in, now.'

Flynn rocked back, glanced at Santiago. The expression on her face truly disturbed him. 'What do you think?' he asked her.

Her nostrils dilated. She stared at Romero.

'I know what she thinks,' Romero offered. 'She thinks she has to take me in. She is a cop. She believes in justice. She is weak and so are you, Mr Flynn. The moment of threat to me has now passed.' Romero sneered as he spoke.

Flynn watched Santiago.

She said nothing.

Romero's own gun was on a work surface in the small kitchen. She reached for it, cocked it, strode over to Romero and placed the muzzle against his right temple. Romero tried to remain cocksure and brave. Santiago splayed the fingers of her left hand across the top of his skull, steadying his head.

Then she shot him.

Flynn rubbed his tired, gritty eyes.

It was four hours later and he was sitting on the balcony of a tiny apartment in Puerto de Mogán that he and Karen Glass had once used. It was a nice apartment but since it was a rental it was quite sterile and there was nothing to remind Flynn of their stay. It was in a great location, though, with a view towards the marina.

He had paid for the rental with Bashkim's cash, a wad that was becoming very depleted.

He sat alone. It was almost noon but even so he had a glass of scotch in front of him together with a bottle of water. One was to take the edge off, the other to rehydrate.

Inside the apartment he could hear Santiago in the bathroom.

He knew she was sitting on the floor of the shower, letting hot jets of water swill away the grime. He did not interrupt. He knew she had to wallow in her feelings, start to come to terms with what had happened – the taking of a man's life.

After the shooting, Flynn had eased the gun into Romero's hand and curled his index finger around the trigger to try to simulate a suicide scene. Flynn knew, though, that any half-competent pathologist, forensic scientist or even detective would be able to figure out that Romero had not killed himself. There would be no gunshot residue on his fingers, no back-spray of blood from the wound. Flynn had tried to cover this up by rubbing Romero's

287

hand in his own blood, even though he knew a tenacious cop would be able to piece together what had really happened. That would be a bridge to cross, he thought philosophically. At first glance it would appear to be suicide and when the video was viewed Flynn had to hope that any anomalies would be overlooked – or missed. Hope that good cops would just be happy that a corrupt one had taken his own life.

'Flynn!' Santiago called him from the shower.

He swallowed the whisky, made his way to the bathroom.

She was still in the shower but now standing behind the steamed-up door. She wiped away the condensation and looked at Flynn through the streaks with her big brown eyes. He stripped and stepped in. The water was still hot to burning. She wrapped her arms around him and pressed herself into his body.

'I've killed a man,' she said softly, and began to sob. 'When will all this be over?'

For the life of him, Flynn did not have an answer to that.

They slept for a long time that afternoon, way into the evening, before dragging themselves groggily out of bed, back into the shower, then dressing to go down to the port to eat at one of the hidden-away restaurants behind the marina.

It was a quiet meal, little said until later when they strolled through the flower-festooned streets hand in hand and reached the end of the quayside.

'I can't keep running, Steve, not now. I haven't been back to my own apartment in Las Palmas for weeks. I had cheese and chicken in the fridge.' She sighed. 'I just want to go home.'

'I get that, but we still have a problem – who do we trust? We could end up being thrown back to the wolf pack and torn apart if we're not careful. If Romero is just the thin end of the wedge of corruption . . .'

She nodded in agreement.

'First we need to know that Romero's body has been found and that it's being treated as suicide. If they think it's suspicious, then we'll need to be really vigilant. I know I warned you to be careful, but it might be as well to keep in touch with that all-hearing friend of yours in admin.'

'She doesn't really know that much . . . just grapevine stuff.'

Flynn tensed up and squeezed Santiago's hand. A cop car cruised through the junction ahead of them. But they were on a poorly lit street full of tourists, just another couple mooching through the bougainvillea.

'And handing ourselves in isn't the only problem we have,' he pointed out.

'Do you really think Bashkim would be stupid enough to come after us?'

Flynn gave a snort of a laugh. 'We have singed the tail of a tiger – well, a wolf – and held the damn thing in the flames, actually. Let's see . . . Bashkim's son dead.' Flynn visualized the bait knife skewering Dardan's carotid artery. 'Plus seventy-five million dollars and a few million pounds' worth of coke up in flames; four of their guys in the UK dead. We've taken on a violent Albanian crime family and rubbed their noses in shit. Of course they'll come for us. They kill people who stand in their way. If we reappear on the grid, we'll be sitting ducks at some stage.'

Santiago was silent.

Flynn gave her a reassuring hug.

'That said,' Flynn went on, 'Bashkim killed the three most important people in my life.' He swallowed, composed himself. 'And that means only one thing, my love.'

'What's that?'

'One way or another, I'm going to take it to them. I have to. I can't sit back and wait for a bullet in the back of the head.'

Santiago regarded Flynn with horror.

'I don't know how, yet,' he admitted. 'I'm not great with plans, as you know.'

She reached up and cupped his face with the palm of her hand. 'I'm coming, too.'

Shocked, he looked into her eyes, about to argue the point – but he could already see there was no way of winning that one.

She went up on tiptoe, he bent slightly and they kissed slowly and passionately until they were interrupted by the mobile phone ringing in Flynn's back pocket. It was the one he had taken from the gunman in Glasson Dock; he had only turned it back on tonight. It said 'Number withheld' on the display.

'Flynn.'

'Ahh, Mr Flynn,' came the cheese-grater voice he recognized instantly.

Flynn's eyes locked with Santiago's. Instantly she knew, going by the look on her face. Flynn's silently mouthed 'Bashkim' was superfluous.

'Good of you to call.'

'I see you have already moved against my associate.'

'I don't know what you mean.'

Bashkim chuckled. 'It was well done, I grant you that. Suicide.'

'Whatev—'

'You are a worthy adversary,' Bashkim praised him. 'But now that has to stop.'

'You sound like a Bond villain.'

'Oh no, I am much, much worse than that, because I am real.'

'So we're friends, eh?'

'Do you recall what you called me when we first met?'

'Er . . .' Flynn hesitated. 'Nancy-boy?'

There was a pause as Bashkim worked that out, but he was in no mood for joshing. 'You called me a wolf.'

'Oh, yeah, I forgot that.'

'And you have done a great deal of damage to me personally and professionally, Mr Flynn. Do you know the consequences of that?'

'A Nobel Peace Prize?'

'Your flippancy does you no favours, Flynn.'

Flynn resisted the urge to say, 'Oh, flippin' 'eck.'

Bashkim went on, 'You have unleashed the wolf pack and very soon you and that little bitch of a cop will be dead, ripped apart, because I will hunt you down.'

Flynn found his teeth were grinding. He didn't want to get into a threat-trading squabble but could not hold back from growling, 'Nah . . . you ever heard the story of the three little pigs? Well, spin it on its head, you fucking country hick, because this little pig's going to come and burn your house to the ground, with you in it, innit?'

Flynn hung up, tore open the phone and ripped out its insides, threw them to the ground and stamped on them. He looked at Santiago.

'Looks like we might have our work cut out here.'

Nineteen

'It's a hovel, but it'll have to do.' Flynn responded to the expression on Santiago's face. She'd looked around the bedsit located in Blackpool's South Shore, under the shadow of the Big One, the huge roller-coaster ride on the Pleasure Beach. The Meccano-like structure was just visible from the window and Flynn, in a slightly philosophical moment, saw the ride as a metaphor for his life at present: a long, slow, easy ride up, followed by a plunge into insanity.

'Places like this really exist?' Santiago said. 'I was right when I said people on the run live in holes in the ground.'

'Seems so,' Flynn replied.

It really was a shithole of a pad, tucked under the eaves of a large terraced house divided into tiny flats, with peeling, damp walls, an electric fire, a camp bed and a kitchen that consisted of a single hob, a tiny fridge and a toaster. Flynn had reeled away from the fridge when he'd opened it. There was definitely 'something' living in it, but Flynn wasn't courageous enough to touch it in case it attacked him.

'But it's cheap and incognito, cash up front and I know the landlord – once arrested him for dealing, and he owes me a big favour because he's not banged up. So I got a good deal for it.'

'You were robbed, whatever you paid for it.' She sat down heavily on the bed, which creaked dangerously. 'We live like tramps.'

'But look!' Flynn opened a door. 'It's got its own toilet and shower room.'

Santiago was seriously unimpressed.

It was one week later.

The two of them had been dropped off in Tenerife by Flynn's friend, sportfishing skip Tomas; from there they'd travelled by ferry to Cadiz and then by coach up through Spain to Santander, where they boarded the overnight ferry to Portsmouth, managing to book an inner cabin.

Flynn was again nervy about using their own passports, but there was no option. Neither had the contacts, time or resources to source forged ones, so each time one had to be produced they expected the hand on the shoulder – but it never came. Customs and Immigration continued to be lax and frequently they were just waved through by bored-looking officials.

They then 'coached' it from Portsmouth to Blackpool, where Flynn hired a small car. When they turned up on the landlord's doorstep he took Flynn and Santiago up to the room and swiftly pocketed the handful of notes that Flynn offered.

Santiago tested the bed but jumped off when a spring jabbed her in the backside.

'It's only for a short time,' Flynn promised her.

She had become very withdrawn and morose on the journey, particularly after she spoke to her friend in admin, who told her she was no longer a murder suspect and Romero's death was being treated as the suicide of a depressed man. The police, however, did want her to hand herself in and had appealed for that on local radio.

Flynn had gently challenged her about her resolve, which seemed to be wavering, but she said she was determined to see it through – whatever 'it' was – at least until her tattoos had all faded.

'If you want out,' he offered . . . and not for the first time.

She shrugged him off. 'I'll stay with you to the very end,' she said ominously. Flynn hoped it would not be a tragic finale.

The afternoon was spent nipping around to various shops, including three different super-stores, two DIY stores and an electrical ware-house. They carried their purchases up to the 'penthouse', as Flynn began to call the bedsit. It was just a matter of perspective, he argued. It was on the top floor, had a view of the sea if you crawled out of the window and stood on the roof, so case proven. It was just a bit *bijou*, but he also argued that a pad like this would have cost over £300,000 in London.

'Still doesn't stop it being a shithole,' Santiago countered.

Flynn could not contest that.

On their return with the shopping, the first thing Flynn did was fix a heavy duty padlock on the outside of the door. That done, he laid out his purchases on the floor and smiled proudly at Santiago.

They ate at a seafront café before Flynn – as evening drew in – drove them on to the Shoreside council estate in the Marton area of Blackpool. It was Blackpool's largest and poorest housing development. Many properties were boarded up, what looked like a bomb site occupied the spot where a row of shops had once been and there was a general air of neglect, poverty and hopelessness.

Flynn had spent a lot of his time as a drug squad officer in and around the estate, which was the hub of dealer activity in the resort.

But that day his business was not with drug dealers. He needed to speak to someone much more low key and subtle, and he hoped the guy hadn't moved since Flynn had spoken to him many years before.

He circled the perimeter of the estate and stopped on Sea View Crescent outside the home and business premises of one Tommy McCann.

There was a light on in the house.

'What's with this guy?' Santiago asked.

'Guns, mainly – and ordnance.'

Flynn got out, marched to the front door and thumped it with the side of his fist.

Inside he heard someone muttering, the scuff of footsteps, the door opening on a heavy chain.

Flynn was already prepared for the reaction.

'Fuck!' the man behind the door shouted and began to slam it shut immediately on seeing Flynn, who just as immediately threw his shoulder at the door. The chain held, though it gave way ever so slightly, and Flynn repeated his move, crashing the whole weight of his body against it a second time – and this time the chain was torn from its fixings and Flynn burst through.

The man – McCann – had already turned and fled.

Flynn propelled himself down the hallway after him.

McCann reached the kitchen door, went through and tried to slam it in Flynn's face but did not succeed. Flynn powered through and the door, instead, slammed into McCann's forehead, inflicting a vertical groove from the centre of his hairline to the bridge of his nose.

Flynn was on him, spinning him around and pitching him to the floor, then dropping heavily on to him with his right knee on his spine between his shoulder blades. Flynn pinned both of McCann's arms up his back, took his weight off the spine and placed McCann's hands under his knee to hold the guy in place while he zip-tied his wrists.

Only then did Flynn raise his eyes to look around the kitchen, which wasn't actually a kitchen at all, not in its truest sense.

There was a cooker and fridge and all those accoutrements, but actually the room was an arsenal.

Santiago entered behind Flynn.

McCann moaned. His face was crushed out of shape on the tiled floor.

'Have we come at an inopportune moment?' Flynn asked.

'You could say that,' McCann said through his distorted lips.

* * *

McCann sat sullenly watching Flynn and Santiago inspect the hardware on display, like an ironmonger's, though in this case it was a weapon-monger. It was a nice, well set out display, awaiting the imminent arrival of a client.

Six handguns, six machine pistols, four pump-action sawn-off shotguns, all ranged across the kitchen worktops. And ammunition to go with each weapon.

Also on display by the kettle, sitting in what could have been an egg box, were four grenades. Another box contained four percussion grenades alongside two hand-held Tasers. And, wrapped like blocks of butter, a dozen slabs of plastic explosive together with detonators, wiring and timing devices and half a dozen light modern bulletproof vests made of Kevlar.

'Well, well, fucking well,' Flynn said, drawing in his breath. He looked at Santiago and then gestured to the seated McCann. 'Meet Mr McCann . . . started out as a spotty lad running parcels for drug dealers, then gravitated to sourcing packages himself and getting shitty guns for shitty crims to pull shitty jobs. Bit by bit he expanded, didn't you, Tommy? Still low level, as all such cockroaches are, but – hey – some of these things are quite new and nice.' He ran a fingernail down the barrel of a machine pistol. 'So, who are these for, Tommy?'

'Up yours, Flynn. What is this shite? You're not even a cop now.'

'Which is why I can do this.' Flynn smacked McCann open-handed, but hard, across his face. He had big fingers and a big hand and a lot of power went into the blow. McCann's head snapped round. Immediately his face started to swell to the exact shape of the imprint Flynn's hand had made on his jawline. 'Who are they for, Tom?'

McCann shook his head to try and clear the blurring of his vision. 'Can't tell you.' Some blood and saliva dribbled out of the corner of his mouth.

Flynn backhanded him this time, jerking his head the opposite way and leaving a line of four red indentations where his knuckle tops had connected.

'No need for that.' McCann spat more blood and could feel loose teeth now. 'I don't deserve this.'

'You deserve every smack I give you.'

Flynn pretended to be about to hit him again and McCann hissed a whistle of fear and cowered. Flynn's hand stopped a centimetre from McCann's face.

He glanced at Santiago, who had watched the slapping with detachment. 'Take your choice,' he said, pointing to the display.

McCann's head shot upright. 'What? What're you doing?'

'Helping ourselves.' Flynn selected a pistol, tilted it admiringly.

'No . . . no, you can't do that.' There was a real tremor in McCann's voice.

'I think you'll find I can do whatever I want.'

Santiago browsed the weaponry as if she was drifting through a clothes shop. She chose a semi-automatic pistol and one of the shotguns. She slid them into the holdall brought along for the purpose, together with magazines and boxes of appropriate ammunition.

'Look man . . . guys,' McCann whined. 'These are for a big time crime family. They're due up from London tonight. If I haven't got their order, they'll nix me.'

'Nix you?' Flynn queried.

'Cut my fucking throat.'

'Oh, that nixing,' Flynn said. 'Who are they?'

'The Smiths.'

'Ahh,' Flynn acknowledged. He knew of them. Very organized, controlled some key areas in central London. Very bad people. 'You've gone up in the world, mate.'

'Yeah, yeah, so you see,' he slurped, 'I'm knackered if any of this stuff disappears . . . c'mon, give us a break. I'll cross your palm with silver. They've got a big job coming up apparently, a bullion thing, I've half-heard.'

Flynn appeared to listen sympathetically, then smacked him hard across the face again. 'Best not to let them get their grubby little paws on this lot, then. Prevention better than cure and all that.'

He chose his weapons and ammunition and a Taser, then added all the grenades, four blocks of the PE plus detonators and timers.

'Bastard,' McCann dribbled.

Flynn loaded another pistol, cocked it and gave it to Santiago. 'Point this at him and if he moves, shoot him in the foot.'

She nodded.

Flynn then got to work.

Five minutes later he had dragged McCann out of the house and was sitting alongside him in the back of the car, with Santiago at the wheel, the pistol now in Flynn's hand. They were parked about 200 metres from – and out of the line of sight of – McCann's house.

Flynn checked his watch, one he had bought that day from Tesco for £8. 'Now let's see how accurate your little timing devices—'

The final word of the sentence was cut off rudely as the kitchen at the back of McCann's house exploded with a huge yellow flash of fire and black smoke. They could not see the explosion from the car but heard it, and it buffeted their ears.

'Oh, you absolute bastard,' McCann said.

Flynn kicked him out of the car. His hands were still tied around his back and he dropped to his knees and started to cry as plumes of black smoke and tongues of flame licked up from the kitchen window and the whole house caught fire. Within moments it was ablaze.

'You will get me killed,' Jerry Tope said, and not for the first time.

He glanced nervously around the restaurant section of the Fairfield Arms, situated just off the M55 motorway close to Kirkham.

Flynn and Santiago sat side by side at a table in an alcove.

Tope – after coming in and wandering around the place for a minute before locating the couple – sat opposite. The words about his future death were the first ones he spoke before looking properly at Flynn, then Santiago – at which moment his jaw sagged and his mouth popped open.

He was completely enraptured by her, yet also slightly repelled.

He could see she was stunningly beautiful, yet

the shaven head and tattoos made him gulp. She reminded him of a young Sinéad O'Connor.

His head flitted back and forth between the two and he was unable to speak.

Flynn grinned and said, over-dramatically, 'May I introduce Maria Santiago?'

'I . . . er . . . jeepers . . . you never said to me she . . .' Tope stuttered, then got a grip of himself.

'Was a woman?' Flynn completed the sentence for him.

'No . . . a beautiful woman,' Tope said, then looked at Flynn. 'Did I just say that?'

Santiago smiled and reached across the table, proffering her hand. Tope shook it and held on to it a few seconds longer than was appropriate.

'*Hola*,' he said in a deep creepy voice. '*Cómo está?*'

'*Muy bien, gracias*,' she said seductively.

'Oh, fucking hell, get a room,' Flynn said, interrupting the moment. 'Or in your case, a tissue will do,' he said to Tope. 'Now, what've you got for me?'

Tope turned angrily. 'I thought you said you wouldn't be bothering me again? You actually promised.'

'I'm a fibber – what've you got?'

'Uh, first, was that financial stuff any good to you, all that banking?'

'It was.' Flynn did not elaborate.

Tope waited, saw nothing was on offer, then said, 'Oh, OK . . . as far as the Glasson incident is progressing, all the dead people have now been identified. The SIO is sure there were others involved,' – Tope looked meaningfully at Flynn

301

– 'but they can't be sure. Someone will be coming to interview you, Steve, because you are registered as the owner of the boat that exploded . . . yeah, yeah, I know, you lost it in a card game. That's your story and I suggest you stick to it.'

'What about Bashkim?'

'Well, all the dead guys had links to the Albanian mafia, but not directly to Bashkim, it seems . . . layers, you know? And re Bashkim, I don't have a lot, to be honest . . . I've looked at passenger lists for airlines and ferries, found nothing. Intel reports suggest Aleksander Bashkim is out of the country, but Pavli might still be here. We don't know for certain.'

'And where do they operate from?'

'Well – various pubs and clubs in the region, as you know already, as well as brothels fed by trafficking girls.' Tope looked uncomfortable. 'I'll die for this . . . again, as you know, the NCS and SOCA have been running long term ops against the Albanian mafia, concentrating on London and not the regions, so a lot of intel that goes on the system just doesn't get followed up, although it's possible the NCS might now be interested in what's happening up here because of the Glasson thing . . . dead bodies and bombs tend to rack up curiosity . . . and money, too. Do you know how much went up in smoke?'

Flynn did, but played innocent. 'Shock me.'

'Hundred mil.'

'Hundred mil what?'

'Dollars.'

Even more than Pavli had boasted about, the little liar, Flynn thought.

302

'Anyway, I digress.' Tope had entered the restaurant with a folder in his hand. He pushed it towards Flynn. 'Do with this what you will – although, can I ask what you intend to do with it?'

Flynn opened the folder and had a quick scan of the contents, then looked at Tope. 'Ever heard the question, how do you eat an elephant?'

Tope frowned, as did Santiago.

'Bit by bit, one chunk at a time, one mouthful after another . . . we start munching away tonight.'

Twenty

Using a pair of thirty-six inch Clarke bolt cutters, Flynn snipped through the chain-link slung across the entrance to the forecourt of the used van dealership in the Plungington area of Preston. The chain fell apart and he ran to the vehicle he had chosen to steal that night. The third vehicle, actually.

There was no finesse in his crime.

He simply backhanded the curved end of a 450 mm steel wrecking bar into the driver's door window. One blow and the window disintegrated and, just as he had anticipated, no alarm went off. He slid the wrecking bar back into the rucksack on his back, which he was using like a quiver. He reached through the gap and unlocked the door, climbing in behind the wheel. From a tool belt he was wearing around his waist he took a heavy duty screwdriver and jammed it into the ignition – a slot which had seen much better days – and turned it.

It was not a pretty crime, but on a fifteen-year-old Ford Transit van for sale for £150 it was effective. Flynn understood vehicles like these. Anything more modern and he would have had problems.

The engine turned over, coughed, spluttered, died. The fuel gauge rose to just under a quarter full, so, if it was telling the truth, there was enough fuel in it for his requirements. He did not need much. He tapped the accelerator, wary not to flood the old engine, then turned the screwdriver again.

Reluctantly it came to life and he drove off the forecourt and was gone.

On Blackpool Road he slotted in behind Santiago, who was waiting for him in the hire car, and they drove towards Deepdale.

There was a definite bum-cheek-clenching moment when at the junction where the A6 dissected Blackpool Road the lights were on red and he had to stop. Glancing in the door mirror he saw a set of blue lights haring towards him from behind. A cop car. As it approached the lights the siren came on and other cars pulled aside; the car slowed at the lights, then edged through the junction before racing on to whatever emergency awaited.

Flynn exhaled and unclenched his arsehole.

The lights changed.

A few minutes later, now leading, he took Santiago on to a large industrial park and drove around the back of a huge disused warehouse where they had already parked the two vehicles

Flynn had stolen a short time earlier, another old Transit van and an equally dated Vauxhall Astra.

Flynn climbed out of the van, Santiago out of the car.

They were dressed in black from head to foot, clothing bought on their earlier shopping expedition.

'You ready for this?' Flynn asked her.

She nodded.

It was time to arm themselves.

They travelled in separate vehicles, Santiago in the Astra, Flynn in one of the Transits. He knew Preston relatively well, although the last time he'd been on the streets as a cop was over ten years before. He could easily get from one place to another across the city, but finding specific streets was more difficult; he didn't have the heart to buy a satnav for what he hoped would be a short-lived visit. Where he headed that late evening was fairly straightforward anyway – towards Preston Docks – and his first planned visit of the night.

The start, he had declared to Santiago, of the onslaught.

Steve Flynn never failed to be amazed by men who paid for sex. He tried to understand it, but could never quite figure it out. And he definitely could not get his head around men who visited prostitutes in sordid surroundings – girls and women who were nothing more than sex slaves and prisoners forced into the life – and paid £50 for a five minute fuck, then came back day after day – hundreds, thousands of men, even here in the small city that was Preston, Lancashire.

Flynn did understand how women were tricked and trafficked and coerced into becoming prostitutes by criminal gangs who turned the victims into junkies; they often did not even understand what was happening to them. They became empty vessels whose lives were destroyed by people like Aleksander Bashkim.

He also realized that he couldn't change the world, but tonight he hoped he might give that vile, degrading trade a bit of a kick in the balls. He knew he was doing it for his own reasons, but if by screwing up some of Bashkim's business he might be able to save a few souls in the process, perhaps he would . . . maybe. What he really wanted from tonight was to draw Bashkim and Pavli out from under their rocks, so he could destroy them.

He was not being altruistic in any way.

These conflicting thoughts waterfalled through his head as he and Santiago sat about 200 metres away from the entrance to what had once been an indoor skatepark on the banks of the River Ribble in an industrial estate to the east of Preston Docks that had seen very much better days. The skatepark – inside a huge warehouse unit – had once thrived, but had gone bust and lain empty for years.

Now it had a new lease of life.

Flynn and Santiago were in the Transit on a road leading to a swanky motor park, with the Astra behind them, watching a steady stream of cars passing along the track leading to the unit-cum-brothel.

'Why don't the police or the council close this place down?' Santiago wanted to know.

'Maybe the local guys don't know about it. It's fairly discreet, off the grid, behind a gate, there are no neighbours to worry about. Punters come and go and it's not doing anyone any harm – on the face of it,' Flynn argued reasonably. 'No public order problems here.'

Santiago's face was as hard as stone in her disgust.

'And it's not a priority. Stuff like this rarely is. The police will be lucky to put out three mobile patrols a shift here, maybe a couple of bobbies on foot and some PCSOs.'

'PCSOs?'

'Cheap copperin' . . . don't go there. It's all about money. Even when I was a cop the force was being squeezed by the government, and it continues to be so.'

'No excuse.'

'It's the supply chain that needs closing down,' Flynn said. 'Squeeze the bastards at the top, the snake-heads . . . the ones who arrange all the trafficking . . . as if . . . it's unwinnable.'

A heavy silence descended between them.

Two cars drove past towards the unit, a lone male in each. Flynn knew there was a manned gate about halfway down the lane with a couple of heavies sitting indolently in a shed, checking people entering.

The first hurdle he and Santiago would have to jump.

'Are we going to give it a go?' he said.

Santiago nodded.

She clambered over the passenger seat into the back of the van, crawled to the back doors and sat with her arms locked around her knees.

'Ready,' she said.

Flynn checked his watch: eleven thirty p.m.

He drove slowly along the lane towards the warehouse unit. He had previously looked at the place on Google Maps on a computer belonging to the landlord of his bedsit and knew it stood alone, surrounded by a high mesh fence and fields, not overlooked by anything. It was two miles from the city centre but could just as easily have been in the middle of nowhere. The brothel equivalent of a McDonald's drive-thru.

He drove the van slowly, under no illusions about this or any part of his plan. It could all easily go very wrong. He expected it to do so, because the main problem with the plan was that he was winging it.

The two men emerged from the shed. One stood in the middle of the track and waved him to stop with a torch and hand signals.

Flynn complied and leaned on the always open driver's window.

The man looked lean, tough and craggy. Six feet tall at least, athletic build and dressed in the outfit of all heavies the world over – in 1960s TV dramas, at least. Black roll neck sweater, black jeans and trainers, with a black bob cap on his head.

'I don' know you,' he said to Flynn in accented English. East European, maybe Albanian, Flynn thought. In recent times his ear for such accents had improved dramatically.

'I know. I don't know you, either.'

'Fuck off, then. Turn round, fuck off.' That sounded very Anglo-Saxon.

'I don't think Aleksander would want you to talk to me like that.'

The name had some effect on the guy.

'Aleksander who?'

'Mr Bashkim to you . . . special delivery for this unit,' Flynn said. He jerked his thumb over his shoulder.

The guard went on tiptoe to look over Flynn's right shoulder into the back of the van, seeing the small female shape in there. Santiago had drawn her knees right up and tucked her forehead against them, hiding her face.

'No one told me about this.' He flashed the torch beam over her.

By this time the other guard had joined him, similarly attired.

'What's happening?'

'This guy says he has a new hooker for this place.'

'Hot bitch from Kazakhstan,' Flynn said luridly.

The second guard also peered over Flynn's shoulder.

'Want to see?' Flynn offered. 'Maybe one of you guys could be first in there . . . she hasn't been fucked out yet, or so I believe.'

The two men exchanged glances and the first one said, 'Let's see her, then.' To guard number two he said, 'You check it out.' He made a phone gesture with his hand, thumb to ear, little finger to mouth.

'OK.' The guard started to take out his mobile phone and both of them shuffled to the rear of the van. Flynn dropped out and followed. At the back he opened both doors for them to see.

Santiago raised her face as the first guard

309

flashed his torch beam at her. She looked up big-eyed, sad, as though she had travelled in hope but ended up in hell. She had purposely rubbed mascara and dark make-up around her eyes to assist the overall impression.

'You're right,' the guard said approvingly. 'Hot bitch.'

'I knew you'd like her . . . now are we OK?' Flynn asked. He eyed the second guard who was still tabbing through his phone's menu. Flynn paused as he found the number, then pressed dial.

'Hey boss, you expecting a—?'

The first guard was still ogling Santiago, who was trying her best to look terrified.

Flynn nodded slyly to her, then stepped sideways and peeled the phone out of the guard's hand. The guard looked questioningly at him – but only for a moment before Flynn drove his fist into the man's face as hard as he possibly could, dropping him instantly.

At the same moment Santiago burst into life. She leapt forward in a blur of motion, striking like an uncoiling leopard, grabbing the hand-held Taser hidden between her thighs and jamming it into the first guard's chest. It sizzled as the connection was made and slammed 50,000 volts into him. He fell in writhing agony as the electricity seared through him and momentarily closed down his system.

She jumped out of the van and got to work with the pre-prepared strips of duct tape stuck on the inner van doors. She covered the guard's mouth, flipped him over and bound his hands behind his back, then tied his feet together. Flynn was doing the same with the other. Then Flynn and Santiago dragged them behind the shed where, much to Flynn's delight, there was a drainage ditch into which they rolled both trussed-up guards.

They ran back to the van which was still ticking over lumpily.

Flynn fish-tailed it towards the warehouse.

'Hot bitch?' Santiago questioned him, pulling on a black ski mask.

'Yeah, my hot bitch.' He swerved into the car park at the side of the unit, where there were half a dozen cars. He took a few moments to tool up with the items he thought he would need for the next stage of this operation, then pulled a ski mask on.

Each brandishing a machine pistol, they ran towards the entrance and crashed through. Inside was a short corridor with a counter to the left where clients booked in and paid. Behind it lounged a rotund middle-aged woman who was busy counting money by hand, lots of it.

She looked up.

Screamed.

Santiago scaled the hatch like a high jumper, smashed the stock of the machine pistol into the side of the woman's skull, silencing the scream and felling her. She toppled off her chair. The cash flew out of her hands as if she was releasing a cloud of huge butterflies. As she fell she caught her head on the top corner of a radiator before hitting the floor, stunned.

Santiago stood over her like a mini-colossus, kicking away a lead-ended club from under the woman's chair.

Flynn had moved along the corridor, emerging into a small waiting area where four men sat drinking beer from bottles. From their horrified expressions he guessed they were punters who had paid and were now waiting their turns.

He brought the machine pistol around into a firing grip and panned it across the men.

'Out,' he screamed, 'get out of here.'

None reacted so, to gee them up, he fired a short burst into the false ceiling above their heads. The polystyrene tiles disintegrated like snow around them and as the echo of the gunfire died away he screamed, 'Out!' again.

Santiago appeared from the office at that moment, pushing the rotund receptionist ahead of her with the barrel of her firearm.

The men moved this time, with Flynn still screaming behind them, kicking backsides.

As the last one left Flynn got his bearings, turned left and stood at the head of a long narrow corridor with six doors on either side. It looked as though it had been built separately and dropped into the warehouse like a complete prefabricated unit.

This was the place where the business was done.

One door opened. A man appeared, frightened face, pulling on a shirt.

'Out,' Flynn yelled.

The man hurried out, yanking up his pants, fastening his shirt, his shoes in one hand. Flynn gave him a kick up the rear, too.

Flynn looked back at Santiago with the receptionist still in front of her.

'How many women are there here?' he demanded.

She looked at him defiantly. Blood had run

312

across her face from the cut on her head. She was woozy, but still managed to scowl at him and say, 'Go fuck.'

He levelled his gun at her. 'How many?'

'Twelve,' she blurted quickly, not that woozy any more.

'How many customers?'

'Maybe six now.'

'Keep her here,' Flynn told Santiago.

He started to make his way along the corridor. He booted open the first door and found a man on top of a girl, his backside slamming in and out. Underneath, the girl, maybe fourteen years old, took the abuse with her eyes closed and a drugged expression on her face. Flynn hauled the man off her and jostled him out into the corridor towards Santiago and the receptionist. Santiago pulled the woman out of the man's path.

Flynn watched him go and nodded to Santiago, who screamed, 'Flynn!'

He spun at the word, realizing his back was exposed.

Two men had appeared at the far end of the corridor, armed with handguns.

Flynn dived into the bedroom as they opened fire.

Santiago ducked and shoved the receptionist down the corridor with a powerful heave, then she too dived sideways, taking cover.

Two bullets hit the woman, stomach and chest. She slumped sideways.

Flynn pivoted out of the room and sprayed the corridor with a long burst from the machine pistol, taking both men down with a diagonal line of bullets, rising across the gut of one and

313

the chest of the other. They fell against each other into a tangled, bloody heap on the corridor floor. Flynn ran up to them and kicked away their guns, not sure if either of them was dead.

Santiago stepped back into the corridor and strode over to the twitching body mass of the receptionist. She was alive, and looked pleadingly at her.

Santiago stepped over her and then she and Flynn began to work through, systematically clearing the rooms, watching each other's backs as they did.

They actually found only nine more girls, all aged between thirteen and seventeen, three with customers who, to a man, were quivering, wilted wrecks, cowering in the corners of the squalid rooms. Each was relieved to be given a pass-out by the masked duo. They ran for their lives without complaint. There was no trace of any others.

Then started the slower process of collecting and herding the girls out of the premises. Each was high on drugs and they were like ragdolls to move and manipulate. Each was also naked, and trying to wrap them in their grubby bedding – since there was no sign of clothes anywhere – took precious time, which Flynn knew was valuable. Every extra second spent was a danger.

The two worked silently and efficiently until finally every girl, from every room, was sitting huddled in the back of the van.

'You keep an eye on them,' Flynn said to Santiago. 'Give me five minutes.' He picked up his rucksack and sprinted back into the warehouse. He had pre-prepared the explosives, going for the simple option of 125 gram slabs of PE with timer detonators set so that when he snapped them they would begin to work, giving him ten minutes to get clear. It was simple, effective, not rocket science. The only possible thing that could go wrong was the timers, which could be unpredictable, but he had randomly sampled three while preparing the bombs and all worked perfectly.

He had prepared four for use that night. He placed one on the reception counter, two in separate rooms and the fourth in the waiting area. The explosions would be big enough to destroy this particular area within the warehouse but not the whole building, unless it happened to catch fire – which he hoped would happen.

The point was to make a point.

Happy with what he had done, he looked down the corridor. The two men at the far end had stopped moving, were dead, as was the receptionist, who was lying there with her eyes wide open. He snapped the first timer in one of the rooms, then quickly worked his way back doing the same with the others before finally snapping the one on the reception desk, then sprinting very, very quickly to the van.

Santiago ran up to him, having removed her hood.

'There's another girl in there,' she gasped.

Flynn blinked in disbelief. 'What?'

'One of the girls says her sister is still in there . . . she's drugged up and slurring her words, but that's what she's saying.'

'Shit.' He calculated: two minutes gone, eight left. 'Fuck!' Now three minutes gone. 'Where is she?'

'She said in one of the rooms.'

'Didn't we search them all?'

'Well, we can debate it,' Santiago snarled urgently. 'There's still a girl left in there.'

'I'm on to it.' Flynn forced his machine pistol into Santiago's hand, spun and ran back into the warehouse, cursing as he ran past reception, glancing at the bomb on the desk. It looked harmless, like a slab of butter with a pencil stuck into it.

He would have liked to have been able simply to pull out the detonator, but now cursed himself for a smartarse because when prepping them he had fitted a simple anti-tamper device which meant that if some poor sod thought all he had to do to disarm the bomb was pull out the detonator, he would be fatally mistaken. A wire running from the inserted tip of the detonator had been attached to the PE and would blow the bomb via a secondary detonator if it was pulled out.

It would have been easy for a bomb disposal expert but not for a numpty working for the Bashkims.

He could have disarmed the devices too, but because of the care required and the time it would take – about two minutes for each device, not including the time it would take to get from one bomb to the next – he could not do it.

And he only had seven minutes remaining to search for, find and evacuate the last remaining girl.

'Fucking smarty-pants,' he berated himself as he skidded into the corridor where three people lay dead. He looked in the first room, checked under the wire-framed bed, found himself saying, 'Clear.'

Next room: 'Clear.'

Next: 'Clear.'

He entered the fourth room: 'Clear.'

Five minutes remaining.

He bobbed out of this room intending to dive straight across to the one opposite, but he was stopped dead.

'Is this what you're looking for, Steve Flynn? I'm guessing it's you.' It was a voice he recognized with a cold shudder of dread and in a parallel thought he scolded himself: Winging it, you stupid bastard.

He froze, turned slowly, his chest heaving with exertion.

'I'm assuming it's Steve Flynn – remove the mask.'

Flynn complied, dragging it slowly off and dropping it by his side.

He looked all the way back down the corridor at Pavli Bashkim, standing there behind the body of the receptionist with a thickly muscled arm around the neck of a thin, bony wisp of a naked girl, held in front of him like a shield. His bicep was under her chin, forcing her head up, crushing her windpipe. She gagged sickeningly but had no fight in her.

Pavli pressed the muzzle of a pistol to her head.

He wore a terrible, cruel smile of victory.

'It had to be you,' he stated. 'No one else would dare.'

Four minutes, Flynn thought.

'You were right,' he said. 'It's me.' His pistol was tucked into the waistband at the small of his back.

Pavli seemed to read his mind. He removed his

gun from the girl's head and pointed it at Flynn's body mass.

'Take off your jacket.'

Flynn did: three minutes thirty.

A knowing look crossed Pavli's face. 'Now the vest.'

Flynn was wearing one of the light ballistic vests under his jacket. He ripped open the Velcro tabs and dropped it to his feet.

Pavli then threw the girl aside. She crashed down against the wall and slithered to her knees, gasping and clutching her throat. Pavli gave her a contemptuous look and swung his gun in her direction.

'No!' Flynn screamed and took a step towards him.

The gun came around in Flynn's direction.

'I was in the back room, in case you were wondering.'

'Can't say I was,' Flynn said.

There was perhaps four metres, just over twelve feet, separating the men.

Three minutes.

'Do you see what you did to me?' Pavli tilted his face sideways and showed Flynn the horrendous, slimy, oozing burn-flash across the side of his face.

'Not Mr Handsome any more.'

'You are more trouble than you are worth, Flynn. I knew we should have killed you when we had the chance, but my father wanted to use you first . . . and then you did that.'

'Confetti and snow.'

'One hundred million dollars, and twenty million dollars' worth of cocaine.'

'A lot of confetti and a lot of snow,' Flynn said, weighing up the distance, the angles, and realizing that, simply, he was defeated and was going to die.

Two minutes forty.

Just keep him talking, he thought. Let's both go to hell together.

'Incidentally,' Pavli said, 'I never told you. Your girlfriend was a great fuck. I tore her insides to shreds.'

'Not with your dick, presumably.'

A strange growl came from Pavli's throat at the insult.

Two minutes.

'So now I'm going to kill you, then go outside and kill that Spanish bitch. Then I will bring all the girls back in and have the place up and running within an hour . . . so you know you've failed before you die. You can take that knowledge to hell with you.'

Flynn shrugged.

One minute forty-five.

Pavli rested the butt of his gun on his left hand, made a triangle with his arms and looked along the sights at Flynn, who instinctively tensed his stomach muscles and imagined a nine mm slug slamming into his chest, shredding his heart and lungs.

'I stole some of your money, by the way. While you were having a shit after you'd fed Carlos to the fish.'

Pavli grinned. 'I'd be disappointed if you hadn't.'

'Just one packet. Quarter of a million dollars in it, I guess.'

'Good for you. Not much use in hell.'

Flynn saw Pavli's finger get comfortable on the trigger and his shoulders settle.

'I will never enjoy killing anyone more than you.'

'I have that effect on people.'

Pavli steadied himself. Flynn's world slowed down, sound distorted.

There was just the faintest blur of movement behind Pavli and simultaneously the bang of a shotgun being fired and the front of Pavli's face exploding outwards in a terrible gruesome mushroomed mess as the round fired at him from the sawn-off in Santiago's hands entered the back of his head, then exited, removing all of his features with it. He dropped and fell flat and behind him Santiago brought the weapon down from its firing position.

There was no time for anything then.

'We need to move,' Flynn shouted. He ran down the corridor, stooped to scoop up the naked girl in his arms and negotiated the two corpses in his way. With Santiago ahead, they ran to the warehouse exit. The back doors of the van were still open and Flynn had to throw the girl in on to the others huddled inside. Santiago was already behind the wheel, crunching into gear. Flynn scrambled into the passenger seat as the van moved forward and slapped the dashboard with his hand.

'Go!'

She almost stalled it, but after a few kangaroo lurches got control as she fought with the unfamiliarity of right hand drive, a nooky clutch and heavy steering, as well as the added pressure of Flynn looking at her with his best 'What the fuck?' expression.

320

They had reached the guards' shed on the lane when the warehouse erupted, rocking the van.

Flynn watched the building through his door mirror until Santiago skidded on to the road.

He looked at her again. 'Not a bad start to the night.'

Twenty-One

Three months later

Flynn sat at the café on the first floor of the commercial centre overlooking the marina in Puerto Rico. He was eating his usual full English breakfast accompanied by a mug of strong filter coffee. The sun was a quarter of the way up in the clearest azure sky.

Jerry Tope sat opposite him in his work suit, hot and sweaty. Detective Maria Santiago sat next to him, also in her work suit. Cool and fabulous.

Tope had been doing most of the talking.

'So, Lancashire Constabulary were left with two vans full of' – here Tope tweaked his fingers – '"working girls", who were also in the country illegally, brought in by an Albanian gang, according to them. They were deposited, half-naked, in the car parks outside police stations. The force was also left with three warehouses – one in Lancaster, one in Blackburn and one in Preston – which had been blown up and razed to the ground, and the one in Preston had four dead bodies in it, all shot to death before the fires. The warehouses had all been used as brothels.'

'Crikey,' Flynn said in mock awe. 'And what are the cops putting it all down to?'

'Gangs at war . . . going to take some real unpicking, I can tell you.'

'I assume because of all the research you were able to do, you could point the lead investigation officers in the right direction?' Flynn probed.

'They think I have a crystal ball,' Tope declared. 'I even managed to point the Metropolitan Police to a crime gang in London called the Smiths who were about to pull a big heist. Imagine that!'

'Well, good on you, Jerry. More power to your arm.'

'The powers that be were so impressed that they sent me on this jolly – the first proper one I've ever been on.'

'Really – and the point of it is?'

'To liaise with the cops here over Karen Glass's death and also to interview you about boat ownership.'

'As I told you, I lost my boat to an unknown gambler in a card game.' Flynn sliced a sausage and slotted it into his mouth. 'And, as you suggested, that's the story I'm sticking to.'

'Good. I'll need a statement to that effect.'

'No worries.'

Flynn looked at Santiago, who was Tope's point of contact for the local cops. She gave him a secret smile.

She was looking much more like the Santiago of old, the one Flynn had first met when she and Romero had turned up at the scene of Adam

Castle's shooting in the villa. The temporary tattoos had faded and her beautiful hair was growing back, now in a shiny bob-cut that Flynn thought accentuated the structure of her face and shape of her eyes. The skinhead had been nice, but not something he could have lived with for ever.

The past months had been a harrowing period for both her and Flynn.

After the 'night of the fires', as they called it, they carefully disposed of any evidence that could have linked them to the warehouses and deaths. Clothing was destroyed, firearms damaged beyond re-use and disposed of, and explosives made safe and sent to the bottom of the Irish Sea.

They then returned to Gran Canaria, where Santiago made contact with the police chief and took it from there. She was reinstated within a week, back on active duty within two.

All of which sounds like plain sailing, but she'd had a very hard time of it, mostly because of her conscience. The fortunate thing for her was they brought in an anti-corruption unit from Madrid who took over the investigation into Romero's suicide and his connection to crime gangs. This elite unit was also investigating the Bashkim crime clan on a much wider scale, working with Interpol, other police organizations across Europe and the FBI and DEA in America. Romero's connection, as it transpired, was only a minor facet in a much larger ongoing scenario of which Santiago was not aware, and nor did she want to be. This helped her in that they were not really interested in her and Romero because they were just tiny pieces in a 5,000 piece jigsaw.

The anti-corruption squad also quizzed Flynn about Adam's death at the villa. Flynn openly admitted having to kill Dardan in self-defence, which was the absolute truth, of course. He maintained that he had never met Dardan before that and did not know anything about the Bashkims wanting forty-nine per cent of *Faye* – the boat he had lost in a gambling debt, he also maintained. They questioned him further about Adam's business dealings, which he also said he knew nothing about – again true. He was happy to share some truths with them, but not everything.

When pressed about the bomb underneath his Nissan that killed Jose he said he knew of no reason for it. He expressed surprise that the story had come out that the Bashkims wanted half of his boat and suggested that possibly they had thought of him as a stumbling block to this and simply resorted to their usual tactics of killing people who might stand in their way, but had killed Jose by mistake. Flynn maintained that the only Bashkim he had ever met was Dardan, who had tried to kill him when he stumbled on Adam's murder.

His story and that of Santiago tallied with regard to the shooting of the cop who had been escorting them from Puerto Rico to Playa del Inglès and how Santiago had been on the run from Romero in a panic, not knowing what to do, terrified of turning herself in because of Romero's undoubted sphere of influence and his ability to manipulate evidence to suit himself. It also transpired that the other officer who had been driving Flynn and Santiago had disappeared and was suspected of involvement with the Bashkim clan.

Flynn got the impression that the cops were glad of some information and speculation, but that it didn't really help them very much in the overall scheme of things. They had bigger fish to fry.

He took the opportunity to visit Jose's widow, which was a very different type of meeting. She was in total grief and was now virtually penniless without Jose's income from the boat. As Flynn left her he pushed a sealed envelope into her hand and said, 'This should help you through. I know it won't bring him back.'

He embraced her and left.

Next he flew to the UK, where he attended the double funeral of Adam Castle and his sister, Karen Glass.

The service was conducted by a Humanist preacher and during the eulogy Flynn pressed his hands to his ears because he wanted to remember them both as he knew them best.

Back in Gran Canaria, he and Santiago spent time together which varied from loving to furious, but he knew that, unlike him, she was having problems coming to terms with what had happened to her, the life and death situations she had faced and, ultimately, the lives she had taken. It was mashing her mind. She was laid back one minute, brittle the next.

Flynn recalled one particular moment that he thought was the key to helping her move on. They were spending a hot afternoon on Amadores beach, had hired two sun loungers and were dipping in and out of the warm water lapping up on the manmade crushed shell beach, just trying to do something normal for once, even though there was nothing normal in their lives just then.

Santiago was distracted, far away in her thoughts. Even when they were in the sea, fooling around, she wasn't really there with him.

Finally, they were lying on the sun loungers. Flynn became aware that she had moved because of the creak of her lounger.

'Flynn?'

He squinted sideways. 'Yes?'

'Just tell me one thing, please.'

'Go on,' he said softly.

'Did I do the right thing, taking men's lives?'

He propped himself up on one elbow and removed his sunglasses. He reached across and removed hers too. 'Yes, you did.'

'Thank you,' she replied. She put her sunglasses back into place and lay back. 'In that case, it's time to move on.'

'And,' Jerry Tope was saying, bringing Flynn's focus back to the present day, 'the body that turned up on the beach in Conwy was eventually identified from DNA as Carlos Esposito, Mexican drug cartel guy. Thanks to my brilliance, they've linked the money and drugs from Glasson Dock to him and Bashkim. Seems Bashkim was going to launder the money for him in Europe, but Bashkim got greedy, wanted it for himself and' – Tope zipped his forefinger across his throat – '*adiós* Esposito.'

'My, my,' Flynn said admiringly. 'You know so much. And as for Bashkim?'

'Looks like he's gone to ground.' Tope shrugged. 'Word is he's back in the Albanian hills, and if he is, he's pretty untouchable.'

'Some you win,' Flynn said philosophically. 'Any update on Tracey Jayne?'

Tope nodded. 'She had a visit from Merseyside Police . . . they're taking up that particular gauntlet.'

'Good.'

Tope and Santiago exchanged a glance.

'Time we were going,' she said.

'Meeting with the anti-corruption unit in Playa del Inglès at ten,' Tope said with *gravitas*.

They stood up. Tope shook hands with Flynn, pulled him towards him and whispered in his ear, 'Really – no more. Don't ever contact me again. My blood pressure is fit to burst and I really don't want to lose my job.'

'Deal.' Flynn patted his arm.

Santiago kissed Flynn on the cheek. 'See you later.'

'When the cows come home, hopefully,' he said with a wink.

The two detectives left the café, going downstairs and over to the car park where Santiago had left her police SEAT Ibiza. Flynn leaned on the balcony rail and watched them drive away. Santiago gave him a little wave and blew a kiss.

Flynn looked over to the marina where *Faye* had been moored in between the other sport-fishing boats. Her space was still there – but not for long. Flynn had told Pavli the truth about stealing a pack of money while the Albanian had been using the toilet. Although risky, it was one of the things that Flynn had to chance, like laying explosive charges on *Faye* (because there was no way he would ever have let her fall into Bashkim's hands). He had walked off the boat with it in his rucksack.

It had contained exactly $250,000 – half of which he had given to Jose's widow. He intended to invest the remainder in a new – second hand – sportfisher. Enquiries were already under way to that end.

Leaning there thinking about the future, Flynn became vaguely aware of a figure standing a couple of metres away from him, leaning on the rail as he was. He paid no heed until the person turned towards him and slowly removed the hood from his head. Flynn's look of distant dreams changed to one of present nightmare.

'Did you really think you had seen the last of me?' Aleksander Bashkim said.

Flynn gawped at him. His face, like Pavli's, bore the scars of the explosion – but worse. He looked as though a bucket of hot ashes had been thrown into his face, and then it had been pushed into a gas ring turned on full blast. He had no hair and his mouth curled unnaturally because his lips had been scorched off.

There was a small calibre revolver in his right hand. He was leaning on the rail, pointing it casually at Flynn, who remained motionless. In his left hand was a mobile phone.

'Do you know what it's like to lose loved ones?' Bashkim asked.

'Well, only a dad could love sons like Dardan and Pavli, I guess.'

Bashkim snorted. Flynn saw he had no eyebrows either.

Bashkim said, 'This is your forte, isn't it, Mr Flynn?' He waggled the phone and Flynn's mouth went dry. 'Wiring up bombs and making them

328

explode by means of a phone signal, and killing loved ones.'

Flynn was certain that his heart had stopped.

'Watch this,' Bashkim said. He gestured with the gun towards the town of Puerto Rico and the direction in which Jerry Tope and Santiago had just set off in the car.

Flynn turned.

Bashkim pressed a button on the phone.

Flynn's hands balled up into tight fists.

Nothing happened.

He glanced at Bashkim – was the fucker teasing him?

'Just keep watching . . . it's a terrible signal around here.'

Flynn heard the boom of the explosion, saw the mushroom of smoke and flames rise, felt the waft of air on his face.

Dumbfounded, he turned to Bashkim again.

'So how does that feel? Fortunately for you, you won't have to live with it, as I have. How I regret not having you killed straight away. Mistake – now about to be rectified.'

Bashkim raised the gun. Flynn saw that his hands also bore the marks of the explosion, waxy burns like silver flashes up the back of them, the hair singed off for ever.

Flynn braced himself. There was nothing else left to do. He closed his eyes.

The gun fired.

Flynn flinched, tensing the stomach muscles, expecting the punch of the slug into his belly – but at the same time it occurred to him that the sound of the discharge from the weapon was not what he was expecting to hear, because with it was the clatter of a slide and then the ejection of a shell casing associated with a semi-automatic pistol, not a six shot revolver.

The first bullet hit him in the chest.

The second in the side of the head, the third in the neck.

They were all fired in quick succession so that the noise was almost continuous.

Flynn opened his eyes.

Bashkim was on the floor and he was clearly almost dead, certainly mortally wounded, as the blood pooled from the particularly horrendous wound in his neck that gushed red through a jagged rent in the flesh.

But just to make sure, the man with the pistol ran up to him and fired two more into his head. Then he was definitely dead.

The *coup de grâce* of a professional.

He was a tall, broad-shouldered, beyond handsome man, as big as Flynn, dressed in a casual polo top and chinos. He looked as if he could once have been an all-American boy, with the square chin of Superman and steel grey eyes.

'You,' Flynn said.

The man grinned, nodded at Flynn, gave him a lazy salute, then was gone, down the back steps of the café.

Flynn sat down slowly, tore his eyes away from Bashkim and looked towards the town, where smoke and flames now licked up to the sky and there was the sound of sirens and two-tone horns in the distance.